THE WORLD *of* RAE ENGLISH

THE WORLD *of* RAE ENGLISH

Lucy Rosenthal

Black
Lawrence
Press

www.blacklawrence.com

Executive Editor: Diane Goettel
Cover design: Pam Golafshar
Cover art: Robert Daniel Ullmann
Book design: Amy Freels

ISBN: 978-1-937854-39-3

Published 2014 by Black Lawrence Press
Printed in the United States

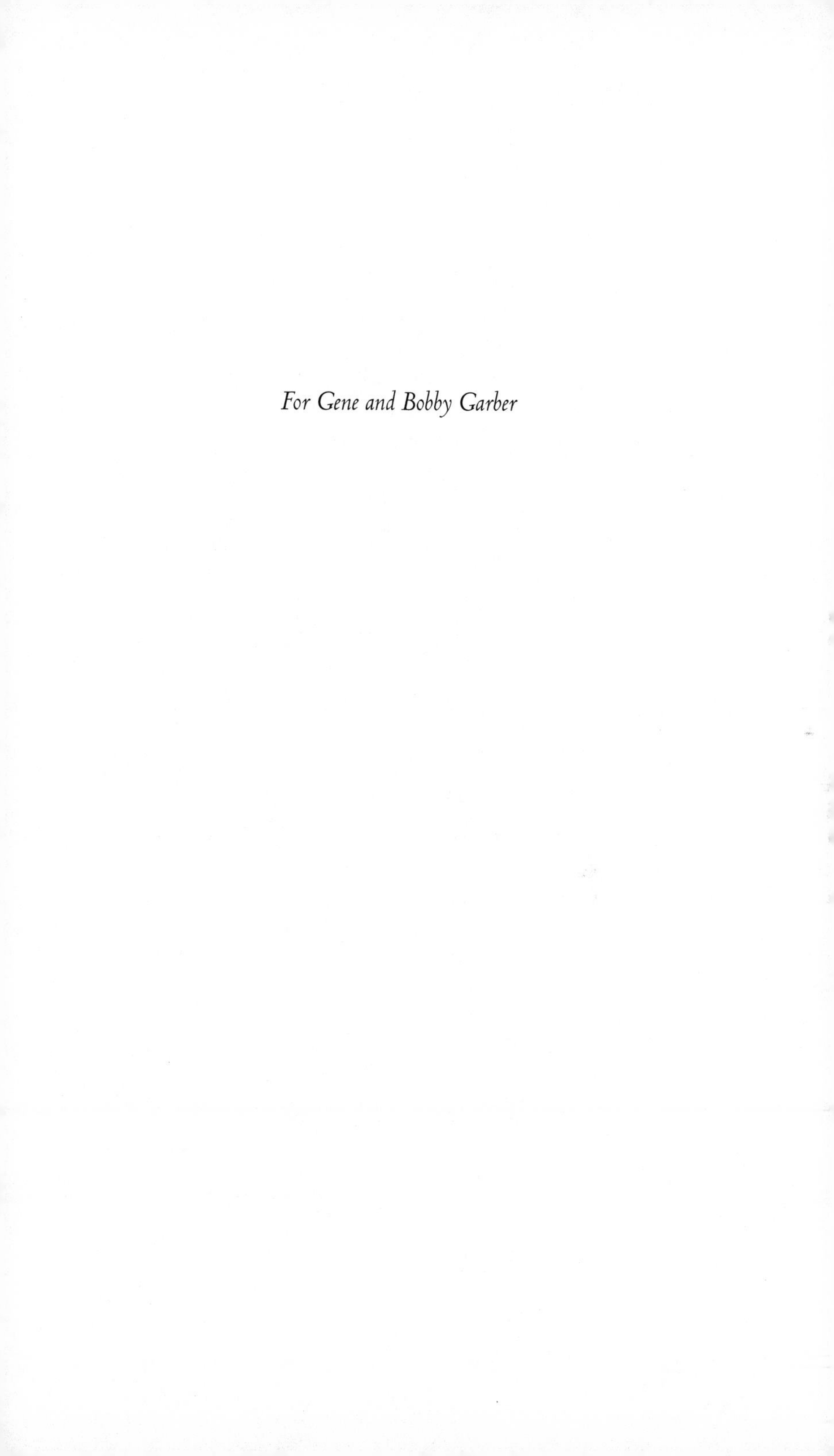

For Gene and Bobby Garber

Acknowledgments

I am deeply grateful to the many friends and colleagues who offered me generous editorial and moral support as this book unfolded. I am especially thankful to Diane Goettel, at Black Lawrence Press, who could not have given this book a more caring and welcoming home, and to the talented people at BLP: Amy Freels for the interior design and full cover, and Pam Golafshar for the jacket.

Many thanks to Bob Wyatt for his long-standing and unfailing support. For their insight, encouragement and warmth I am grateful to Carolyn Ferrell, Myra Goldberg, Gilberto Perez and Diane Stevenson. I am indebted to Greg Mertl for his invaluable editorial suggestions. Fran and Sam Klagsbrun have my gratitude for their early readings and suggestions. For history, many thanks to Bob Spitzer. I am grateful to Judith Glassman, who mediates between computers and humans, for the rescues she performed and the advice she gave. Thanks to Judith Weber, for the original paperweight and more.

I am grateful to Joan Long for her friendship and unerring artist's eye. George Cavey's thoughtful reflections on the sixties gave shape to key scenes.

Special thanks to the Virginia Center for the Creative Arts where this book was written and rewritten over several residencies. I am deeply grateful for their support.

This book had many friends, not all of them named here. The list goes on. I hope you know who you are and how thankful I feel.

Contents

i Prologue: F : a debriefing 1

1. G-Man 4
2. Pussywillow 24
3. Border States 56
4. Barbecue 71
5. Sweet Nothings 101
6. Overshooting the Runway 127
7. Search Party 146
8. Across the River 162
9. Dead Ahead 180
10. Lanyards 203
11. R 224

Prologue

F : a debriefing

I dreamed of F last night, my ex-husband, who was masquerading as someone who tells the truth. It's said that you dream of the people you've loved when you're ready to say goodbye to them. It's a comfort to think of F pushing his way into a dream only to be bounced. I'd like to believe it—but it certainly takes practice. I've tried erasing F's name, thinking of him as his initial only, or as *former husband,* a generic brand, filed under *ex*. I can't keep him at bay, hard as I try—by shunning his book signings, putting a block on my caller ID, curtailing (if only for myself) his television appearances with the mute and power buttons on my remote.

He's on a book tour, promoting his second book, a memoir titled *The Pitfalls of Deceit*. His first book, *The Confined and the Released,* was on prison reform; in it he argued passionately—F has passion to burn—for the rights of convicts, present and past. (I don't know yet if the new book mentions his field work—the research he did while serving his sentence on location. Of course, in his first book, he did come clean. That was the point.)

F is friend to the downtrodden. The oppressed minority of *that* moment was felons. I'm not sure what it is now. As a pundit—he has worked hard to become one, he was always ambitious—F champions his minorities on a pick and choose basis. Notoriety helps—though he's become known more for his generous nature than his record. As the dark cloud recedes, he's gained in authority; even concealed, the murkiness is compelling; you might even take it for an aura. You know he knows things—from the cosmos to politics and back again—and you want to know them too. He's been a regular on talk shows—Chris Matthews, Bill O'Reilly, Piers Morgan. Often he's paired with John Dean.

I pay a price for my curiosity, but—

I've been reading his memoir. Not least because I'm in it. He calls me 'Inga Redmont'. To protect me, I suppose, and himself as well. He writes, "My ex-wife who is full of secrets has made me hers." I think that makes him very proud.

It's true. He has long been my secret. The skeleton in my closet—or one of them. They don't get out much. Even on Halloween. Don't ask, don't tell.

Furtively, I carry the book around with me, like contraband, from room to room, in a plain wrapper. (I've turned its dust jacket inside-out.) No one should know. Flipping through its pages, I discover things about Inga that I never knew: She figures in what the kids would call "the sexy parts". F is pleased to tell the reading public that he was Inga's first man. Reportedly, once, in the middle of one or another of their pleasurable interludes, he heard her murmur *'Adam'*. Yes, he acknowledges she said it out of romantic innocence, and when she alluded to it later it was with an edge or irony—but still! He has never forgotten it. I have. He goes on: Though inexperienced sexually she was a quick study. Otherwise, she was bookish. She drew the name *Adam,* she told him, less from Genesis as from a story by a southern writer she much admired, Katherine Anne Porter; she said the story broke her heart. He got that part right.

They grew apart, he and Inga; they separated, and went their separate ways. Quite a story. He neglects to mention that the way he went was to jail. I've had my share of misadventures but they were this side of the law.

I had to put *The Pitfalls of Deceit* aside. The book seemed filled with heavy hints about who I was really. A question I've been asked before. We'll get back to you as soon as we know.

After a while, I picked F's book up again, of course. I've always been fascinated by misinformation.

And yet—I can cut him some slack: He may have been the first man of my adult life, but he was not the first liar. And I've told more than a few.

Chapter 1

G-Man

But it is time to set the record straight. I am not Inga. And I can tell my story better than Frank.

The story begins with two friendships: my childhood friend Norma Povich and my father's friend Ricardo whose last name I didn't know. Ricardo came to our house for eagerly anticipated visits all the time; he would sweep into our house bearing brilliant flowers for my mother and playfully pretend to kiss her hand.

Norma, on the other hand, visited just once—and after that, never again. My mother did not welcome Norma. You might even say she threw her out. Politely. At the time my mother said that Norma was not normal. Whatever that meant. In my adult life it came to mean that you formed your close attachments on the sneak and, whether you had a family or not, you stayed out of its house.

My friend Norma's departure, so sudden, broke time in half for me. I was six, going on seven, and I didn't get it. From then on, the events of my childhood seemed to take place across a divide: Before and After Norma—and her expulsion.

I remember our final conversation. In a spooky undertone, she said: "Who do you think you are?" I think she must have known that I no longer had the answer to that question.

Before, I could have explained simply that I was descended from royalty—or occupied some other high station (exactly which one was a technicality) and in short order, I would have believed it myself.

Because I'd known for a fact, before, that my father was the most important man in the world. I had no trouble marshaling the evidence.

What else to make of my mother's hushed reverence for him? And how attentively she cooked for him, and the beautiful way she dressed for him? Or the ritual solemnity attending his retreats to his study (though one didn't know exactly what he did behind its closed door).

Even after the arrival of my sister, who seemed to consume my mother (they named this distraction Marta) he stayed at the center of our world. My mother, though preoccupied, continued worshipful; and I worshiped him too. I didn't know whether he was the President or God—after a while, I took for granted that he was one or the other or both.

That he favored me consoled him, I think, after Marta came, and misappropriated my mother. I hung around him all the more, making sure he knew *my* feelings for him were unchanged. I worried that any transfer of my mother's devotion to the unworthy baby would hurt him. I kept an eye on him and, as much as I could, on my mother. Sometimes I could see her steal a worshipful glance at him from the endless round of feeding and bathing the baby and changing her diapers. But more and more, her glances were fleeting.

I began to tell myself that her worship of him must now happen behind the closed door of their bedroom where they retreated together every night—and that somehow, that way, the family hierarchy, along with an orderly universe, was restored. Though they would emerge every morning without looking at each other, they seemed content, as if they'd settled something between them. It was then, I think, that I began to think of the night as a time of secret and devout transactions.

I met Norma Povich sometime around then, when I was delivered over to the first grade of the local public school. My mother got me ready—saw me into what she decided was a pretty dress (I thought it was frilly and too short) and looped my braids together with a bow that was unevenly tied; the asymmetry was deliberate; she set great store by my not looking like anybody else. My father, holding my hand, walked me to school, a short walk, very slowly, I thought so that I could keep up with him. But sometimes it seemed that he didn't want to let me go, and I began to wonder if there wasn't some other reason for their sending me out of the house, though once we were there he would rush away abruptly.

Sometimes I envied Norma Povich whose mother knew how to dress a six-year-old so that she didn't look like a Christmas tree. At least Norma's homespun, ordinary clothes covered her, as clothes were meant to do and let her go with the scenery. I thought it highly desirable then to go with the scenery, which for me, meant basking in my father's reflected light.

I would tell Norma about my father, whom she would glimpse sometimes in the mornings when we would arrive together, hand in hand. I managed never to notice exactly whose hand *she* was holding—I assumed it belonged to some nondescript, but serviceable adult, one or the other of her parents. While my parents were distinguished and glamorous, hers I was sure were pasty lookalikes. Norma got a better sense of my mother, who came every day after school to pick me up, dispensed a friendly word or two for Norma like bonbons before we went our separate ways. Which my mother managed to telegraph to me were *very* separate. Norma lived far enough away so that we never visited each other's homes or played together in the playground where my mother would take me after school.

My day was framed by them, my father and my mother. That he took me to school and she came and got me became for me a law of nature—as inevitable as the phases of the moon or the rising and setting of the sun. What we believed in was each other. One day, a few years later, I woke up knowing beyond any shadow of a doubt that what was profane was to believe in one's self.

But that took a while. Meanwhile, with Norma, I made the most of the time we had together, getting as much mileage as possible out of recess and lunch. Norma looked up to me. I loved telling her stories about my home and family, how they were grand and special, my father most particularly in ways I couldn't go into, though I was full of heavy hints.

The hints had to do with World War II, now in progress. In the service of the war effort, I told her, my father was entrusted with secrets; probably they had to do with ridding the world of Hitler and other evil men. My mother was Jewish, I rattled on, and my father's mission while on earth (by this time I'd promoted him to some more elevated realm) was to save my mother's people from the Nazi scourge. (I'd hedge my bets about whether my mother's people were my people too. Anyway, I was pretty sure I'd never need saving.) Oh, and another thing, I told Norma, helping myself from her lunchbox to a sugar cookie my mother had assured me would rot my teeth, I had a younger sister who was very sick and not allowed out of the house. In fact, I said, in a loud whisper, she was *deformed.* (Which seemed fair enough since she was small, squirmy, and given to yelling.) Apart from that one tragedy, and the added danger my mother was in from being Jewish, we were as a family aglow with the rarest kind of happiness. I wiped the cookie crumbs I'd spilled on myself and Norma with my sleeve, while she hung on my every word.

That fall I learned to read. I remember, sitting on the sofa between both parents, all of us poring over my reader, when the letters suddenly became words and the words had meaning. "I am a gingerbread man," I said, "I am, I am." I was so proud. So were they. Even the information, conveyed with unusual firmness by my gentle father, that "gingerbread" was not pronounced with a hard "g" did not mar the moment.

He said, "Repeat after me," he said, and I did as he asked, soft g's and all.

I went on, "I can run," I said, "I can, I can." Not that I'd ever want to.

In the spring, when Norma and I were promoted to 1B, the reins my parents kept on me were loosened. I was nearly seven and, they told me, I could begin going back and forth to school by myself. Soon, Norma followed suit. The absence of our parents somehow made us more like equals. Norma herself had gotten bigger, I noticed, bigger than me, though I still felt sure I had the upper hand. Still, from time to time, Norma acted bossy; now and then I detected a swagger. I began to notice that my fabulous tales of my life at home held her less and less in thrall. I needed to find some new way to excite her interest.

One afternoon, inspired by a comic book I'd examined before it was confiscated by my parents, I told her that my father was a G-Man. He worked for J. Edgar Hoover, the head of the F.B.I., to whom he reported personally, I told her breathlessly, and waited for her to ask me what a G-Man was. *Geee,* I said, drawing it out, letting my lips pucker. Norma said nothing. It was, I notified her, a soft G, as in gingerbread. A hard G, I went on learnedly, would be the G, as in, "Go away!" I saw a slight recoil. "Oh Norma," I said, tugging at her arm with a jolly impatience, "I didn't mean anything." She shuffled closer. Pausing from time to time, for breath as well as to make sure that she was listening attentively, I went on to tell her that a man who regularly came to visit my father was, in fact, sent by J. Edgar Hoover to transcribe information obtained by my father, the spy. The visits were secret, I told her, she mustn't tell anyone. Promise? Getting her to promise took some pestering. "Do you swear?" I nagged.

"Yes," she said sourly. I also got her to promise not to tell anyone that the man's code name was Ricardo and that he too was a G-Man. I was beginning to believe it myself.

The real Ricardo was not only my father's best friend—he was, in fact, his only friend. He was handsome, beautiful, I thought, tall and dashing; he wore a trench coat and *looked* like a spy. I looked forward to his visits, they were like holidays. They made my father happy. As a small child, I would make my way through and around the forest of their legs as they, Ricardo and my father, greeted each other. My mother would take Ricardo's flowers, arrange them in a vase and set them as a radiant centerpiece on the table. Often she would dress up and look especially beautiful, at dinner sitting quietly, then leaving them alone, my father and Ricardo, to talk long into the night. In the morning, though he was gone, his flowers were still there.

I got to thinking Ricardo was my uncle. I thought that for a long time until my mother told me curtly he wasn't.

But that day in the schoolyard I didn't tell Norma about the real Ricardo. Instead I went on to regale Norma with my tales of doorbells and telephones ringing mysteriously in the night, all in support of the war effort. As I finished, I saw that she was looking at me, bright-eyed. And she had a question.

"What," Norma asked me, "is a G-man?"

All at once, I realized I didn't know. To cover it, I said impulsively, "You'll find out—come home with me," forgetting everything I'd need to hide, including my perfectly healthy sister and the picture I'd painted of our house as a citadel against stormtroopers whom only the goodness of my father kept at bay.

Home was just around the corner. When we got off the elevator, my mother was standing in our apartment's doorway, holding a vase of withering flowers. Abruptly, she set it down on a side-table; I saw the petals floating in the cloudy water. She looked at her watch and then, sternly, at me. I'd broken the commandment against dawdling after school.

Drawing us into the apartment, my mother sat Norma down, and quizzed her about where her parents could be reached and her phone number. I kept my eyes fastened on Norma who was, I thought, looking glum. Quickly I decided she was also looking pale and sickly. I felt briefly proud to have brought home someone who might possibly qualify as a waif, since we set great store by good deeds in our house. I hoped that my mother would be impressed and feel sympathy for Norma too.

But more and more, Norma—squirming on the plush upholstery of our sofa and making small kicking motions with her feet—

was losing my sympathy. As she mumbled answers to my mother's questions, her indifferent gaze would wander here and there, fixing on one or another of the furnishings, as if she was sizing us up. Suddenly, our richly woven rug, the end-tables with their cunning curves and fine-grained polished wood, our walls hung with pretty pictures—all of this, seen through her eyes, began to look shabby, shrunken. Her largeness loomed, threatening to overtake the room, and it was suddenly brought home to me that I might not live in a hallowed elevator building that doubled as an eastern outpost of the White House.

When my mother, armed with Norma's telephone number, left the room, Norma rose, and began poking around in earnest. Spotting a stray flower petal on the floor she picked it up, and studied it as if her thumb was a Petri dish, and flicked it back on to the floor. Then she began fingering a paperweight, a prized gift from Ricardo, studying its blue-green depths, opaque but glistening, turning it over and over in her hands as if its contents were liquid.

"There's no water in there," I told her. "It just *looks* like the ocean. It's a paperweight."

"What's that?" she asked.

I explained to her what it was.

"Oh," she said. "How come there's no paper?"

"It's so pretty," I said, and advised her that owing to its prettiness we used it solely for decoration. She was shaking it, waving it, holding it up to the light, passing it from one hand to the other.

"Put it down," I said, suddenly afraid; any minute, my mother could come back in and find alien fingerprints all over it.

"It doesn't look like any ocean," Norma said. "It looks like dishwater." She plunked it back down on the coffee table; it skittered a little.

I swallowed; I didn't want to look at it. Now she was gazing up at our bookshelves, pretending she could read the titles she wasn't tall enough to see. What was she looking for?

Finally, she said, "Where is he?"

"Who?" I asked stupidly; I really had no idea what she meant.

"Your father."

"In his study," I said.

"I don't believe you," she said.

"Well, he is!" I cried.

Coming back into the room, my mother gave me a warning look. "Norma," she said, formally, "Your mother's coming to get you. You girls can wait for her downstairs." I was hanging back. "Go with her," she said, adding, "When Norma's mother gets here I want you to come right back up." I turned to look at Norma; her stare was making me uneasy.

"Mama," I said, "Where's Daddy?"

She looked at me impassively. "I'm not sure," she said. She repeated, "Go downstairs."

I felt a sudden, illogical jolt of fear that he had gone and taken the baby with him; the house was oddly silent; the sight and sound and smell, even of the baby, would put things right. But before I could frame another question (about the whereabouts of the missing members of our world-famous family) my mother closed the door behind her.

Standing in the vestibule alone with Norma, waiting for the elevator to take us down, all I knew was that I couldn't wait for her to be returned to her tribe. The elevator touched down at the lobby, the doors squeaked open, and Norma and I, eyes averted from each other, walked out into the late afternoon's fresh air.

"You don't have a father," she said to me as we cooled our heels on the sidewalk. I did, I protested. Hadn't she seen him bring me to school?

"That's not your real father," she said.

"Yes it is!" I said.

"Well, if he is," Norma hissed, "he's too scared to come out of hiding."

Stung, I said I was sure he'd been in his study where he was hard at work discovering radium or tracking Nazis, if not writing some great book. "We have to keep everything secret," I told her. "There are things he can't even tell us."

Norma said, "I bet you don't have a sister, either."

I began anxiously to look up and down the street to see if I could spot someone who looked like Norma's mother, who up to now I knew as someone who had no looks at all. "Of course I have a sister," I huffed.

Norma said, "Babies cry. I didn't hear anybody crying."

"My sister doesn't cry," I said, "she's too sick."

Norma said, "Maybe she's dead."

I shrieked, "*No!*" Who was this creature? I wondered if the Norma I'd known at school had a wicked identical twin.

"I think your father's the one who's sick," said Norma.

"There's nothing wrong with my father!" I said.

Then Norma said, "I bet he's *deformed*."

For a dizzy moment I wanted to hit her (I'd never hit anyone in my life), I wanted blood to come running out of her ears. Out of the corner of my eye I saw a cop standing halfway down the block; I pictured him coming to catch me before I finished killing her, saw myself in handcuffs (and not the toy ones I'd gotten at the five and ten and was saving to use on Marta when she was bigger). I took a deep breath. "I bet *your* mother's dead," I said.

"You're a liar!" she said, which was not untrue, but that didn't stop me."Otherwise she'd be here," I said airily. Her face was flushed, she looked wild.

I took a step back, she closed in for her kill: "You think," she said hoarsely—I could see her teeth, tongue, "your father's like the Mayor—or the President!"

"Well, he is," I said, adding in an effort to be gracious, "He's just as good as they are. Maybe better." I decided not to reveal to this mere mortal just *how* much better he was.

Then, a figure so faded and indistinct that she could only be Mrs. Povich seemed to be trudging toward us. I jerked at Norma's sleeve and pointed. "Isn't that her?" I asked."Yes," said Norma, icy. Her courage was up, which worried me. I didn't want her to unfurl lurid tales of persecution at my hands.

Her mother came directly to where we were standing, in front of my house. She glanced at me and frowned. Then she kneeled down. She asked, "Norma, why are you alone in the street? It's almost dark. Are you all right?" She had some kind of accent, like my mother's; it had a fainter music than my mother's.

"Mrs. Povich," I trilled, "I'm Norma's friend—"

Norma poked her head out from the folds of her mother's skirts: "That's not her name. She's not *Mrs. Povich*."

"Isn't she your mother?" I asked, bewildered.

"We live with my stepfather," said Norma. "My father lives someplace else."

"Where?" I stammered. I wanted to know that—and more—why had she never told me? I had a sinking, sick feeling. Norma had two fathers. Though it had never before occurred to me to question my own father, I wondered if that was better than having only one. I couldn't find words for my other questions. My tongue stuck to my teeth.

"Come on, Norma," said her mother and took her daughter's hand. Norma and her mother were big people; together, they took up the whole sidewalk. I watched them as they walked down the street away from me, hoping they'd fade or vanish, like the fireflies we saw in the country, whose split-second light would flicker out. At the end of the block, while they stood waiting for the light to change so that they could cross the street, Norma slowly turned and, looking straight at me, she stuck out her tongue.

As I rang the bell to our apartment (I wasn't old enough to be given keys), I could hear the familiar and reassuring sounds of Marta's squalling. Now, why couldn't she have done that while Norma was here? My mother appeared, holding her, this wriggling bundle; with her flashing green eyes and fringe of pale red hair, she was finally beginning to look like something: us. I regarded her with fond disdain. "Oh, shut up," I told her brightly.

"You've been told not to say 'shut up,'" said my mother.

"I was talking to *her*," I said, pointing.

"Your sister has a name," said my mother. Then she asked, "Did *your friend's* mother come?" I gathered from this that Norma didn't have a name, not at our house."Yes," I said. "Her mother came."

My mother said, "Sit down. I want to talk to you."

She went to put the baby down while I sat gingerly down on the sofa where Norma had recently been fidgeting. The sofa didn't feel or look like itself; I could barely look at it.

It was the last thing I wanted—to be here where I'd been sitting when I learned to read. If I looked at Ricardo's paperweight now, I'd see bugs, I thought, and closed my eyes.

My mother swept back in; for some reason she had changed out of a blouse and skirt with muted colors into something more festive, something with the floral splash that often heralded a visit from Ricardo. Ricardo! All at once I knew what could wipe away the smudge of Norma: his presence, his flowers, that he was my father's friend. I heard my mother say with icy disapproval, "We don't like your friend." I knew then there would be no rescue by Ricardo and that the brightness of her dress was not for him.

I blurted out, "She's not my friend. Not anymore."

"Why? What happened?" my mother asked.

"She stuck her tongue out at me," I said, flushing, ashamed.

"Oh," said my mother, "That wasn't nice."

"I hate her," I said.

"You don't have to go that far," my mother said, after a pause. She added, "You can feel sorry for her." The thought of Norma was making me sick; so was the thought of feeling sorry for her.

I whispered, "Why don't you like her?"

"She's not a good friend for you. She might not be—" my mother hesitated, "—normal."

I didn't know what that meant; maybe the information I'd picked up on the sidewalk had something to do with it.

"Mama, her mother has a different last name and she has a stepfather."

My mother said, "Oh, poor thing. Is her father dead?" The question chilled me. It made me worry about my own father.

"I don't think so," I told her seriously. "He just doesn't stay with them. He stays somewhere else."

"Probably," said my mother smoothly, "they're divorced." I needed to have that explained and she went about explaining something that I hardly listened to. I watched instead her pursed lips, her frown line which fascinated me (mid-forehead and equidistant from both brows—I couldn't take my eyes off it), and the expressive flutter of her hands. "And some Daddies," she was saying, "turn out not to love Mommies, so the Mommies send them away."

I interrupted: "Are you going to send Daddy away?" I asked her.

"Oh no!" she said laughing, "Why would I? Sometimes," she went on, and now there was a scratchy quality to her voice, "the Daddies just leave." She paused. The house was still. "Either way," she said, as if she were polishing off one of Aesop's fables or some other bedtime story, "It's called divorce."

All I could think of at the end of this oration (the longest since her account of how babies were born) was that I could end up like Norma, not normal, and with an unspeakable name.

I whimpered, "Is Daddy going to leave?"

"Never!" she said, with her bell-like laugh. "You know Daddy!"

And there he was, large and stooped in the doorway, smiling his reticent smile. His face bore the creases of sleep, though he didn't look rested; I knew that in sleep he rested his fervid, astonishing brain. I was overjoyed to see him, but I knew better than to bound across the room to hug him (though, always, it was what I wanted). Shyly, I inched toward him. I was reaching for his hand when my mother, big on cleanliness, abruptly told me to go wash my hands.

Something was wrong, I knew, even in sleep, it was too early for these sounds, for any sounds. I listened—grating sounds too deep and growly for the baby, maybe not even coming from a person. I kept hearing it, it came and went. I climbed out of bed, opened my door cautiously and peered down the hall. A light, coming from the living room, threw shadows on the opposite wall. I went padding toward the living room; a door slammed somewhere; and then I heard the sound again, awful, wheezing and guttural, but mesmeric, drawing me in like a moth to a flame. I cried out for help—*Daddy!*—and stumbled into the living room. A ruined joke, looking like someone who had once been my father, was slumped over on the sofa and I understood at once that Norma was a wicked fairy whose still-hovering spirit had cast a spell. The horrid, metallic sounds I'd been hearing all night were issuing from my father, coming up from his chest and throat. I went up to him and as I stood there, stationed between his knees, I saw simply that he was crying.

"Daddy," I said, "don't. You'll hurt your throat." I touched his cheek; I thought I'd soothe his tears, dab at them with my fingertips, as he did with me. "Daddy," I crooned, stroking his face, glad and astonished that he was not pushing me away. I wished for him to stop crying, but I didn't want *this* to stop. "Daddy," I said, "don't cry anymore, I'm here." He lurched forward and grabbed me and crushed me against his chest. "Everything's okay, Daddy," I began to say, "Don't be scared."

I kept on saying it, while he held on to me tightly and said over and over again, "Do you promise? promise me please, don't go away, I couldn't bear it, promise me."

"I promise, Daddy, don't cry anymore." I was glad I knew exactly what to say. His weeping went on without sound. He seemed to forget I was there. I sat down on the rug at his feet. From time to time I'd look up to show him I was there. "Daddy dear," I'd say, and say again, liking the sound, the definiteness, of the two *D's*. "Daddy, dear," I'd whisper, "I love you." I wanted him to answer me. I like to think he did, but my memory has an empty space in it.

My mother came after a while and took me back to my room, my bed. I pleaded, "Don't turn out the light."

She said, "I'll leave a light on in the hall. Go back to sleep."

I couldn't remember having been asleep. "Daddy?" I said.

"I'll take care of Daddy," my mother said and drifted out. I lay there for a while, listening to their mingled disembodied voices echoing down the hall. I thought of Norma and her two fathers, the real one and the other one—Daddy, Daddy, I thought.

The next day, at breakfast, nothing was said. My parents packed me off to school as usual. It was as if nothing had happened, nothing at all.

Years later, in one of the rare times I allowed myself to think about it, I realized that the events of that night were elongated in my memory; they seemed to stretch over decades—the wounded cries, the stranger who only *looked* like my father, the desperate embrace which never happened again. Looking back, with the eyes of an adult who had known real time, lived in it, I understood that all of it might have taken place in a span of thirty minutes, no more, though it isn't over yet.

That morning I walked, as slowly as I could, down the block in front of my house and then around the corner to the school. I wanted never to get there. I wasn't even sure why, but I knew when I got there at the first shrill sound of the bell. It was the signal to march to our classrooms, which we did on the buddy system, two by two. Norma had always been my buddy. Shaky, I looked around to see who else

I could get to walk with me and fell in beside a skinny girl, Julia Payson, whose father had just died.

As the day wore along, past reading, penmanship, spelling, and arithmetic, I'd catch glimpses of Norma who woodenly refused to look at me. A loneliness settled over me, heavy, dank, and clammy. And by lunchtime, as I watched Norma heading resolutely for the lunchroom without me, my desolation was complete. I trailed slowly after her, taking a seat several tables away from her alongside some classmates I barely knew. I put my brown lunchbag on the table in front of me; it had spots of grease on it; I was sure that whatever was inside it had gone bad. I took a bite of it; I wanted to spit it out; it had no taste, it was like chewing paper. I sat there, huddled, trying to disappear; I prayed that no one would talk to me and was glad when no one did. I waited in the lunchroom until everyone, including Norma, had gone. I dropped what was left of my lunch into the wastebasket, and started for the classroom. Gingerbread, I whispered, as I climbed the stairs—giving it a hard G, giving in to a sudden, wild notion that my father had been wrong.

I kept it up in class when we opened our readers and it came my turn to read aloud; the teacher kept correcting me; what was the matter with me, she wanted to know—I was mispronouncing words. I wanted the afternoon to end—except that I didn't know what would happen to me when it ended. I only knew *I* didn't want to end.

When the bell finally rang, I thought of a way to avoid going down to the schoolyard with my classmates and I offered to stay and help the teacher put away the erasers and chalk. But she had already chosen Julia Payson, the girl with no father, and so, with shaking knees, I went downstairs, and there outside was Norma, the girl with two.

Briefly, I toyed with the idea of sticking my tongue out at her, but seeing her, then walking toward her, I had an overpowering sense of relief. She looked as she always had, *so* familiar to me; it was as if nothing had changed, and maybe all of this could be undone. I forgot to be afraid of her, I forgot everything. I don't know what I had in mind to do or say as I walked up to her; I think I was intending nothing much more than standing around companionably before we fell to our usual clowning and telling of secrets. "Hi, Norma," I said, preparing to make faces, giggle.

She stepped back. "I'm not supposed to play with you."

"Why not?"

She said, "Because my *mother* says so!"

A bolt of fear went through me. Her mother had power.

The possibility had never occurred to me. And here was Norma wielding it.

"Please, Norma," I heard myself say. "Please."

"Go away," she said. It was what I'd said to her in my erudite account about G's (*hard, as in 'Go away'*), but I'd been joking and Norma wasn't.

"C'mon," I said—now I couldn't stop myself—"Let's just walk around the block, okay?"

"My mother's coming," she said, tossing her mousy curls. "She won't like it if she sees me with you."

I said again, "Please." She loomed over me, smiling her snooty new smile.

"Beg me," she said. She gave me a little push and I lurched back unsteadily. All I wanted was for her to be my friend again, which would cancel yesterday and put the world right. "Beg me," she repeated and I sank to the ground, hoping that would really worry her, but it felt as if that's where I belonged.

"Norma please," I said, getting on my knees. I had the habit of worship and it stayed with me and it didn't matter whether they were false gods or true. I should have been more on guard—It is a mistake to forget how swiftly—in a heartbeat—the habit of worship can change into the habit of begging.

Looking up, I saw her smiling down at me. If I stayed on the ground, I would shrivel. I scrambled to my feet, thinking I'd find safety at eye level. But she was still taller than me—and her smile was no friendlier. She seemed, in fact, to be regarding me as a creature trespassing from the pages of a horror comic book, not frightening because fake. Speaking with quiet scorn, she said to me: "Who do you think you are?" I couldn't answer because for the first time in my life I didn't know.

As it turned out, she didn't take me back; I believe those were the last words she spoke to me. I got good at pretending I didn't care. I would skip past her with my nose in the air. After a while, I didn't have to pretend.

When the term ended Norma and her ragtag family moved away and I never saw her again. Sometimes I wondered if her real father stayed behind or went with her, but there was no one to ask.

It seemed to me after that more and more my father would disappear behind the closed door of his study. My mother, however, blossomed; she glowed with a new contentment, a new satisfaction; she seemed to be more confident even in her own elusiveness.

It was around the same time that Ricardo's visits ceased altogether. "Where is he?" I would ask my mother, in a whisper. She never answered.

Two friends: Two vanishing acts.

But Norma and her questions lingered, like the Cheshire cat's smile. With her question, "Where is he?" she'd diminished my father, her credentials presumably being that she had two. I had no answer to that; I must have sensed a light dimming. That, like Ricardo, he could fade too.

"Who do you think you are?" she'd asked me.

I am trying to answer her question now, not because I owe her anything, though I might, but because I have more sympathy for a child's curiosity and she was the first to ask.

Here is the short answer:

My name is Rae English. My father used to call me Rae of Light.

Chapter 2

Pussywillow

The cat, Pussywillow, raked its blunted claws against the wire-mesh screens of Ted Gobisch's kitchen. Pussywillow is dead now, but Ted Gobisch, who was allergic to her, loved her.

When I think of him, of Iowa City, sometimes that's what I see, what I remember most of all.

The first time he took me home, a week to the day after Val and Andrew (his chairman) introduced us, Pussywillow was there to greet us; she nuzzled Ted's leg, and then leapt into my lap, where she disposed herself contentedly and purred. She even followed us into the bedroom, and was attempting to join us as we settled in the bed when Ted began to sneeze, the sneezes coming in such rapid, convulsive succession that, propped on my elbow, regarding him with growing alarm, I could hardly sandwich in the words, *God bless you.*

"I don't believe in God," he managed to reply, in the middle of his paroxysms.

I was rather widely experienced with men at this juncture of my life, but this was a new one to me. The man was an Associate Professor of Religion.

"Just bless you, then," I said smoothly, wishing I had a local girlfriend to tell this to.

But neither my blessings nor the aplomb I was manifesting seemed to do him any good. I listened to his sneezes and gasps with growing dismay, thinking that what I was hearing was probably the death rattle. It began to occur to me that I hardly knew this man, and that he could die at any moment with me in his bed, and then what would I do—I'd already, instinctively, shut my eyes so that I wouldn't see him turning blue. I didn't feel one bit like Florence Nightingale, I wanted to run back to the homely room I'd rented, where I'd be safe from death, illness and other entanglements. Surreptitiously, I groped for my panties. The other articles of clothing, thank heaven, were near at hand on the chair.

He saw me. "Look, don't do that," he said. "It's the damn cat."

"What?"

"I'm allergic to it."

He'd begun to sneeze again.

"What shall I do?"

"Get her out of here. Not outside," he said weakly, seeing me pounce upon the creature—*So, Pussywillow! You—It was you, all the time!*—"The pantry," Ted directed me weakly. "And close the door."

"You," I muttered to the cat as, half-naked, I carried her through Ted's unfamiliar rooms, illuminated by the Iowa City full moon. "Do you know how long I've been waiting for a night of love? You've destroyed that poor man, not to mention my hopes." The cat was purring. "Idiot," I whispered, as I deposited her on the pantry floor and raced for the door.

He was lying on his side, waiting for me. "Come back in," he said, patting the covers, "and get warm."

I *was* cold, I realized, as I crawled in alongside him. All I wanted now was to get comfortable, never mind the jolts of pleasure I'd been anticipating, ever since Ted had taken my hand, at the beginning of the evening as we ordered our steak dinner ("walking rare," he'd said) at the Jefferson Hotel, looking at me with ardor, just before he'd poured the wine.

"You okay?" I said, making every effort to mask my glumness.

He kept patting the covers, indicating I should come closer. I obliged, though I had absolutely no wish to snuggle.

"Comfy?" he asked. A quaint midwesternism, I thought—*comfy*—feeling mournful about my dead and gone desire.

Ignoring his question, I turned toward him, and said, "Let me ask you something—Why do you keep her?"

"What, Pussywillow?"

"Yes, Pussywillow, if she makes you so sick."

He was rattling on, something about his loneliness when his wife, Georgina, left with the two little girls, there was only Pussywillow—I braced myself for an onslaught of his self-pity, when he broke off suddenly and said, simply, "I loved her. And since I hadn't been allergic to her before, I thought it would go away. Actually, I get these attacks less and less. Haven't had one for a long time."

How disingenuous he is, I thought, doesn't he know what he's telling me? (I'd learned a thing or two, though probably no more than that, from the Freudian analysts I'd seen in New York after I was well separated from Frank.) As if I give a damn, I thought, about the frequency of his attacks. I slumped against the pillow, prepared to lie awake with jangled nerves till morning.

"So," I said, keeping my voice light, might as well continue to be civil, "did I have the honor of bringing this attack on? In collusion with the cat?"

"Maybe," he said, looking at me seriously. I wished I had a potion that would put him right out, wasn't enjoying this conversation. He went on, "You know what Kinsey says a sneeze most closely resembles? An orgasm. It's nearly identical, physiologically, to a sneeze."

The word stirred me a little. I sighed and smiled. "Very learned. Must be the scholarly discovery of the year."

The flat of his palm was against me, under the band of my underpants. "Take 'em off," he said.

"You take them off," I said. My eyes were closed and I was screening him out, preparatory to enjoying him. "I don't want to work."

I felt him withdraw. So, I thought with an inward shrug, he doesn't like them bitchy.

"Rae," he said, "open your eyes."

I obliged, reluctantly.

"Raise your hips," he said. I did, arching, looking at him with longing, uncomfortably aware of the frankness in my gaze. He was pulling off my panties, gently, seriously, slowly. "Don't play games with me, Rae."

It was said matter-of-factly, without reproach. He was kneeling over me, tentatively; his eyes were very bright. My breath caught, and I took him into my arms.

We lay like that for a while, arms and legs and torsos and tongues pressing, the sheets and the blankets thrown back, the breeze from Ted's vegetable garden coming in through the screened window. I wasn't cold now, dots of perspiration were forming on my body, I could feel them between my breasts.

"Salt," Ted murmured, his tongue in a hollow of my shoulder.

He was inside me, his thrusts were nervous, I thought to slow him down—this lean, tense, compact body, that seemed on loan to me. Ted, I whispered, my heels pressed against him—

"Shh," he said, sounding uncommonly anxious for a man engaged in a pleasurable act. I decided, not having much confidence in his ability to exert any mastery over the dissipating currents of my desire, to contribute a few moans to this enterprise.

But the moan I uttered was so unexpectedly pitiable and had such yearning in it, that he paused—at the same time that I went slack—and he said, in a voice full of tenderness, "*Rae, honey*—don't cry, dear, dear, my special girl."

Promptly, a tear spilled.

"Don't, don't, sweetheart, you've made such a difference to me, I want to make you happy, let me, let me." Then he bent down and kissed my lips, and burrowing down, shyly placed impassioned kisses all over my breasts. "Rae, honey, tell me what to do?"

"You're doing fine," I told him, which infused him with such confidence that—even if it was, in part, a lie—it was worth it. And the unhappy echoes of the word "happy" in my history died away, as he began to do things, and so did I, which left me afterward, as we were subsiding, in a pool of pleasure.

As a way of remaining faithful to Frank, I had been faithless with numberless others. But as Ted held me, spent and making muttering little sounds of gratitude, I thought *I do not want to hurt this man.* I was grateful too; the more adept and generous I became with my body, the more stingy with sentiment I'd gotten. I had a witty sharp tongue that curdled feeling. (*Tell me about happy,* I'd say, stealing a line from a movie, *Nothing makes me sick!*) Increasingly, I'd gotten as little tenderness as I'd given. It didn't surprise me; I didn't expect it. But here was this sweet man, with his arms still wrapped around me. (I used to clock it, the arms would vanish within moments of the boyfriend-of-the-hour's climax; oh, maybe they'd hang around in a desultory way for mine. In a manner, may I say, reminiscent of my mother.) Now many minutes had gone by, and Ted still held me.

"Oh..." I said softly, pulling back a little, taking in the juncture of his thigh and hip, which I kissed.

One week earlier, I'd stood leaning against one of the counters of Valerie Cort's big, cheery ramshackle kitchen, while outside dusk settled and the wind shrieked through the giant trees. Andrew had picked me up in town and driven me out to the farm, as he and Val called it. The reason for its being called a farm eluded me, since I never saw any animals, except for the requisite dog and cat, but I chalked it up to country ways, and let it go. The kitchen was alive with preparation; oils were being poured, condiments sprinkled, water flowed from faucets, and sounds of sizzling issued from the stove. Briefly, I felt all of this activity was in lieu of bathing and oiling and powdering me.

"Ted's been divorced four years now, or is it five?" Val had drawled, while she fixed the salad—Andrew was doing the martinis—"and he's still cautious. You know how divorced men are."

"Uh huh," I said, leaning against the kitchen counter. I was dressed to the nines—in a black skirt whose hem came to an abrupt halt at mid-thigh, set off by a black sleeveless sweater, black ribbed stockings and penny loafers. A coed with a difference. My hair was so tightly yanked back and tied—with a black velvet ribbon—that it appeared to be piled on top of my head. I must have looked like a glamorous crow. ("She's from *New York*," Ted told me Andrew had whispered, by way of explanation. I think about the same time it came out that I was Jewish. There's the concealment factor of *English*, my father's name.)

"Five years," said Andrew, "and maybe she doesn't 'know how divorced men are.' You jump to conclusions." He had gotten up a big pitcher of martinis, which he carried over to the refrigerator and was leaning into it, looking for shelf space.

"Try the top shelf," Val said dryly.

"Her method," Andrew said, with an edge. "Have a whole pitcher ready, so you'll never be without."

"How you run on," Val said equably, gathering up the assorted discard peelings and wan lettuce leaves scattered over the sink and depositing them in the disposall.

As the disposall whirred, and they kept on, back and forth, I noted that everything they said to each other was said with a smile, and it recalled to me the affectionate banter of my parents.

(Annette: *"Don't you dare turn your back, I'm talking to you!" He: "I thought you were finished." She: "What made you think that?" He, testily: "You'd made your point—" She: "Edward—" He: "Two, three times." She: "You! Shut up, you!" He: "It is thee, who must shut up." Sound of door slamming. He, under his breath: "Stupid bitch." She, yelling: "And to think* I *could have married David Sarnoff!"* Or, depending on her mood, a famous Indian mystic, a noted middleweight Jewish boxer, a dashing Arab met in Rome while gazing raptly at Michaelangelo's Sistina, or some movie star like Rudolph Valentino.

When I was very small, and agitated by my parents' openly conducted quarrels, my mother knelt down and, thinking to reassure me, explained that the worst of spats were always repaired when the participants went tenderly to sleep with each other, in the same bed, like two dolls. My mother was very beautiful then, she had piercing blue eyes, and a wonderful, deep enveloping voice, and I was mesmerized by everything she said. To this day, Slavic voices, husky with music, go right to my soul.

My Dad was from the South and sometimes had a drawl to show for it, though he'd lived in New York City, with my mother, then us, for many years. I thought he had, as a human being, special definition, though he went around in life as the tip of the iceberg. Marvelous iceberg, marvelous tip. He died, unforgivably, when I was sixteen. I forgave him; I just never forgave whoever, whatever had allowed it to happen. I believe he died of some grief. I didn't know what it was, but it never left him and it never left me.)

And now, feeling almost as sacrificial as the food, I was listening to Val's gravelly voice, flirting, placating. She was the first woman I'd trusted in a long time. I sensed that she loved me, that I filled some need for her (her twin daughters were away somewhere and rarely referred to), and it helped that she was not beautiful. Though I found her ruddy weatherbeaten face, with its crinkly smile, lovely in its way. Her directness, her way of listening to me, to Andrew, her seeming unflappability and humor were very individual. Rock solid. She'd been an Army brat who'd lived all over. She had a drawl.

"Rae?" Andrew was saying, "Did you ever date a divorced man?"

I'd never told them, not even Val, about my marriage. My mother and Marta were, between them, the repository for that erased chapter of my life. I almost never thought about it anymore.

"Not for any length of time," I lied glibly. (It wasn't something I really considered a lie; since I'd erased a portion of my past, it was necessary, of course, to invent it.) "A good friend of mine did, though; the guy ended up going to prison."

Val's gray eyes were alive with interest. "Wonderful. What did he do?"

"I think he embezzled some of his firm's money," I said with a laugh, getting into the spirit of the entertainment.

"Did she date him before or after?" Andrew inquired briskly.

"Before, I think. He was in rotten shape after his divorce, though I think she really cared about him and she helped him pull himself together," I yattered on. "But prison was too much. She couldn't see herself being faithful—"

"To a felon," Andrew concluded cheerfully.

"That's right," I said, grinning back.

"Look, honey," said Val, "Ted is a very sweet guy who's been badly hurt. He wouldn't harm a fly."

"Something must have made Georgina fly the coop," Andrew said easily, at the stove, stirring one of Val's cauldrons.

"We don't know anything about it," Val said, "except that Georgina was a very restless girl."

"She means promiscuous," Andrew said, pointing with his stirrer for emphasis, while gravy dripped on to the linoleum.

"I didn't say that. I've never said that," Val murmured, taking a swipe with a paper towel at the spots on her floor. "She was intellectually restless. Wanted to go off and get another degree."

"Oh sure," said Andrew. "So she became a vegetarian and went off to live in an adobe hut outside Santa Fe—"

"Oh, I don't think an adobe hut. She took an apartment."

"And those two little girls—" Andrew rattled on—

Valerie broke in, "—whom Ted rarely gets to see—"

"He sees them once a year, in the summer," said Andrew, "The rest of the time they live with their batty vegetarian mother."

Listening to Val and Andrew go at Ted and Georgina with relish, two things, simultaneously, began to occupy my brain: The first was that Iowa City held a richness of gossip, it was a staple activity, owing its rare vitality, I felt, to the fact of there being in those days just two movie houses, and only two television channels (occasionally, when the weather was clear, three), and to the fact that you were somehow stuck there. People needed to use one another for entertainment. The nearest good restaurant, I'd been told when I arrived, was several hours away in Des Moines—and though you could walk the mile to the airport, and the bus station was around the corner, and the train passing by in the night made the houses shake, you couldn't get out of town.

That was all right, because I didn't want to. I'd been places and I had nowhere else to go.

The second thing was Ted.

When I came to Iowa City in the fall, until I met Val, I'd been sick, you see, with loneliness; I thought I might die of it. The fresh start I'd planned loomed as a false move, and I went around with a certain dread. I'd had an adventure or two in my life, I'd risen to arduous occasions, but this had never happened to me before. Far from being an adventure, it was a stoppage: I was unknown, you see, in a place where I knew no one and no one knew me. I wouldn't have told a soul, even if there had been anyone to tell, but I began again to have nightmares, I hadn't had them since Frank and they were not about Frank. One in particular kept recurring—I'd be by the phone, my hand, sweaty, clutching a piece of paper with a pencilled list of names and numbers, old friends all, they were supposed to be, though their names were unknown to me, and I soon found that they'd never heard of me either and wouldn't talk to me. They'd say, *Sorry, my husband has just left me, and I'm lying down; I can't talk to you, I'm about to swallow Clorox bleach #2; I can't talk to you, the goat's loose, I have to tether the goat.* The excuses would vary, but the refrain was the same: I can't talk to you. I grew maudlin (inwardly—of course I never showed it). No one to tell me I looked nice, or didn't, or that I looked well, or not. It was so hard. With no one to reflect me back to myself, I began, childishly, to miss my mother, and my sister, married now and living on the west coast and expecting a child of her own. I missed the men I hadn't loved. In Iowa City, they weren't there for the easy plucking. Everybody was young, even my fellow Workshop students were younger than me, most of them by a good five years, and older was the one thing about being first-born I hadn't liked. Thirty years old, old, older than God. My only contemporaries were married faculty, exempt from the shames of age and solitude. I felt I was in solitary confinement in a woman's prison, my solitude was so thick I could smell the dampness of the cell's cinder blocks in my small over-furnished rented room. From the chill of the walls, I'd get bad sore throats. It was in this condition, which I was adroitly masking (a habit I'd had plenty of chances to practice in my coming of age) that I met Val and then Andrew—and at their cozy house two months later, I let my defenses slide a little, a calculated risk. Val and Andrew both sympathized lavishly, but it was Andrew who was moved to action. "I'd like to say I thought of it," Val told me on the phone, "but it was Andrew. The guy is divorced, he's been alone for four years now. An assistant professor in Andrew's department, he teaches the Bible. Nice, and rather cute. About thirty-five. Andrew said, 'Have her to dinner, have Ted too, let her sit in front of our fireplace with her legs crossed'—Andrew likes your legs, you know, he is very pious about them—'and look him over.' So would you like that, honey?"

I said yes, of course, and with alacrity. He'd be here, any minute, the only eligible man in Iowa City, they'd told me, and a nice man too. Ted Gobisch was his full name. (Perhaps not as elegant as Chase, my married name, which the instant the marriage was over became repugnant to me.) But Ted Gobisch was, I was picking up from Val and Andrew's cross-currents of interchange, still living with shades. And how was I going to feel about a man who lived in his past and so openly?

"She's gone far away," said a crooning voice. Val went on to say, "You can set the table, if you like, child. The plates don't all match, I have just discovered, but it scarcely matters."

"A martini, kiddo?" Andrew asked amiably. He was snapping his fingers, for some reason. "Get a headstart?"

"It's a lovely thought," I said, crossing to the cabinet to take down Val's dishes, "but no thanks. I think a headstart might muddle my head."

"She needs her wits about her, Andrew darlin'," Val was saying. "Place mats, honey," she said, handing me an assortment. "Choose the ones that best match the plates."

"You can tell my wife is an official hostess, can't you," said Andrew, fondly.

For a moment I saw the formal drapes, the elegant table illuminated by candlelight whose flicker made the newly polished silver gleam. The easy, well-scripted chatter of guests, men and women with white hair. I saw Andrea and Nye Cowan. I saw a face framed by brown hair well teased and sprayed, and a thin body zipped into a tight off-white brocaded dress, giving a fine aristocratic hint of cleavage, and I saw Whit Chase, the host's brother, taking it in with approval.

"Wait," said Andrew, "until she starts slinging the grub." His bass voice had resonance. I couldn't place his cultivated accents, exactly. They reminded me of some movie star's playing a great orator—a politician, maybe—he could assume them at will. His voice and speech were his assets; supple instruments, they gave him his charm, they certainly served him as chairman, and in his own kitchen, in shirtsleeves, commandeering at least half of the cooking, he could be downright hilarious.

I was laughing with abandon, I thought.

But Andrew, looking at me, said, "You know, you have such dignity, Rae. Even giggling like you are, you're contained."

"Don't make her self-conscious," Val said mildly, mopping her brow with a tissue. "Now, where is my lipstick?"

"When she declined my offer of a drink, she was regal, you know?"

"Andrew, dear, take her into the living room and sit her down by the fire. You look fine," she said, turning to me. "You don't need to freshen up, do you? Go on."

Andrew's arm was around me, it felt nice, sturdy and protective. I sat on the sofa. The fire was lit; he stoked it. I was reminded of no other fire, my brief fugue state was behind me. (I had such lapses from time to time, even monitoring myself closely, and I learned simply to accept them by forgetting about them.) The smells of food were in the air, delicious, and I relaxed.

I heard the car pull up, the fire crackled and gave off heat, and I heard Val open her front door.

"Hi there, Teddy!"

I heard a response, something that sounded like a yodel, Yoa! Oh!, and a stamping of feet, Val laughing, "Oh come on in, Teddy, it isn't even snowing."

"An icy wind, leftover snow, I'm warming up, I do believe you live at the North Pole. Good evening, Andrew."

"Come in Ted, we've got a guest and a fire. Say hello to Rae English."

You see, it couldn't have been more auspicious. He came in, ruddy from the cold, slight, wiry, wearing horn-rimmed glasses. Very like a grown-up bookworm. It made him slightly absurd, a youthfulness, almost a juvenile quality, that didn't appear professorial, a tense slicing of the air with his hand, a laugh that could be too loud. But he was friendly, and attractive in his way.

As he sat down, awkwardly, Val gave him a tray of cheeses to balance on his knee. Introductions were performed, and I reached across the cheese tray to shake his hand. "Writers Workshop, huh?" he said, with a sort of racy grin.

I nodded, demurely.

"I don't think she's into that," Andrew said.

"Into what?" I inquired.

"Oh, the Workshop has a horrible reputation," Ted said.

"It has an excellent reputation, I thought," I said. "Best place for writers, they say."

"I don't think Ted's talking about that," said Andrew. "Ted's talking about wild parties."

Ted nodded, and smiled at me; he *had* meant that.

"Oh," I said. "I wouldn't know. I haven't been to any."

"Count your blessings," Ted said. "Have some cheese."

Where were all these cliches coming from, I wondered, biting into a cube of cheddar. Count your blessings. I was doing some comparing: Ted's immediate predecessor had been a neurologist, rugged, brilliant, cold, a man of few words—but when he did talk, what he said was original, and that was extremely pleasurable for me. We'd ended things some months before I came to Iowa City. I didn't love him any more than he'd loved me, but we'd been companionable, connected sporadically, for a long time, dating others—*bedding them, you mean, said Marta acerbically, shortly before she became engaged*—then trying not to, trying in the last few months to be together. Early on, all night on that November 22 when President Kennedy died, I'd sobbed in his arms, and that grief—he'd cried too—cemented things, as much as they could be cemented between him and me. But who knows what lay behind the floodgates that the murder opened in us separately? We may have been weeping over other deaths, the annihilation of our idealism and youth, but I'd mourned those things before, and his youth and whatever prior losses he'd had were different from mine and different to mourn. And three years later when we broke up for good, I was relieved at first—no further need for the pretense that we had things in common. And then, to my surprise, I became depressed. For the first time since Frank, I couldn't summon the wherewithal to hunt up another stranger. I was twenty-nine and didn't like it. I went to and from my job—I was assistant to a dean in the college where my father had taught—and to and from my apartment. I did my exercises. I ate salads. I wrote at length in my journal about celibacy. I spent a lot of time with my sister, who had fallen in love with an assistant professor of botany at the University of Washington in Seattle. And as their courtship got underway, I tried to coach her. I was successful; she was an apt pupil, Marta. I think the idea that Marta would be moving so far away gave my mother a lot of pain, but I was occupied with other things like wondering whether I'd ever have anything in common with anyone. I wrote in my journal about that too. And my sister, meanwhile, was occupied utterly with Keith Benedict.

On one of these ordinary evenings, I got home late from work and on an impulse, phoned a neighbor who did haircuts. Normally, I'd let it get as wild as possible, and then drop in at a cheap hairdresser on a side street near where I lived for a bargain cut. "Chop it off," I'd say. When Rhoda rang my bell, shears in hand, I said to her decisively, "Chop it off. I want it short."

"That beautiful hair of yours?" Rhoda said. "You want to look like a boy?"

"Yes," I said. "It would go with my name." Growing up with the name, I was sure people without seeing me took me for an abbreviation or a boy.

"Nothing doing," said Rhoda. "I'll shape it." Then she added, "I wish you'd get over him."

"Which one?"

"You know which one," said Rhoda. She meant the neurologist, but skipping Frank entirely, I suddenly, with an ache in my heart, thought of my father.

"What would you think about my getting married?" I put the question to Rhoda, who was, with her shears at work, studying the shape of my skull like a phrenologist.

"To whom?" she gasped. "Someone I know?"

"Perhaps," I said, cagily. (Hadn't always been cagey. Thanks, Frank.) "Actually," I said to Rhoda, coming clean, "there isn't anybody right now. But I've begun to think about it. Hey—my hair looks nice."

"I know," said Rhoda, patting it.

I had begun my new, ordinary life stoically, then, discovering that as a free agent—owing nothing—I had access to the extraordinary pleasures men could furnish. So I gave myself permission to go from Frank's to other beds and felt myself, in nights of convulsive couplings, to be an outlaw, a sexual subversive. But now, with my cruel and intelligent doctor gone, I found myself unable to want a successor, and I knew that for me, the ordinary life lived alone would be a slow death. From now on, it wouldn't give me what I wanted. I wanted to stop being an outlaw. I wanted legitimacy.

So here I sat, miles away from the origins of my resolve, facing an animated stranger named Ted Gobisch whose gaucherie didn't significantly undercut his charm.

A number of topics were being reviewed, as accompaniment to Val's several hearty courses: Ted and Andrew, for our amusement, held forth on what to do with the lone Jewish student in the department who had recently announced intentions to convert to Catholicism and become a priest. His mother had written Ted, whose Bible course she held responsible, an angry letter, and his father had written Andrew.

"Ridiculous!" Ted was sputtering, "She made it up out of whole cloth. I teach the Bible as myth, as metaphor. I also hint, as you full well know, that my bias, if I have one, is agnosticism." This was said with relish.

"Agnosticism," Val snorted, "more like a fanatical atheist, Teddy."

Ted looked pleased. "Well," he said, piling some salad on my plate—"You do want some, don't you? I thought so,"—then helping himself.

"Still," Andrew said, with a put-on dourness, "the family could sue us."

"You don't mean it," said Ted. I cringed imperceptibly (as they say, at least I hoped it was imperceptible), then told myself it didn't matter if more elegant expression was beyond him.

"They can claim we converted him, in the guise of offering a literature course," mused Andrew.

"Dammit, I teach the Bible as literature!" said Ted. "Isn't it clear that a young kid who wants to go to seminary is having problems with sex?"

"Perfectly clear," said Andrew resoundingly.

"Don't holler, folks," said Val, presiding over her table, "There'll be plenty of time after dessert."

"Over after dinner drinks," said Andrew, looking at his wife, who had taken possession, at her end, of Ted's bottle of wine.

"What haven't we covered?" Val asked. "Rae, can you think of anything?"

"The contemporary application of *The White Devil*," I said, "Who really wrote *The Spanish Tragedy?* Who was with Jean Harlow the night she died?" Ted was looking at me with admiration, I noted. I was set to continue, when he interrupted me.

"An English major."

I nodded. "Barnard College."

"Phi Beta Kappa, I'll bet," said Val.

"Yes," I said, modestly, feeling grateful to Val. In my family, it was not a novelty, so no one boasted. My father before me and Marta after wore their keys. I'd put mine away with my ring. My mother had been denied membership, we were all given to understand, because she had matriculated at a Swiss university where the provincial honorary society had never been heard of.

"I'm impressed," said Ted.

"Thank you," I said. His candor was kind of sweet.

"What do you write? Fiction? Poetry?"

"Fiction," I said. "I don't know a thing about poetry."

"She knows Edgar Allan Poe's *The Raven* by heart," said Val.

"And she can cook!" Andrew said, with mock wonderment, thinking to undercut his wife, in case she might be going too far.

"I'm not much of a cook, in fact," I said.

"Andrew, Shh, *shhh!*" said Val.

"Don't put her on the auction block, Val," Andrew chided.

"Shh, Shh," Val went on, as if she were pacifying an excitable puppy.

"Let me help clear the table," I said.

"Sit still," Val ordered. "Andrew will help me."

Andrew rose, sheepishly, winked at Ted or me—maybe both—and with some semi-scraped plates in hand swiftly followed Val into the kitchen.

"I think your chairman might be in the doghouse," I said, thinking to be sassy.

"I can't imagine Andrew staying there for long," said Ted.

"I can't imagine Val keeping him there for long."

He looked at me in an amiable, distracted way, and said, "So do you write short stories?"

"No. I'm working on a novel."

"That's ambitious," he said morosely. Something in him was being banked. What was it?

(The intelligence came from Val, at a later date: "He has a contract to publish his dissertation. All he has to do is make some changes, and he's put it off for about seventy years, since Georgina left."

"Why?" I inquired, there being no precedent in my family for such slacking off. "Demoralized, I guess," she told me. The message to me, I gathered, was to put it right. Woman's work is never done.)

"It's a challenge," I said, giving him a full smile and showing some dimpled knee. "The short story and novel are really very different forms," I went on, learnedly. "For me to write short stories now would be ambitious. I have my heart in this novel." Saucy tilt of head, to ward off his noticing threadbare heart.

"Uh huh," he said. "Are you going for the Ph.D.?"

Ah, I thought, he doesn't listen; questions were popping out of his mouth at a rate exceeding my ability to answer them. "I'm supposed to be a Ph.D. candidate," I replied in measured tones, hoping a deliberate pace would simmer him down, "but I don't know that I'll do that." I decided not to mention to him that I hadn't come to Iowa City to improve my mind. "That's what's nice about the Writers Workshop. They leave you alone."

"Nice, if you want to be left alone," he said, giving me a look. "You teaching as well?"

I nodded. "I'm a T.A. Do I sound teacherly?"

"Teacherly," he repeated, looking at me as if the candy he'd been helping himself to had an unexpectedly different flavor. "I guess you do."

I registered that it was not clearly a compliment.

"What's your novel about?" he now wanted to know.

"Families," I said, lightly. "The happy kind and the other kind. The family is the original political unit."

He laughed, then asked me something else.

—Yes

—No

—I don't really miss New York

—Manhattan

—Yes, born there, really.

The midwest, Iowa City and environs in particular, were fascinating to me, I lied at one point, why I'd even driven with Val one day out into the country to see the Amanas and their refrigerators. I remembered: the flat outskirts of the city, as we drove along, and the creeks at low tide that looked like swamps. It looked as if I had stumbled into time itself, the edge of the world.

I had stopped listening to myself sometime back, I'd felt muted, as if my answers were coming from the bottom of a well. These conversational forays with this new man were tinny; I was accustomed to deeper registers. Even the colors of the room seemed stripped. But as I glanced up, I saw the unguarded sweetness in his face; he seemed to be looking at me with trust. (More than once, the analysts I'd dropped in on in the last checkered decade had suggested that I was a snob, someone who thought herself too fine for ordinary experience and ordinary men. Did I think happiness was to be found with the charming phrasemakers I was hooked on? Hadn't I learned anything from the rottenness of my extraordinary early marriage? Didn't I know that charm was compensatory, a strategy to mask flaws? Even though I knew my mother and sister would not have concurred, I would accede to this notion now and again, especially in the aftermath of rapier exchanges with this man or that which drew blood.)

I heard merry sounds from the kitchen and Val and Andrew returned bearing dessert.

"You baked!" said Ted, happily.

"And she did it all by herself," said Andrew, uncovering something marvelous looking that steamed and was redolent with a fragrance of warm fruit and brandy.

Covered with a mound of whipped cream that Val had spooned on to it delicately, it was handed to me and then Ted. We smiled at each other and dug into it with our forks and spoons.

"Eat, children," said Val, "you both deserve sweet things."After dessert, after the brandy that had been baked into Val's idiosyncratic version of brown betty, brandy was served straight. I sipped, slowly, feeling the warmth that had begun in my throat spread through my chest.

"A thorough jerk," Andrew was saying contentedly. He and Ted had been in some kind of colloquy.

"Anybody I know?"

"No, honey," said Val, rocking, holding the pussycat in her lap and looking soft and feline herself. "They're talkin' about a cherished colleague."

"Pablo Richter, a hotshot poet," Ted said, looking at me pointedly, "and if you don't know him, count your blessings."

"And stay away from him," Andrew advised, sitting back, puffing on his pipe and looking richly amused.

"I will, I promise," I said, fervently. I was leaning forward, my skirt was hiked up well past mid-thigh, and various knots of hair had long-since worked loose from my ribbon and were curling across my damp and flushed brow. "What's wrong with him—what's his name—Richter?"

"Right," said Ted, "you must have the answer to that before you make rash promises, mustn't she, Andrew? So tell this nice girl what's wrong with Pablo Richter."

"Shh—Shh," Val was shushing them, her lips were pursed primly.

"Valerie, my darling, what is this hissing about now?" Andrew was looking at her quizzically.

"You don't really *know* anything," Valerie admonished. "This is all speculation."

"Oh, for God's sake," Andrew exploded. "One hardly needs police blotter evidence—"

Ted broke in, "Wasn't Susannah's breakdown evidence enough?" Turning to me, he added, "Susannah was his first wife."

"His *only* wife," Valerie said. "Boys, don't play so fast and loose with your facts."

"Only wife," snorted Ted, "what about that common law situation?"

"Oh, rumor—" said Val.

"Rumor," said Andrew. "I can give you chapter and verse about who it was and where they did what."

Valerie said, "And I'm not so sure Susannah had a breakdown."

"Really?" inquired Andrew.

"What would *you* call a suicide attempt?" Ted put it to her.

"It can be a perfectly rational act," said Valerie calmly, setting the cat on the floor. "Andrew, darling, where is Fergus, do you know?"

"I don't know where that frigging animal is," Andrew told her. "More brandy, anyone? Rae, honey?"

"No, thank you," I said, demurely, suddenly aware that anyone sitting at almost any angle away from me and minded to could probably see up my skirt. I did some smoothing of skirt and hair.

"None for me, thanks." said Ted.

"Andrew, honey, please take a look around for the dog. I haven't heard his crazed barking for at least an hour, and I am worried." She didn't sound worried, she sounded as if she were shooing us home. I cast a sidelong glance at Ted.

"Okay, okay," Andrew was grumbling. "Just let me get into my jacket, will you?"

"The dishes, Val," I said softly, "can I help you?"

She looked at me as if I had just earned honors in criminal stupidity, and in tones of deep reproach replied, "No. No you cannot."

"Come, young miss," Ted said, holding out my coat. "I'll drive you home."

"Oh, and please keep an eye on her, Teddy," Valerie implored. "She can be so flighty, that one, just a little girl from a big sinful city lost among us good honest folks in the midwest."

We were at the door. I braced against a bitter wind.

"I found the dog!" Andrew yelled, from somewhere around, and then he and Fergus, a mixed-breed with the overall demeanor of a basset hound, appeared in the moonlit snow. "Fergus, hold still, or I'll feed you to the chickens." Some mournful, credulous barking.

"Our dog," Valerie said, with a long-suffering sigh, "has such a low IQ. He believes everything your Chairman tells him."

"Don't we all, honey," Ted said, giving her a kiss. "Thank you so much, G'night now, G'night."

"Such a wonderful time, Val," I said, hugging her. "Splendid evening, splendid dinner."

"Yes, well," said Val, "don't embarrass me, you're both so welcome. Drive carefully now, Teddy."

He had taken my arm, Ted, as we made our way across the snow toward a beige Volkswagen. "Here's my buggy," Ted said with a certain breathlessness, holding the door open for me, "Okay now? Wait, let me throw that on the back seat. Okay, now." I slid in, shivering.

"I'll get us warm in a minute," he said, getting in on his side. His teeth were chattering too.

After a moment, we were bumping down the Corts' driveway. "Ice," he muttered. "Look over there," he said, slowly pulling on to the road, "see that ugly shack over to your right?"

I made out a shadowy structure, framed by the snow and the nearly pitch dark sky. "I see it," I said. "What is it?"

"Pablo Richter's place," Ted said, as it passed from sight.

"Is he really as bad as you all were saying?" I asked.

"He eats screwed up young women of all ages for breakfast," Ted said. "Yes. Really as bad."

"Does he do it over there, in that house?" I whispered. It all seemed so innocent, somehow, a wicked witch (male, as it happened) out of Hansel and Gretel, living off in the woods somewhere, eating babes. Since I knew none of them, it had the character of some other child's bad dream, and I could nibble at the story's edges, it being no more real than a gingerbread house.

"Here, there, everywhere," Ted said. "He is rarely zipped into his pants."

I felt a little dart of lust at the thought of the filthy things Richter had done and was doing all over town. How did he find time to write poetry?

Ted, turning the corner on North Linn, drew up in front of my house. At once, my landlady's light went on.

"Oh God," I groaned. "Mrs. Gillette. I'm going to *have* to move."

"What have you got, a little apartment?"

"A room, and it was hard enough to get. I rented it by mail before I got here. I didn't know I'd have a live-in landlady and a moat."

"Well," he said, anxiously, "don't be too quick to move out. It's hard to get a decent place around here."

"I know," I said, refusing to think of the places I used to live. I was looking at him hopefully, planning to mount no objection to a deep, goodnight kiss. "I'm settled in here for now. I have a hot plate."

"The girl who has everything," he said, looking at me with a certain melancholy. "Try to think of this as your suffering for art. Come on—I'll walk you to your door. Will that rouse your landlady some more? Does she pack a shotgun?"

"Probably," I said. We climbed the porch steps. He extended his hand. I shook it. "What a good, firm grip," he exclaimed. Our words were whispered. I didn't tell him my handshake was second-nature, that I'd been schooled by an expert.

"I'll call you," he said.

"I'll look forward to that," I said. I flashed him my best smile. From inside the window, Mrs. Gillette's iron goose-necked lamp cast a narrow arc of light.

He stood for some seconds, squinting at me in the half-dark of the porch. My muscles felt knotted; I became aware of a dull soreness in the small of my back. I was very tired, I knew. I saw him move toward me in the shadows. He gripped me, he pulled me away from the lighted window to the side of the porch, we were against the railing, he wrapped his arms around me, there was a shudder in my knees, and as he kissed me I heard the whimper of an animal, and then I became helplessly engaged by the active movement of his tongue, it muffled the cry, and I held on to him, aching and dumb with pleasure.

When he released me, I saw his smile. He saw mine too. (Unique to our species, as they say, along with the foreknowledge of mortality.) "Very, very nice," he said tenderly. His finger brushed against my cheek.

"Yes," I said, gently; I stroked his hair.

He pressed me to him again, briefly; he sighed, "Oh my."

He did call, two days later, explaining to me that this was Ted Gobisch, remember? We'd met at the Corts. Of course, I said, laughing. He invited me to share a steak dinner with him downtown at the Jefferson Hotel on the coming Saturday night. I'd be delighted, I told him. I blurted out, "I really love red meat."

"Glad to hear it," he said dryly. "You'll have to eat your vegetables too." I had a powerful sense of a big indulgent smile.

Tip of the iceberg. Still waters run deep. The family is the original political unit.

What can I say? He made me feel at home.

So it happened that on a Sunday morning in Iowa City, I awoke to find I had not been sleeping alone. Ted Gobisch, propped on an elbow, was looking at me and apparently had been doing that for some time. Seeing me stir, watching my eyes open, he drew me to him.

Odd, how the body has the hang of intimacy. I'd been instructed by an amazing master of pressures and thrusts but the master was long gone and I still knew how to lie in the arms of someone I'd just met as if I'd known him all my life, and be amazed.

My body ran the length of his. I felt his muscle and bone, I felt his hair. I swallowed. He kissed me, just above my right eye. His beard abraded my face. That would show. Good.

The sun was very bright through the curtains, and I closed my eyes. I didn't know whether I wanted to go back to sleep or have him make love to me again. I hugged him tight and waited.

"Good morning," he said, softly. How civilized.

"'Morning," I mumbled back, and opened my eyes. He was half-sitting up now, curved over me, our bodies were no longer in full contact. With the result that I not only was naked as a matter of plain fact, but felt naked, a less simple fact. I maneuvered down under the sheet.

Ted said, "I bet you're hungry."

"Yes," I said, half-smiling. "That must be it."

"Why don't you jump into the shower, and I'll fix breakfast. You like pancakes? French toast? We don't eat meat in the morning around here."

I had thought we'd take a shower together. Well, goes to show, don't leap to conclusions, don't judge one lover by another, remember that you're new in town, strange to the local customs.

"Either would be wonderful," I said, with reference to the French toast and pancakes.

I got out of bed, taking the sheet with me, and standing, I wrapped it around me like a toga.

Ted went to the closet and pulled out a robe. "You'll want this," he said, handing it to me. The fabric was pliant, the color, a dark red, gleamed. "I'll get you a fresh towel," he said, and left the room.

I dropped the sheet and put on the robe, whose caressing softness on the skin brought to mind my childhood; out of old habit, I patted it with my palm and fingertips, a woolly toy.

I stood under a pounding shower and washed the smells and acids of intimacy away. Stepping out, toweling myself dry, I noticed Ted had no talcs or perfumes around; some of the gentlemen I'd known kept a supply for visitors like myself, making the place seem quite like a hotel. That Ted made no such provision was interesting information.

I slipped on the robe and, emerging from the bathroom, I was greeted by the inviting smells of breakfast. I heard the screen door open and close, probably Pussywillow being shooed out, and Ted appeared in the hallway and handed me a dried flower. "Ted. Thank you."

"From my garden, last summer, best I can do," he said. "Come."

"I thought I'd get dressed," I murmured, looking at the preserved blossoms.

"No, no," he said. "Everything's ready. Come."

And he led me into breakfast.

"Last night," he said shyly, regarding me across his nicely set table—

"Yes?" I was pouring maple syrup from a pitcher; my eyes were lowered.

He whistled.

I looked up and was about to laugh (my ribald throaty laugh), but he was looking so utterly vulnerable and solemn that I reached across for his hand; the thing, for him, wasn't about mirth.

"I didn't know I could—care—for anyone again, after my wife. But—and this doesn't have anything to do with her—I find myself—"

"Ted," I said, swallowing, feeling full of compassion, but also unnerved. I *hadn't* cared for anyone after my husband, I'd made a pretty good career of not caring. And here was Ted, who scarcely knew me, declaring himself and I felt I had to stop him. "Don't," I blurted out.

Instantly, the look of trust on his face vanished, and though we were to become very much more bound to each other, that look never returned. It was as if I'd told him I'd come directly from someone else's bed to his—or that I'd best be going, there was another bed for me to occupy waiting just across town.

"Ted," I said softly.

Were there tears in those eyes that wouldn't meet mine? "You don't have to say anything," he said.

"I had a good time too," I said, wanting to repair the damage, not sure why I was feeling quite so culpable, nor why my lip was trembling.

He laughed, his nervous, mirthless laugh, and taking hold of some plates rose from the table. "It was," he said, with a kind of ruefulness, "pretty high-voltage bliss. Georgina's words," he added, by way of explanation, and went into the kitchen to do the dishes.

Nice touch, that reference to the ex-wife. I'd been about to take my place at his sink, but as the water ran, and suds were being produced—the sounds indicated that dishwashing and cleanup at Ted's place were a major production—I thought, dammit, dammit, what am I doing here amid his domesticity and skeletons, and biting my lip in a fruitless effort to stop what was happening inside me, I thought of the ex-wife and her bounty of two small daughters and began to weep soundlessly. Three minutes or so of this, and it seemed stupid. (The evidence, moreover, pointed to the absence of a comforting hug, all very familiar. Cut your losses. So what if you were shown the two girls' photograph to admire last night?) I took up my napkin, blotted up my tears and blew my nose hard and went in to assist the new boyfriend (or whatever) in the kitchen.

"Ha," said Ted, setting the hot water on spray and turning it up full steam. "I've improvised a manual rinse cycle. Not so dumb."

"Not so dumb at all," I said.

He turned, and blinked at me through the steamed lenses of his glasses. "You been crying, or something?"

I nodded. "Something."

"No, don't," he said, "It makes me feel so bad. Rae, honey, don't, come, let me show you my garden."

I was wondering how that was going to be accomplished with my bare feet and snow on the ground.

But he led me on to a screened porch. "See over there," he said, pointing. "In the spring, you'll see." He grew tomato plants, peppers both green and red, and bell-like radishes. And then there was his flower garden. He went on, eagerly, to tell me about it. He liked to grow things.

I said, "You're so open."

"She didn't think so," he said, looking at me. "She thought I was a closed-off sonofobitch."

I felt the brief blast of someone else's ugly marriage. Determined to be spared, I said, "Please, Ted, let's not talk about her. Not this minute, okay?"

"It upsets you," I added.

His expression softened. "Tell me," he asked me gently, "why were you crying?"

"Oh, I was envying Georgina," I said lightly, with a practiced little shrug and smile.

"No, no," he said, "Don't do that. Not her. You're nothing like her."

"Not to worry, I'm completely over it," I said briskly. "I better get dressed, and get home."

He looked at me quizzically. Increasingly ignorant of the customs of the natives, I was testing. I knew about morning surliness, and the recoil of a lover unwilling to acknowledge that anything special had taken place the night before, and I knew about a morning's refreshment of passion too. I remember waiting, standing barefoot and chaste in Ted's robe, my toes curling against the cool linoleumed floor. "Don't do any getting dressed and going home yet," he said, taking my hand. He led me then into the bedroom, he undid the belt of the robe, he kissed each breast, devoutly, as a church bell rang somewhere, and as I began to sigh and shudder, he pulled me on to the bed, where we grappled, at first sweetly, and then with powerful, fierce effort.

For a while, afterward, all I could hear were the merged sounds of our hoarse, spent, jagged breathing. My heart was beating very hard. He had cried out that he loved me, loved me. His pleasure had astonished him so.

What an awesome act, I thought, one could die of it.

"Must you leave?" he asked me, at length.

"I don't have to," I said.

"You'll spend the day with me, then?" He was ardent, eager.

I nodded. "Stay there," he said, "don't move." Naked, he went to the window, opened it a little and drew the curtains so that daylight came in. "I'll be right back," he said, throwing on a pajama top. I lay waiting, contentedly, and then, chilled, I reached for his robe—it had been flung at the foot of the bed—and slipped it over my shoulders. The sun was bright, and I could almost see the vivid colors of the garden as they would be in spring and summer, the green of the surrounding grass; I'll be here, I thought, and I'll kick off my shoes and the blades of grass will yield under my feet.

He came back into the bedroom, and as he sat down beside me, I saw that he held a fat, succulent tomato. "One minute," he said, and began to rub it gently with his pajama top till it shone. "Let's get it clean," he said. I waited, expectant. Then, he stroked my cheek, and held the tomato to my mouth. "Here," he said, "Take a bite."

I laughed. "Ted, it'll drip on your beautiful robe."

"Eat of the fruit," he said.

Its juices were sweet on my tongue.

Chapter 3

Border States

So his arms enfolded me late into that Sunday, as a smoky, frozen twilight supplanted the cold brightness of the Iowa City day. It was as if I'd crept into a painting or frieze, as still as the girl ('unravished bride of quietness') on Keats's Grecian urn. I felt cradled—a cradling I hadn't known since Early Frank—and before that since sometime back in the Pleistocene Era before Annette, my mother, stopped crooning *Rockabye Baby,* and down I'd come, cradle and all. This was a comfort surpassing even the waves of pleasure still lapping at me from the lovemaking we'd concluded, Ted and I, a few hours before. I wanted to spread over this shy and generous man the warm and fuzzy blanket of my gratitude.

Except that I had no idea of how to go about that. I sighed. Ted started, and asked instantly, "Are you okay?" Was he *always* this jumpy?

"Of course," I murmured, "I'm just drifting…drifting," I murmured. "Sorry." The moment called for a light kiss. Offered; accepted.

Then Ted said, "Just don't drift too far."

I'd have to learn to mask my bouts of inattention better, so that he wouldn't feel deserted. "What about you," I said softly.

"What about me," he broke in, with a corrosive little laugh.

"Where've *you* been."

He said, "Georgina," and added, "I've been far away too. Thinking about her." He flinched.

"Tell me about her," I urged him, proud that in the last twenty-four hours I'd scarcely thought of Frank at all (let alone any of the others). "Sorry about this morning—making you stop." It was true; I was. "I know your talents better now," I murmured, wondering uneasily as I said it if it wasn't something I'd read somewhere or lifted from another bed.

"She was very, very pretty—and sexy too," he said, rising from this bed with surprising swiftness. "I'll show you her portrait." I pictured an oil painting, with its face long ago turned to the wall. But he began rummaging in a drawer and unearthed instead, from under some socks, a photograph, handsomely mounted, of a well-scrubbed wholesome-looking girl with a cloud of neatly combed fine hair and a knowing faraway look. She was giving the future the melancholy look of someone who already knew none of it was going to happen. I could have been looking at myself.

"She *is* pretty," I mumbled, disappointed not to be contemplating something more like the picture of Dorian Gray. Turning, I saw Ted's eyes still fastened on her, filled with pain. "Give it to me," I said, softly, "give it to me," and reaching for it, I took it out of his hand.

"Now where do you want it?" I inquired. Standing half-naked before his open bureau drawers, picture in hand, I riffled dexterously through his things. "Under your shorts, socks, where?" He laughed nervously.

"You do that snooping very well," he said. "You would make a good spy." He was looking me up and down with an alertness I took for admiration.

I went on: "Where? Should I take it away with me? Toss it?" I persisted, "Just tell me where."

"It doesn't matter," he said, grinning, watching intently as I lobbed it into the drawer and slammed it shut. Together, we scrambled back onto the bed.

His hand glided along my knee, first one, then the other, reverential and solemn, as if he'd played a part in the fashioning of this miraculous arrangement of sinew and cartilage. "She was promiscuous," he said abruptly.

"Oh," I said, making a little hissing sound that could have been mistaken for disapproval. I said, "Go on."

"Now?" he asked and his hand became a fist; he must have thought I meant about Georgina.

"No time like the present," I murmured decorously without skipping a beat, shifting my weight onto one elbow and chastely sitting up.

"I don't think there was a significant faculty bed she hadn't slept in," he said.

"You knew?" I asked, shifting uneasily.

"Yes."

Then in a muffled voice, he said, "Well, maybe not Richter."

Then, warming up, he went on, "She moved out and took the girls with her. We were married exactly five years."

A crease formed between his brows. "Let's see, she could have been sleeping with Lars Olmstead then. Or was it Duane Wheeler?"

I leaned over, a little clumsily; my lips grazed some hollow of his shoulder. I knew about Lars Olmstead (whose class I was taking); he was a local writer with a notably knotted up and glacial style, who'd headed the Workshop until last year when he'd gone on leave after winning some prizes which sewed up a long-sought national reputation. As a student, it was his reputation I was drawn to. I was no slouch when it came to hanging out with celebrated men, though Georgina also seemed no minor leaguer. "Who's Wheeler?" I wanted to know.

Ted said, "Then he was a hotshot resident in Psychiatry. After that, Chief. He's doing some fancy research now. And he still sees a few handpicked upper-echelon regular patients, at the hospital and in a private practice. I guess he's made quite a stir."

"She slept with both of them?" I was feeling a certain grudging respect.

"Georgina likes them flashy," he said.

"What kind of research is he doing?"

"Something government-funded on pedophiles—child molesters. He calls it 'dirty work'; he makes house calls at prisons." Ted's hand lazed in the hollow between my legs.

"That's who he treats," he said after a while, "Some well-heeled academics and a prison population. I think Georgina's drawn to outlaws. She's reckless enough to find all that exciting."

At least Georgina's outlaws didn't go to prison themselves.

"Sometimes I think Wheeler's still gunning for me," Ted said wistfully.

I said, "Why would he do that? After all, *he* wronged *you*."

"That's exactly why," said Ted. "That's the way it works. Some people—like Wheeler—are very good at disliking the people *they've* harmed."

He went on, "Besides, who knows what Georgina told him about me. I know she poured stuff into his ear. And she has a rich imagination."

"Lies?" I asked, hoping to sound horrified.

"Well," Ted said, "let's say embellishments. Or exaggerations." He sighed. "I guess the affair ended when they realized I'd found out. Our marriage broke up, she left town, so he must resent that. He probably thought he'd had a convenient arrangement. Sex with no strings—You'd think a brilliant psychiatrist would know it doesn't work that way." His voice broke.

"Was it okay with her? The 'no strings'?" I asked quietly.

"Who knows? Maybe it was," he said. "By that time." He shook his head.

"How in the world," I asked him, "did Georgina get mixed up with someone as nice as you?"

"I don't know," he said ruefully. "Something in the barometric pressure, the stars, the constellations. Something unlucky, I guess." He paused. His declamatory style had loosened. "She wasn't knowingly looking for trouble. She was a virgin and I was pretty puritanical too, which suited her." His voice had thinned; for a second or two decibels hardly seemed to be registering at all. "One of those late fifties, early sixties upbringings. You know—Nice girls wait until they're married and all that."

I allowed as how I'd heard something about such quaint antediluvian assumptions, nodding twitchily and making some squeaky sound, all the while trying to banish the memory of Frank on our wedding night, gazing in triumph at the flecks of blood on my thighs. ("Terra cotta thighs," he'd murmured approvingly, studying them.) I had the eerie feeling of being elsewhere, even though I lay alongside Ted on the bed, saw and heard him, was cognizant of being conscientiously patted and touched. I felt one of us at least—if not both—was all alone. Okay. Even if our common bond turned out to be a shared capacity for self-erasure, wasn't that better than nothing? "She ended up," he was saying hoarsely, "flat on her back, in this makeshift two-by-four apartment, sick as a dog, a sick, shaking puppy, with two badly frightened little girls."

What a badge of failure, a comedown, this represented for a late-fifties, early-sixties girl like Georgina, like me—two quaking untended children, and a sick, unruly dog. Hadn't Jacqueline Kennedy said at the beginning of the new decade that if you fail at the job of caring for husband and children, nothing else mattered?

"So I'd go over there everyday and bring groceries and take care of her and cook and clean for her and the girls."

"And feed the dog," I added softly, to round it off.

"Nope," he said, puzzled, "there was no dog, it was Georgina, Georgina was sick as a dog." He was blinking owlishly, shaking his head over the pale joke of my misunderstanding. "She had pneumonia." Modestly, he said, "I nursed her through that."

"Oh," I said, "How nice..." I felt a sigh forming deep inside my chest.

"And all those luminaries she'd been surrounded by—that circle of studs—were gone, of course." He paused. "From the beginning," he said, "I should have known." He looked at me; his eyes were bright. "After our wedding, we went directly from the Church to the mausoleum to lay her bridal bouquet before her father's urn."

"My goodness," I said, awed as much by Ted's telling of it as by the thing itself; he was becoming bardic. "Georgina did *that*?" But it sounded in fact like the extravagant or melodramatic sort of thing

I could have done, part and parcel of my own genetic inheritance, though I'd learned in my selective and spotty way to rein it in.

"Let's quit talking about her," he said abruptly, and leaned over and began intently to stroke my hair. "It's so long, so long," he said, sounding wistful.

"And snarly."

"No, no," he said. "Shh..." he whispered soothingly. I resisted a passing impulse to shake him off and yielded to his tense caressing hands.

My hair was rebellious, brown and wiry; when left unattended for twenty minutes it fell into untameable knots. When I was growing up, in its nearly chronic disarray, it served chiefly as a reminder of my stubbornness and defeats. But Frank, my politically aspiring husband—then the Speaker of the New York State Assembly—knew about the campaign uses of good looks and loved it; he asked me to let it grow long and I did; he encouraged me to see it through his eyes, I saw how dramatically it photographed, it became my trademark. Over the course of an evening's gathering, of politicians, idealistic civic leaders, others, at the house in Albany or our apartment in New York, bobby pins kept falling out of it; Frank would collect them after all the guests had left. One by one, he'd pick them up methodically; he called them my trail of breadcrumbs. *"Catch you in a minute," he'd say, as we passed each other, going to and fro along plush carpets, and then he'd go into the bedroom, place the pins on the night table for the morning, and get undressed and wait for me.* The cause to which he'd pledged himself, his energies and resources, was Civil Rights. He made it sexy. Not only for me. People were drawn to Frank. Throngs. In the aftermath of these evenings, my idealism and my desire were fanned interchangeably by his ardor. I was remembering when he first confided what lay in his political stars: the governorship—and beyond. His current office—the Assembly speakership—was only a stepping stone. He was shooting for the top, he'd told me. That meant the presidency. (Allowing, of course, for a minimally decent number of years to pass. As presidential candidates go, he was, after all, still young.) *Would you like to be First Lady, my darling?* he'd murmured, as believable as he was handsome. I'd said, *I've I always wanted to be first.* It was on the eve of our wedding, my dress was beautiful, and I was charged with the excitement of appearing in it, stepping for this deeply desired ceremony into a widely refracted public light. As he told me about this, talking about the nuts and bolts of it, tactics, strategy, timing, I nodded, but I wasn't there, I'd leapt into my future, where I saw the succession of Frank's inaugurals, and saw my mother, wan and admiring, an aging figure who though much diminished commanded respect; and my sister—with that impish look in her eye but with her overall definition blurred as she stood beside some doleful academic who, trapped in Frank's shadow, looked rumpled and shapeless. It was not only the Republicans who'd been defeated.

Hell with it, I thought, coming back to the doleful academic now lying beside me tenderly and earnestly stroking my hair. Why summon after all this time the twenty-year-old girl I'd been, vintage Snow White, standing beside her latter-day prince in a place where Disney flowers opened coyly, their petals spreading for pollen, with cartoon birds and chipmunks chirping and chattering against the backdrop of Frank murmuring to me about love, the governorship and Civil Rights. It had seemed so real. The only thing real was Frank's disgrace—and I was to go to any lengths to keep it from becoming mine. (For starters—I resolved not to have his baby—after visiting him in prison—when I knew I would leave him.) He'd come a long way from our wedding night in four years. He'd been diverting contributions from the civil rights organization he'd founded—to his campaign fund and, also, for his personal use. It was called mail fraud, a federal crime. He'd executed it so smoothly, he must have thought no one would notice; after a while he must have kept it even from himself. They came with handcuffs in the middle of the night and they manacled his hands. He was indicted and the year after that tried, convicted and sentenced to jail.

I'd been blissfully ignorant of all of it, eyes averted while playing house, daydreaming about how wonderfully my marriage combined glamour with virtue, with my husband an amalgam of Adonis and Martin Luther King. I was, I believed, becoming saintly by association, standing pretty as a picture at Frank's side while he performed his good works. I'd come a long way too. A ruined Snow White.

"Oh Ted, she was a fool," I said.

"Who?" he asked.

Reddening, I said, "Georgina, who else?" and put my arms around him.

"Wasn't I the fool?" said Ted.

I hugged him tighter; he took it for *no*, my answer and, shuddering with relief murmured in a drawl I'd never heard before, "Dear, sweet thing." Something at once familiar and remote had crept into his speech. Another register, an altered cadence, no longer regionless and nondescript, it was a voice of smoke and honey, liquid and inviting, and I wanted to disappear into it. I whispered urgently, "Say that again."

"Don't pounce!" Ted said, playfully, giving me a swat. "Will you settle for the generic *honey?*"

I breathed, "Where're you from?"

"Does it matter? I've been in Iowa City a long time."

"Tell me."

"I'm from Kentucky, dear, sweet thing, a border state," he said, explaining that it had been riven by divided loyalties during the Civil War, and went on absently murmuring something about my hair. "Lovely, dark," I heard, "... Swell tangles."

"My father was from there," I said faintly. "Kentucky. He used to call me Rae of light."

"Rae of light," he murmured, "Lovely," he said.

(One day, when I'd been mourning the catastrophe of my name, my father drew me with ceremony into his study. There, standing some distance away from me, his elbow propped against the bookcase—he told me that my name was associated with the light and that it was good. My initial—R—was one I shared with his friend, Ricardo; and before that, he murmured, he'd had another friend, a man named Roger. This was before I was born. R, he repeated, as in are, the verb to be. You want to *be*, don't you? I whispered, I don't want to *not* be. He was facing slightly away from me, but I saw him smile with his eyes. Instantly, I felt a radiance conferred upon me. He began to call me "Rae of Light.")

"Rae of Light," Ted repeated, drawing back like Edward, my father, his lips brushing diffidently against my hair.

Between the two of us, supper was somehow gotten together. Steaming, inviting plates of pasta were carried on tarnished trays (leftover wedding presents) from Ted's kitchen to his small dining alcove. I did my part, finding condiments, doing a salad. Ted, meanwhile, went on doling out segments of the story of his life.

"So then I went to Louisville Male High School and graduated from college and then the Korean War broke out and I started applying to graduate schools to avoid the draft. A lot of guys did that, you know." His mouth looked slack; he was even stuttering a little.

Promptly, I said, "I don't blame you, it was like Viet Nam is now, a lousy war. I think it was just fine to stay out of that war," I went on coolly, dispatching in the same breath Frank Chase, decorated Korean War hero. I no longer trusted war heroes, or any other kind. Lying beside Frank in my long-ago and shelved life, I'd wonder at the untroubled innocence of his face in repose, after each day's hectic scramble. I'd try to imagine—never quite making it—what he must have looked like in combat, returning enemy fire, grimacing and clenched. Not until he went to prison and I went to visit him there for the first and last time did I see the look on his face I thought I'd been seeking, the look of someone afraid for his life, stunned, as if it had been just brought to his attention that he was already dead. I moved on quickly and, by the time I left him, Frank wasn't news and neither was I. Now, eager not to jump conversational tracks, I said with vehemence, "Every one of you who stayed out of that war did the right thing. Why get yourself killed or wounded or come home warped?" In fact, I'd long since decided that Frank's character had been ripe for warping, and that Korea had had little or nothing to do with it except to delay it, but that was a detail and I was long past bothering myself with inconvenient facts.

"You're very understanding, aren't you?" Ted said softly. He'd evidently been misconstruing my regularly scheduled lapses of attention, misled by my own carefully nurtured brand of eye contact, the rapt gaze.

"I try to be," I said modestly, as I began to stack plates, a prelude to getting up to do the dishes. He rose to help me and we found ourselves in a domestic do-si-do, following each other, back and forth, gathering, scraping and rinsing, between the dining alcove and his kitchen. "I'll wash," I said, donning an apron, probably one of Georgina's, another fifties relic.

Handing him a dishtowel, I tuned out, then in again, in time to hear him announce wistfully, "These days sometimes I wish I'd stayed in the insurance business."

This was startling to one who thought she gravitated naturally only to born high achievers. "The insurance business?" I inquired lightly.

"Life insurance. The family business. It's what I was doing when I quit to go to graduate school."

Had he told me this before? "You don't really miss the insurance business," I said, "do you?"

"It had some of the excitement of gambling," he said, thoughtfully, considering it. "The customer bets he dies, the company bets he lives. No, I don't really miss it. I like *this* life, a college teacher's life. I'm basically lazy, you see, and," he went on cheerfully, "I hate risk. But I don't want to cause trouble or make waves for the department—I don't have tenure."

According to Val, tenure merely awaited the long-delayed publication of his dissertation (on an early twentieth century mystic whose treacly writing had caught on, one of Ted's heroes; my impression was that he was a cut or two above Kahlil Gibran). Andrew had been very patient. But we weren't talking about that, it appeared, in case I thought I'd found the opening wedge for a campaign to nag.

Ted's eyes were lowered, his voice had dropped, he spoke intently and confidingly to the floor. "I don't want to let on to Andrew, but I'm afraid that student of mine, Simeon Levey—the Jewish-Catholic convert—is really screwed up and could be trouble. His parents think he's a boy wonder; they *could* sue."

"Levy," I said softly. "That was my mother's maiden name. My mother is Jewish, my father isn't." I paused. "Wasn't."

Ted wanted to know how, in my mother's case, the name was spelled; so we cleared that up and then he said shyly, "I never dated a Jewess before."

I laughed nervously. "I'm only half of one."

"Sometimes," he said, "I think I'm only half of something too. Does that make us less of what we are or more? Do you think," he asked, "that two halves might make a whole?" He looked at me quizzically. Abruptly, he said, "There's something I want to tell you—something I've been keeping from you—I don't want to keep anything from you—"

I wanted to say, *Don't—please, whatever it is, don't tell me, I don't want to know.* But he so clearly wanted me to know—something. For some reason he'd taken my telling him about my mother, that she was Jewish and I was too, as a significant mark of trust. I braced myself for whatever I might hear, hoping that it wasn't something weighty and awful like membership in the Ku Klux Klan or being treated by Duane Wheeler for pedophilia. "What is it, Ted?" I asked him gently.

"Korea," he was saying, "I ended up there after all. I volunteered—I was a paramedic."

"Oh Ted," I said, drenched in relief, taking his trembling hands into my own. "Is that all?"

"I don't like to talk about it, what it was like there," he said, as if he hadn't heard me. "When you've seen a whole bunch of people gravely ill, when you've seen a whole bunch of people die—"

"I know," I said, though the people I'd seen die had all been my father.

He went on, "They died lots of ways, in Korea. Many people died of pneumonia—fifties penicillin had to be accompanied by bedrest and you can't do that in a combat zone. They died of undiagnosed appendicitis—or blood poisoning. Pneumonia. That's how I was able to take care of Georgina." He shuddered.

"Ted—" I said, interrupting, hoping he would stop—his words had been halting—but he didn't.

"Then—another time—the Red Cross trucks were distributing donuts and coffee. I was in charge of it—I'd gotten something to eat—I don't even remember what it was. I was talking to someone. I don't remember his name. You know, in the course of things I'd gotten to know the indigenous troops, and the prevailing attitude toward them was 'Gunga Din' but this man had been educated here, he spoke better English than I did. There were these moments of calm and we were talking—I was relaxed, amazed, joking—then the racket began, the shelling from the air. I didn't think we were in danger, not immediate danger, anyway—and all at once I was covered with blood and I looked and most of his head was gone. It was arterial blood spurting. And the donuts were still there."

"Where?" I asked, horrified.

"In his hand," Ted said, looking down at my hands, which were holding on tightly to his, as if I could hold him together.

"Oh my dear, that's so good, how come nobody's snapped you up before this?" he said, looking at me gratefully, and muttered, "What are you doing, still single?" and said again, slowly, as if each word were a separate sentence, "Your good firm grip."

"I've had lessons," I said, releasing him. The instructor had been Frank, the subject, how to become a national leader's wife.

"What do you mean?" he said, urgently. "*Tell* me, honey?"

I bit back the impulse to ask him if that was the generic honey he was using, flooded by what I felt as his rush of concern. I shook my head. "Nothing to tell." Embracing him, pursuant to this lie, I said, "I'm trying to take in what you've told me. Let me take it in." I added, "And trust me. I don't have a past."

In fact, it had become easier and easier to jettison the past. Its leading man, Frank, was offstage in a federal prison, serving out a sentence of five years. He was in a minimum security facility, with amenities—lawns, geese, tennis. But he was sealed off from the general population and I could blot him out too, if I made the mistake of remembering him.

Ted, meanwhile, was still enjoying gloomy retrospection of his past, making some pronouncement about the toxic properties of love. Silently, I began composing a pep talk, to be delivered in installments, featuring myself as the antidote, confident that my powers of enchantment could sweet-talk him into a future.

Chapter 4
Barbecue

The day after Halloween, when the last of the tricker-treaters had gone shivering back into their homes, the Iowa City weather turned disquietingly balmy. I had bolted my own door mid-evening. Too many small hands reaching out to me for candy. But the unseasonable warmth had gravitational pull and I, among others, began pouring out of doors.

Students (graduate students in particular), pleased to be liberated from cramped digs, strode around town lugging books and skirting mud-puddles, the residue of the frost. On North Linn, I walked to and fro, over wet, fallen branches, between my place and Ted's. These meetings were beginning to happen predictably, approximately once a week. We'd spend the night, perhaps two, which extended into a loungey, sleepy day, broken by occasional entwinings. There was something courtly and old-fashioned about this, our encounters and the spaces between them—stately, even, a kind of minuet.

When I wasn't seeing Ted, I devoted time to refining my exclusive preoccupation with him. Valerie (my only confidante) one day asked me, "Are you starting to love him?" I shrank from that. I wasn't up for feeling that kind of need, for him or anybody else.

"No," I said. "I don't do love," I said firmly. "It's one of the things I don't do."

But I liked that I had a lover. I liked that very much.

And so, on one Indian summer November afternoon, I waited in my room for Ted to come and get me. He was escorting me to something called a pig roast he'd been invited to just outside of town.

I had taken considerable pains in getting ready for this new, bucolic kind of date, but hearing Ted's familiar step on the stairs, I got cold feet. My last, hasty glimpse in the mirror had shown me a jittery vision in clinging jersey black slacks, and an orange top that clung too. It had a Halloween boldness I liked, a come-and-get-me look, camouflaging the intriguing possibility that I could be a spider. I'd given a quick ten minutes to my hair, nabbing stray curls with pricey bobby pins (Rhoda's going-away present to me), then pulling out two or three hairs that were coarsened and gray. It was a practice begun by my mother, Annette, when my marriage to Frank (fallen prince of New York politics) ended abruptly, crushing her hope that she might one day be mother-in-law to the President. (I'd filed for divorce while he was in jail. I didn't think white-collar crime was so different from the other kind. And wasn't that mean!) My mother would look at me, worried, brow furrowed, eyes searching, searching, as if removing these flaws could eradicate all others. She'd spot the gray hairs on my head and lunge.

("I'm packing a weapon, Ma," I protested the first time she did it, trying to pull away, "so cut it out. Mother? Find another eccentricity—Please?" She smiled and went on plucking.) I pulled out the bobby pins, tugged my hair this way and that, then as Ted knocked, replaced them and went to the door and, with my scalp aching, complained that the idea of a pig roast was too barbaric for me.

"A pig roast—revolting—sounds like the LBJ ranch," I said with a shudder. Vietnam was in the news these days, and though the passage of the President's Civil Rights bill had flooded me with a bittersweet joy (briefly, I took it as a validation of the belief I'd had in Frank), I joined enthusiastically in the gathering denunciations of Lyndon Johnson. At the mention of his name, I'd wring my hands and roll my eyes like everyone else.

"Don't be stubborn about this," Ted said equably. He contributed a further observation. "You know, sometimes you are hard as a rock?" His fluency in cliché was something I was finding more and more endearing, predictable, a comfort.

"That doesn't sound so sexy," I acknowledged. Occasionally Ted was perturbed with me, but his exasperation seemed wholly bred of affection—and his fault-finding to date had missed the point so profoundly that I could have loved him (if I loved anybody) for that alone. If he thought he was getting to know me, he thought wrong; and I was happy to let him think wrong. I knew I just *looked* stubborn. I had become, in fact, deeply malleable. True, I gave certain convictions strong voice, but my politics shifted less with changed reality than with fashion or the politics of whoever I was seriously sleeping with. Mostly, I'd gone for Democrats—like Frank, eloquent and ambitious, with the holy fire in his eye; or the neurologist, whose politics and party affiliation were, I gathered, conferred at birth; and now Ted, whose humanity and idealism were, I decided, byproducts of good character. I liked the generous and unaffected way he cared about people, about me; I liked his steadiness. The sincerity of his lovemaking stirred me; compared to his predecessors, he was refreshingly unadroit and I took his fumbling and hesitancies for authenticity.

"Besides, honey," Ted was saying, "you look so nice, and you did get all dressed up for it. No, it's *not* too dressy for a barbecue, not at all." Then his cheek was pressed against mine. "I just want you," he murmured, "to like my friends."

For a long time, nothing matched a melting tenderness I felt for Ted, even after I became sure that, though he didn't know it, it wasn't me he liked—it was my coverup of hair and clothes.

Perhaps, I thought, looking into his earnest face, I *could* learn to love barbecues. I'd learned to be flexible ("silly putty," the neurologist had dubbed it) in most of the other areas of my life. (I'd learned, for example, to shift gears from possible future First Lady to current felon's ex-wife.)

Ted went on, coaxing. "It's one of the things we do here. It's fun. Yes, Val and Andrew *will* be there." Ah, a drawing card. Val: my touchstone, our guardian angel. He must have seen my face light up. Encouraged, almost jaunty, he went on, "You'll meet our other solid citizens. And," he added, looking at me hard, "let's get some solid food in you. You're skin and bones."

I wasn't sure I liked that, it made me aware suddenly of my too small breasts, to which I tried to give no thought at all.

Thirty years ago the grownups were pushing strained pears—now it was meat.

It was true that pig roasts were a staple Iowa City entertainment. That I had never been to one was an oversight that, up till now, had scarcely troubled me. This one, to which Ted and I now drove over endless stretches of road, with the river on one side and flat farmland on the other, was being held on Lars Olmstead's ranch on the outskirts of town. Lars, my novel workshop teacher, recognized me only when he saw me with Ted. The occasion for his hosting this gala (entailing what I thought would be the on-site execution of an innocent pig) seemed to be nothing more than the out-of-season spring, the melting snow. Anything is cause for celebration here, I thought grimly, the puddles, the mud. Ted said cheerfully, "We're nearly there!" and proceeded to give me a final briefing, repeating things he had already told me or that I already knew. Lars, our host, the sometime Director of the Writers Workshop (and former, not so secret bed-partner of Ted's ex-wife Georgina), had recently returned from a leave he'd taken to finish a novel about duck hunting.

"Did he finish it?" I asked Ted, as we pulled into the long driveway.

"Yes," Ted said, so gloomily I felt sure he was thinking of his own book. About Georgina, Ted was forgiving. I had other things on my mind, like the fact that Lars Olmstead, in his workshop section, seldom connected my name with my face, let alone my writing; that had begun (I told myself) to be fine with me since, more and more, each time before I went, I'd contemplate not going, and in fact was going less and less. I had, actually, just the other day stowed a working draft of *Persephone in South Dakota* in the back of my closet and heaped it over with shoes. I'd given it to Lars, he'd pawed through its pages, and handing it back to me several weeks later, reported, smiling, that he had nothing to say. I took it from him, gingerly, and slunk back to my room at Mrs. Gillette's.

After that, on cursory re-reading it displeased me; there was a mustiness in the interior life of the heroine that seemed to pervade the whole book; it read like something out of Edgar Allen Poe; and I was beginning to suspect that the writing life made me less marriageable, moody and hard to be around. Ted, who had not read it, said he doubted that Lars felt all those things, doubted that he'd given it that much thought.

"What he thinks," Ted said to reassure me, "is that you're pretty and sexy. That tends to drive everything else out of his head."

A sixties compliment and, then, a child of my time, I accepted it gratefully. But afterward I took to brooding. I wondered if Lars had been not so much tongue-tied as offended, perhaps repelled. That he'd seen something in my novel's psychic scavenging like carrion, something no one was ever meant to see. If something had slipped into my novel in a code someone like Lars could crack, even intuit, it was a good thing the book was in the closet before it did any more damage. And I took care to forget about class. My truancy, I told myself, was in the service of the larger public good.

When we arrived, Lars was nowhere to be seen; he was out in the woods shooting birds, accompanied by his literary disciples—five or six male graduate students having in common, Ted explained, their admiration for Lars' work, which they praised extravagantly. It hadn't occurred to me to do that. Naively, I'd been waiting—and waiting—for Lars to praise me. Until this recent whiff of *Persephone* had stung my nostrils and driven me to banish the book to the closet. Where, I decided, hiding behind a remnant of my (formerly photogenic) sunny smile, were it not for Ted, I would just as soon join it. I reached for Ted's hand.

"Wait right here, honey," he advised, disengaging apologetically. "I'll go scout out a friendly face." And he was gone before I could protest. I didn't like being left, I preferred to do my own leaving.

I looked around. Valerie and Andrew were nowhere to be seen. I wanted Valerie the way I'd once wanted my mother until, prudently, after too many years of trial and error, I got over it. I recognized no one; I was standing there alone. Too bad it wasn't feasible to run away from this now, this ranch, my unfinished book, this half-baked town. I was enveloped by the smell of cooking flesh, the pig, roasting somewhere; one could almost hear in the air the echo of its squeals. My knees locked; my feet seemed soldered to the earth.

I thought of how free I'd felt, after Frank, first noticing other men, knowing I could embrace someone, more than one, how I did that, vengefully at first, then brimming with indiscriminate affection, clasping with my whole body, nudging with my hips, my mouth. Until one night, eleven months ago, when the neurologist—the steadiest of them—made a vise of his hands against my head. Take your hands off me, I said, and then, to my surprise, we were both crying. I stopped before him. What's in there? he said. There's nothing there. It's over, I said, as airily as I could, so that he wouldn't hear my voice cracking. Don't worry, he said, I'm out of here, but he came toward me. Made of tin? he said, his ear, then his palm against my chest. Try to resurrect something real in there, he advised. I shook my head. I rather like being called tin, I assured him, drawing up my knees. He smiled. That's a nice long shot of your haunches, he said. I told him that hadn't been my intention. I rocked myself back and forth. When he was dressed, he came over to where I was on the bed. Cupping my chin, he waited two, three beats, then kissed my forehead. I thought that was pretty despicable. (I'd raised my face, my mouth had been open, saliva had gathered, he must've known.) He was looking at me intently. I swallowed. Don't cry again, I said lightly, I may rust. I guess you'd better be careful, he said, putting his set of my keys on the bureau near the door. You better lock up after me. His stethoscope, his black doctor's bag, were in his hand. I locked up after him, and whatever it was, it wasn't tin. To hell with him, I thought, pulling on a pair of mended pajamas; and I turned out the light. Which stayed out till Ted, who through some kind of dumb luck, cared for me.

Now where was he? Vanished into one of the clusters of guests dispersed about the grounds. I looked uneasily around, and saw a mass of uncultivated land, where the levels shifted unpredictably, with bare earth punctuated by spikey weeds and people milling about. One man, whom I vaguely recognized as a disheveled member of the Workshop faculty, a poet, stood talking and waving his arms at the center of a semi-circle of enraptured young women, by a table heaped with platters of food. Gravy from the baked beans was dripping down his torn undershirt.

From time to time, I'd see a bloody thing streak down from the sky. The sky was overcast; the guns reverberated like thunder, as first one, then another, the creatures fell to the ground. I stood there, dazed and queasy. Gravy; blood. My head spun.

Wheeling around, I caught sight of Ted who, with a steady step, was chugging back up the hill. He made his way over to me, accompanied by a large woman, who turned out to be Lenore Olmstead. "Lars' wife," Ted told me with a kind of pleased distractedness, as she warmly pressed my hand. I had already been identified, it appeared, as the new girlfriend. (Val, when I asked her what one wore to such occasions batted her eyes delicately and sniffed, "Lenni will be wearing a dirty dress, with real pearls." She wasn't wrong.)

"Have you seen," Lenni asked me, "our piece de resistance?"

I felt an odd kinship with her. Her broad palm was on the small of my back, nudging me. I turned and there it was, the pig, rotating on a spit in the ground with the apple propped in its open mouth making its expression quite cheerful. I looked at its narrowed eyes, to make sure it was dead.

When I turned, Lenni was standing too close to me. "I've read your book," she whispered. I could almost feel her breath on my neck. Behind me was the barbecue pit, with its hissing and crackling; I could feel the heat of the fire on my legs. "Is that horsey girl from New York the Persephone character?" Lenni was asking.

I nodded.

"Is she *you*?"

"Oh, no," I said, with a modest, friendly shrug, "I haven't been kidnapped lately. And my mother was done with looking for me long ago."

"Well, don't worry," said Lenni, jovially, "We won't offer you any pomegranates!"

I was glad, in a way, my book was in the closet, safe from this chit chat.

"It's an *interesting* idea," Lenni said, "a latter-day Persephone. Kidnapped by the lord of the underworld. Torn from her mother."

I had the impulse to ask Lenni if she'd liked it, something it seemed unlikely she'd volunteer, but I thought the better of it and held my tongue. I'd already been burned by expecting something from her husband.

"Of course, you know *why* she wanders away from her mother?" Clearly, she wasn't waiting for an answer. "Curiosity!" she said. "Plain and simple. The child who seeks and challenges and questions goes straight to hell," she said with a perfunctory nod to Ted—who contributed an interdisciplinary observation: "You mean like Eve and the apple and that?"

I glanced at him, satisfied myself that he was neither biting apples nor burning up, then turned back to her.

In a low, confiding voice, she was saying, "You know, it made me uncomfortable, your story."

"How?" I said.

"The pain in it," said Lenni, matter-of-factly.

This was fascinating, even tantalizing. I wanted to hear more, to ask why, to be taken into the heart of her discomfort with my protagonist's wittily articulated suffering; it promised to be a dangerous place. It was all I could do not to ask her to go on. Now she was saying something about my finishing it, was I going to, something about not being sure I should. Her pronouncements sounded faintly medical, somehow not for the squeamish. I had to strain to hear.

"Stop whispering." The man in the torn undershirt had just strolled over to the spit. "What's the big secret?" Looking straight into my eyes, he put his arm loosely about her waist, and said, "poor animal."

"It's roasting nicely," Lenore exulted. "I better go find Lars." She ambled off in the direction of the gunfire; her dusty black caftan was swaying in the breeze.

"I hope she doesn't get shot by some graduate student with bad aim," said the man, meditatively. "All this Hemingway shit. Right, Gobisch?"

"Right," Ted echoed. He struck me as uneasy. Ted had smooth, clean, hairless arms—as a boy he must have looked like one of your natural sissies—whereas the man in the undershirt seemed covered with fur all over, like a monkey. That, along with a set of rippling muscles, probably made it easier for him to scorn Hemingway.

Now he was examining the pig. "The burial pit looks like the *creche*," he murmured. He was looking at me as if he could see a radar screen of my secrets beneath my skin. Maybe he could. Such as my abortion (illegal), just after Frank was sentenced to five years. The doctor, if he'd been caught, would, like Frank, have gone to jail. Rae Chase (middle-initial E.): Jailbait. Fastidiously, I smoothed my slacks. I didn't want to look at him directly, this local Atlas who at any minute I expected would start scratching, but it was hard not to. He was dapper, an eyeful even in a torn undershirt, with his ropy biceps showing.

"I don't recall your name," he was saying, "Have we met?"

Wondering why Ted was wordless and shifting from one foot to another, I extended my hand. "Rae English," I said, with a wide smile.

"Pablo Richter," he said, leaning toward me as he took my hand. For a moment, I smelled his sweat—pungent, not unpleasant, even friendly, familiar.

Ted, thank God, had stopped shuffling. He began—"Pablo's—"

"Of course," I said, "The poet."

Richter eyed me. He asked, "Did you come together?"

"Yes," I said.

"We—" Ted began. He liked the first person plural, it tickled him to publicize us as a couple, to say *we*. If I was sweet on him for anything, I was sweet on him for that. It was the first time with any man since Frank that I'd allowed myself to go public; I liked keeping them secret, hidden in some way even from myself; to this day, when I think of the neurologist, I think of him as just that—*the neurologist*—the man with no name. Ted was explaining to Richter in some detail, getting caught up in the narrative, his hands moving with ceremony and flourish, that we'd met at "the Corts," just a few weeks ago, at Andrew's and Valerie's farm. Richter, standing still as a statue with arms akimbo, had a look of intent listening, one of my own long-standing trademarks, which if he was anything like me, meant he'd scarcely heard a word.

"Well," he said, cordially, exhaling as Ted finally wrapped it up, "Would either of you care to join me in a martini?"

"I believe," Ted said, "I saw some ready-made in an unwashed gallon milk bottle. So I'll pass."

"I saw that too," said Richter. "Lenni's big heart makes the lack of domestic fastidiousness forgiveable." In his manner and stance, he was exuding a charm that in this setting seemed vintage Clark Gable. "The good stuff's in the kitchen," he notified us, pointing down the hill. "Any takers?"

"I'll have one," I said. "Straight up, with a twist. Actually, I have an ulterior motive. If there's a kitchen, there must be a bathroom."

"Correct. I'll show you. Tiresome, every time one comes here, to be expected to pee in the bushes."

I hadn't come with any such expectation. Still and all, there was something exciting about the unkemptness of the local hospitality; it offered bottomless possibilities. As Richter took my arm, I reached for Ted's. But he was walking away, toward some kid, a student. I called out—"Ted?" He kept on walking.

I said proudly to Richter, "Ted has a big student following."

Richter gave me a look. "That one? I know that one. He used to wear a skull cap," he said, with a grimace, bearing down on the word *skull* as if it were some kind of threat.

"You mean a yarmulka?" I asked, lifting the word from my mother's vocabulary. I wasn't sure I'd heard right.

"Whatever,"said Richter.

While Richter fixed martinis, I used the bathroom, thinking he could surely hear me, the wall between kitchen and bathroom was makeshift and thin, and then the toilet didn't flush. I rattled the handle, thinking *skull cap,* what was that about? Had he said it mockingly? I wondered if it had been the kind of careless disdain my mother would take as anti-semitic and track—after all, even people with the most aristocratic manners (like Frank's nouveau-dowager mother) might feel a pig roast gave them license to take their prejudices out for an airing. Unless Richter was Jewish? I couldn't tell—in this denatured, American-Crisco environment people of various stripes took on protective coloration, so as not to appear exotic. Which would explain why the kid, whoever he was, had chosen not to sport a skull cap at a pig roast; in fact, he was, I later learned, Simeon Levey, the boy from Ted's Bible class; he was no longer wearing a yarmulka because he'd become a Catholic, which was why his parents had filed suit against the University. I wondered if Richter knew any of this. Richter was making me uneasy now, remembering how Ted, his courteous behavior notwithstanding, detested him. And wasn't there a coarseness in the mock gallantry with which, preceding me into the bathroom, he'd lowered the toilet seat? A glance in the mirror, hanging crookedly above a sink fashioned for Lilliputians, told me my cheeks were flushed and my hair wild. Shrugging, I drew on my aplomb—the skin-deep but serviceable kind that might see you through a little dinner at the White House. (We'd had to pass on the one invitation from the Kennedys, which had come just as Frank was about to be indicted.) I unlocked the bathroom door.

"Here," said Richter, handing me a glass. "Cheers."

Whatever made me ask for it, let alone straight up? I hadn't had a martini since I was married to Frank and then rarely. It was hot going down, I hadn't eaten since breakfast, and there was a pinging in my head, a too rapid spreading heat in my belly, and an unsettling awareness that Richter was standing too close. "I think we should go back to the party," I said primly. His mouth twitched; he looked amused.

"Why?" he asked, stepping back a bit, the better, I surmised, to appraise me, a new piece of goods. "You were having that good a time?"

"Yes," I said, adding demurely, "I want to check on the pig. It must be fully barbecued by now."

He chuckled. "Right," he said. "I'll just bet you want to check on the pig. I bet you just loved that snap, crackle, and pop." His hand traced in the air invisible dancing flames.

"That is disgusting," I said quietly. And brought forth a practised shudder.

"Oh, have another martini," he said and began to pour.

"Straight from the unrinsed milk bottle?"

"Just drink it down," he said thrusting a filmy glass at me.

I wrinkled my nose. "That's disgusting too," I said, taking it.

"Who're you kidding," he said, "Something tells me you have a pretty high threshold for disgust. *Salud.*" He raised his glass.

"*L'Chaim,*" I muttered. Glasses clinked. Then I said, "You don't know anything about me."

"Just drink it down, Rae English. Swallow. *Swallow.*" He moved up close and put the flat of his hand against my throat.

"Go ahead. I want to feel it going down."

"Don't do that," I said.

His hips teased against me. "Whatever you say," he murmured. He was running his fingers through my hair. "Thickets," he said, stroking. "Nice."

"I've been told that before," I said coolly, unable to pull away, a feral throbbing had begun between my legs.

"Need any help?" he said. He began unzipping my slacks, smiling quite tenderly at the impolite sounds I couldn't believe were coming out of my mouth. I felt like someone in a movie, drunk with pleasure and wrath and gin.

"I can't do this," I said.

"All right," he said equably, releasing me. "Button—or zip—yourself up." He regarded me kindly. "Are you drunk or just a habitual cock-tease?"

"At the moment? Neither," I said, deciding not to compute how much of this was a lie.

"You're taking a breather?" he said. "Be careful. I've been told there's a high rate of recidivism." Casually, he added, "I know who you are."

I met his stare; it was important that he detect no whiff of my alarm. "So what? Who I am is no secret," I said, with the composure that usually accompanied my lying. What was he talking about? What did he know? That I had an ex-husband, a once-prominent champion of civil rights and equal justice for all under the law, who had himself broken another law and was just now disgraced, in jail, convicted of diverting campaign contributions for personal use? Did he know that Frank's passion for justice had been matched by his amazing good looks? and that the two, for me, had come to seem one and the same? Or was Richter bluffing, talking only about a generic me who'd been about to settle for a quickie in someone else's kitchen. (So far, that me hadn't shown up in Iowa City, where I'd been careful to play against type.)

"I've had you followed," Richter said amiably.

All of a sudden I was bathed in relief; this was no more than talk, a gambit to let me know he had a blackmailer's string on his bow.

"What a big waste," I said, "of your time and money." I went on, "Nobody needs to have anybody followed here. There's no place to hide. No one has secrets here. Everyone's life is an open book," I breathed, drawing on Ted's richly unoriginal vocabulary, a signal to whoever picked up on it that I wasn't making my way through life alone.

"You think that?" he mused. "You haven't been here long. Extend your stay and see what happens. What are your plans? There are rumors that you consider yourself too fine to attend class, that you've jettisoned your book because Olmstead said something to hurt your feelings. So—will we be losing you shortly?"

I snapped, "Where did you hear all that?" I decided not to point out that he'd just handed me proof that the town held no secrets.

He said, "From Edith Bucher. The Religion Department secretary. Also doctoral candidate." He spelled her name for me: "B-u-c-h-e-r. It's pronounced 'Booker.' She knows where all the bodies are buried."

"If she thinks she knows anything about me, she's barking up the wrong grave," I told him huffily, adding, "I'm staying."

He asked me idly, "What's the attraction? Gobisch?"

"That's right," I said.

"Really," he said.

"Well, in that case have another drink." And he began to pour. Handing it to me, he said, "For luck. In case you need it."

Against my better judgment (never, in any case, my strong suit), I took it.

"I'm glad to see that you've lost your aversion to drinking from a dirty glass," he said, with a look of satisfaction.

"That's the splendid alchemy of gin. It makes your pain not real."

I had, in the last five years, since Frank, blossomed in a career of making pain not real, mine or anyone else's. My specialty, in fact, was in not feeling it at all, and that with no assist from alcohol, though this certainly was nice.

"Pablo," I said, between sips, "what kind of name is Pablo?" To head off any reprise of our earlier scrimmage, I was keeping him at arm's length. "Pablo," I repeated, making little spitting sounds, to which the *P*, among other consonants, lent itself. Meanwhile, I'd stopped listening. "What did you say?" I asked him.

"I said it's not my real name."

This was a little spooky. "No? Then what is your real name?" We seemed to have glided into some kind of through-the-looking-glass moment; and the replenishment of the gin was making me dizzy. "Ira?"

"As a matter of fact," he said, "it's Edward. Ed."

"That," I breathed, "was my father's name. Did you know that?"

He chuckled. "How would I know that? Edith's good, but she's not that good. But maybe," he said, coming closer, "I am your father's ghost."

For what seemed a long time I stood there listening for the word "doomed," while tapping my foot arrhythmically.

"Boo!" Richter said.

A split-second later, in an altered tone, he said, "What's the matter?" He had grabbed my arms; he was saying, "What's this, a crying jag? I meant you to laugh."

Jerking loose, I said, "I generally wait till something is funny." Now I felt tears that had apparently escaped my attention earlier.

He stooped into the bathroom to fetch something, and emerged with a square of toilet paper, which he handed to me, solicitously. "Blow your nose," he advised. It was, as a transaction, oddly comforting; and like little girls everywhere, I did as he said. "Maybe it's time to see if they're done cooking the pig. You look as if you could use some food. Or is that what they all say?" he inquired, peering at me. "Wobbly?" he asked dispassionately.

"Not at all," I said, trying to muster self-possession as if it were something that I could slip into as easily as a stocking or glove. For a second, he looked genuinely concerned. Was it possible that beneath this quasi-lizardly exterior beat, secretly, the heart of a sensitive man? I was distinctly tempted to find out; but it would probably be prudent not to do that. "It's time to get back to the party," I murmured, backing away from the hand he'd put out to steady me. "Ted will be wondering where I am."

"I'm sure he's been on pins and needles," he said pleasantly. "We all are."

"It's true what they say. You really are," I said, looking at him, "a rather nasty man."

Smiling, he said, "How would you know nasty from not?"

"You underestimate me," I told him. I had patted down my hair, dabbed at the leftover moisture on my cheeks, and announced to myself I was ready for anything.

"You overestimate yourself." He paused. Then, tapping his chest lightly, he said, "You know if you need anything where to come."

"I'm not planning to need anything you could give me."

"You never know. You might. A thirst for knowledge can lead one to some strange places. Besides, I wouldn't believe everything you hear about me," he said. "I just keep the books. Which makes me an indispensable guide in this particular branch office of hell."

I bit back the impulse to ask him if he was reading his rhetoric from a teleprompter. I'd walked through enough real danger, I decided, to take these stagey warnings as sham. I was defiant; if I were six years old I'd have stuck out my tongue. I would, I told him with asperity, take my chances.

"I see. You miss Gobisch," he said. He opened the door with a flourish. "I know what you want—you want to be impaled on a white picket fence. Happy Halloween."

I pushed through it, past him, wishing briefly that there was a magic carpet handy, even some broomstick I could fly away on. I needed air, to clear my lungs and head, and got it. I took deep breaths, in and out, keeping time to the distant sounds of gunfire. So the boys were still at it, I thought, loitering importantly in the shadow of the Olmsteads' house. Then I heard shouts, ringing cries of *No—No!* while an untidy knot of half-a-dozen or so of the Olmsteads' guests sprinted past me. Had someone proposed a field-trip to the squash court? a round of volley ball? I was more than a little drunk, I knew, as I peered meditatively into the darkness. Seeing me, one of the runners broke away from the pack and came racing over to me.

"What's the matter?" I called when I could make out who he was. It was Andrew.

"Is he *hit?*" someone yelled.

"Bleeding!" came the response, echoing up the hill. So—someone finally had been shot. My knees twitched. Andrew was at my elbow, and began steering me back toward the house.

"Go inside," he counseled. He was out of breath.

"I don't think so," I said. Richter was standing in the open doorway. "What's happened?" I asked.

Andrew said, "There's been a fight."

"I bet I know," said Richter who seemed to have antennae mysteriously able to gather information by remote control. "I bet Simeon Levey took a swing at your boyfriend."

"Ted?"

"Yes," Andrew said. "Simeon Levey, the troublemaker with the litigious parents. It seems he knocked Ted down."

"Punched him, I imagine, punched him to the ground," said Richter who, like Andrew, seemed oddly rejuvenated.

"I better go down and see," I said. Richter had already started down the hill. I watched him. He was light on his feet

"Don't go down there," Andrew said in his resonant Chairman's voice.

"Why not?"

"His head hit a rock," Andrew explained reasonably, "or maybe Simeon threw one. Not an uplifting moment for the Religion Department." He went on, trying to soothe me, making low humming sounds interspersed with indistinguishable words, which translated as "not badly hurt", as "don't worry," which made me worry all the more.

"I need to see for myself," I said.

"Let me take you home," Andrew said.

"No," I said and started walking away. There were things I didn't want Andrew to know, including that I was now badly frightened. Andrew called out, "I wouldn't go down there—he doesn't look so good."

"I don't care how he looks," I cried. A lie; when push came to shove, looks were all I cared about. I ran, ran—

To my Gingerbread Man.

And found Ted, sprawled on the ground, looking up at me; little streaks of blood were matting discreetly in his hair. "I'm not one bit dead," he explained nervously. "Just a touch bloodied." He reached for my hand. I grasped it and, kneeling down, I began to croon, *Teddy, Teddy, Teddy*—to say it over and over, as if it connoted something important over and above his name. I stroked his cheek. "If you say something often enough," Ted told me, "you know, it becomes meaningless." He gave me a weak grin. (*Daddy,* I thought, keeping time to an earlier two-syllable word to have come trippingly off my tongue.)

"I'm not going anywhere," I murmured in an effort to stop babbling. "I'm not going anywhere." He hadn't asked me. But I thought that it all went without saying, as if everything had been spelled out in some original conversation, held long ago, which was not necessary to remember. I asked, "Are you hurt?"

"What do you think," he said. He turned away. Following his gaze, I saw Lars, standing some paces to my right; still looking every inch the capable host, he had the boy, Levey, in an armlock. Levey's shirt was torn. On his skinny, hairless arm I made out the tattoo of a cross superimposed on a Star of David. Ted was saying, in his best I-was-a-paramedic-in-Korea voice, "But I don't *need* an ambulance. My head's fine."

"We need to check it out," Lars told him firmly.

"Remember, you got knocked down and kicked."

Levey, still struggling in Lars' grip, yelled, "I did not kick him!"

Ted glanced up at Levey, then quickly looked away. But I kept staring, drawn by his tattoo; then suddenly he spit on the ground. "Jesus," Lars said.

"Where's Andrew Cort? I hope he remembers to call campus security too," he muttered, tightening his hold on Levey.

The boy cried, "I want my lawyer. I'm going to tell everybody what he is."

"Take it easy, Mr. Levey."

"He doesn't deserve to teach in this university."

"I agree with you, we all deserve better. Don't worry. We'll get Professor Gobisch a nice job at Yale or Princeton. Just hold on."

"Call my parents!"

"Professor Cort is making *all* these calls. Just please try to relax, Mr. Levey."

Andrew came back down the hill. "I sent for an ambulance. The President thinks Mr. Levey should be evaluated at the hospital too."

Lars repeated, "The *President*?"

"*Psych* evaluation," Andrew mouthed.

Lars grimaced.

"I'm suing this university," Levey broke in.

"Wonderful," Andrew murmured, looking down at Ted. "First his parents, now him. Just what all we need, another good suing."

Pablo Richter emerged from the shadows. "I see it," he said scanning the horizon, "the ambulance. Here it comes."

"I'll ride along with you, Ted," I said, all of a sudden convinced that it was the nicest thing one person could do for another. (Once it had been done for me.)

"No," Ted said decisively. "We're not going in any ambulance." He was making an effort to sit up. "No ambulance. No."

"Which 'no' is it," I said, in a jokey way, leaning over him, hoping to humor him into acting sensibly, "No to me or no to the ambulance?"

Looking pained, he said, "No to the ambulance." And got to his feet.

Suddenly, Levey was shouting. "Arrest him!" he said, wresting his arm free from Lars and pointing at Ted. Then his gaze lowered; he subsided; he stopped flailing and the agitation seemed to drain away; and, slowly, Lars released him. Standing there, unrestrained, alone, he looked transparent. "What is it, Simeon?" Lars asked, almost tenderly. "What is it?"

So softly we could hardly hear him, Simeon Levey said, "He's a faggot," and for a moment, I wondered if he was going to cry.

"Ted?" Lars said, incredulously. His expression was quizzical, his eyebrows were raised, he shook his head. I suppose he thought the psych evaluation ordered for Simeon could come none too soon. Richter's lip was twitching; he looked amused. Almost at once, Andrew was at my side, murmuring things designed to reassure me and anyone else who would listen, the gist of which was that my presence as Ted's girlfriend, coupled with my sexy good looks (even when bedraggled, as now), gave the lie to this assertion. Everyone seemed to concur that this went without saying. But I hardly heard him. I couldn't take my eyes off Simeon, now weeping soundlessly.

The ambulance pulled up, in fulfillment of Richter's prophecy, with Lenni Olmstead running alongside it, waving the paramedics to their destination; her stained black dress was billowing in the wind. "It's the young man over there," she said breathlessly, pointing to Lars and Simeon, "the one with my husband." Lars was easing a ragdoll called Simeon to the ground, where he sat hunched, his arms wrapped around his knees. From where I was standing it was hard to see anything but his knees. Then the paramedics surrounded him and I couldn't see him at all. They were taking charge—two hayseedy, sweet-looking young men who looked barely old enough to drive. One of them, apparently at Lars' prompting, went over to check out Ted who, standing some paces away from me, was looking more and more his old self—cautiously animated, on the road to recovery from a succession of assaults.

"You see," said Andrew, still beside me, "Ted's *fine*."

"How peachy," muttered Pablo from the shadows; he now seemed more absurd than sinister, just another sylvan clown.

"Over here!" said Andrew, beckoning, as Ted made his way toward us across the patch of ground that had been set aside for triage, and into my arms.

"Let's go home," he breathed, kissing my neck. He held me tight.

"Do you want to wash up first?" I whispered, brushing my fingers lightly over the traces of blood in his hair.

He looked a little dazed. "I guess," he said. "Let's go on up to the house. Come." As he took my arm, Lenni Olmstead came running over. "Stay to eat something!" she said. "It won't be long. The pig's ready to be carved and we're about to serve."

"It would," said Ted, smiling, "be an overstatement to say I'm not hungry. But do feed Rae. She's been through more than I have. Go on, honey. I'll meet you all at the barbecue pit."

The prospect was hardly mouth-watering, Lenni presiding over a gathering of straggly carnivores. But once again she had her hand lodged in the small of my back. It was as if I were captive to the Vulcan mind meld or nerve pinch, both recently inaugurated on *Star Trek*. I was, almost against my will, being propelled up the hill by Lenni, cheerful and panting.

"I haven't seen Val," I murmured, because it was true and because I was discriminating about the women I allowed to lay motherly paws on me; and Val was all of them.

"Such a chaotic afternoon," Lenni said. She gave me another push, "Go ahead, dear. She must be around somewhere." We were nearly at the top of the hill. She looked around, as if her glance, sweeping, could take in vast acreage and there we were, in the center of a convivial gathering, before the barbecue pit. One young man, whom I recognized as a graduate fiction student currently on leave from duck hunting, was brandishing an oversized carving knife. Lenni took it from him, and stepped forward. A couple of other budding literary luminaries seemed to be the pig's self-appointed pall bearers; lifting it from the pit, they transferred it to a large platter and set it on the long wooden table. Ringed by used napkins and half-empty plastic cups, still quietly sizzling, it rested there.

"Carving ceremony," someone murmured learnedly behind me. I turned; it was Richter. "Get yourself a plate," he advised. "You're so hungry you don't even know it. Trust me. You are *hungry*. Paper or plastic?" he asked me, fingering the Olmstead crockery. The carving had begun.

"I don't know," I said. "Either would be lovely. But you're wrong. I am *not* hungry."

"Not even for vegetables?" he said.

"What have we got? Cole slaw? And at room temperature. Baked beans? I'll fix you a plate. You really ought to try some pig. Don't move. I'll be right back."

To humor him, I'd pretend to be hungry. I'd stand there, trying not to look at the party's centerpiece being stripped from its bones. Its skin was tough, leathery, like a rind. The important thing was not to look. I didn't know what I'd do when Richter returned, bearing plates. Something to think about tomorrow at Tara. All of a sudden, at long last, I saw Val, in profile, hovering by the far side of the table, and excitedly began to push my way over to her. Even when the ground was level, the land dry, it was hard to maneuver; this terrain was an obstacle course; great distances yawned between Point A and Point B. "Excuse me," I murmured sweetly more than once, and then, catching sight of Andrew, I called out, "Val!"

Lenni looked up and put down her knife. She said quietly, "Val couldn't come. Didn't you know?" she asked.

"I just saw her," I said. *Footsteps,* I thought, *I hear footsteps,* going into Ingrid Bergman mode while Charles Boyer, in Lenni's persona, was assuring me there were no footsteps.

"She couldn't come," Lenni repeated. "Have you had anything to eat? My instructions from Ted are to feed you. Now don't tell me you're not hungry."

"Pablo's bringing me something," I muttered dispiritedly, wondering why it was so easy to persuade me that the Val I'd seen had been a mirage.

Pablo reappeared and, with him, food, deposited, slapdash fashion, on a plate; it looked as if its placement had been facilitated by a shovel. Resolving to stash it as soon as I could under some tree or out-of-the-way bench, I took it, thanked him, and moved away, in quest of Val, now alleged to be an optical illusion. Once, turning to see if Richter was following me, I spotted him already in a voluptuous huddle with a woman whose face I couldn't see. I set the plate down; I had tried not to look at it, not to smell it. No sign of Ted. But there was Andrew, standing where I had last seen him, leaning over someone who, I could see as I got closer, was not Val. She looked odd, slouched, athletic, both languorous and ready to spring. I walked over to them. A strange tableau which re-choreographed as they caught sight of me. Andrew waved me over. "Rae honey," he said, "I'd like you to meet someone. This is Edith Bucher."

"Rae," she said, smiling. Then she extended her hand and with a smooth and practiced sullenness added, "I knew Georgina too."

"I remember," I said. I remembered nothing; anything was possible, but I remembered nothing. What I knew of her I knew from Richter and what registered now was that her name scanned like his.

Edith Pablo Bucher Richter. I leaned against the table, to steady myself against this fresh onslaught of mix and match.

Edith was asking me something. She wanted to know if this was my first pig roast.

I nodded, suddenly woozy, unable to speak. This was one first too many. Things were getting blurry; everyone was beginning to look and sound like everyone else; not one face or voice was familiar.

"Don't answer that!" I heard, and there, bless him, was Ted, his voice as always unmistakable, ebullient and off-key. "And her last. Her last barbecue!" he said ringingly, the party's sole surviving standout; his arm encircled me, a band around my waist.

"Oh, I hope not," murmured Andrew. Edith was looking at me intently.

"Next time we want a good meal we'll drive to Des Moines or Chicago," he said, with a nice, emphatic flourish. Turning to me, he said, "Right, honey?" and yanked at my arm. He said, "We're going home."

I grabbed his hand, we linked arms; and I felt a rush, a thrill of belonging, tinged with just a little vengefulness, source unknown but adding to the exultation. Decamping with Ted to the getaway car, I knew I was being returned to an orderly universe. Ted, the tour-guide, would see us safely home. Then, in lockstep, we'd be walking on air. The pig was dead and gone; the others, Andrew, Edith, Pablo, Lars, Lenni, were all receding, their outlines bleeding into each other, indistinguishable, like the cross and Star of David on Simeon's interfaith tattoo.

Ted pulled into his driveway. A sea-change had taken place en route; we had not exactly ascended to heaven alive. Instead, two earth-bound invalids crept out of the car. I followed the invalid-in-chief into the darkened house, whose stillness was interrupted only by the pathetic yowling of a certain cat marooned in the outlying garden. Ted switched on the light. "I need to feed the cat." He declared, "I am both mother and father to Pussywillow."

"I'll feed her," I offered. "You look beat."

"Her dish is in the kitchen. Can you find your way out there?" he asked, pointing nervously in the direction of the back door.

"Sure," I said. But I wasn't sure. The house was unfamiliar in the meager light; in fact, I didn't know it well, not enough, anyway, to find my way around in the dark; and I was feeling strange myself, which was not so surprising given the last few hours' medley of ingredients—beginning and ending with barbecued pig and laced with gin. Not to mention, in between, crazy Simeon, Ted bleeding quietly and uncomplainingly on the grass, and Pablo, the poet who, gifted with the outlaw's knack of converting pleasure to humiliation, knew exactly how to touch me. I stepped back, suddenly aware of Ted's scrutiny, which had a certain medical keenness. There were some things I'd just as soon he didn't know, like my being grateful not to have been carsick and for this narrow escape to have gone unnoticed, though I needed to be careful; there were fleeting indications that the outcome might still be in doubt.

While Ted showered, I went out into the garden with the cat's dish, fetched from the kitchen. The air now was chilly and fresh, nearly raw; I took deep, gratifying breaths. The dish, illuminated by the porchlight, was painted gaily with flowers, rose and pink rosebuds, with splashes of yellow and blue for sun and sky. It must have been a child's once, Erica's or Danielle's. As I set the dish down, Pussywillow bounded over to me. Crouching, I watched her, as she went at the food, with her hint of teeth and burrowing, energetic tongue. From somewhere inside, Ted called out, "Don't let her in the house!"

"I won't," I answered. I paused, listened to the hum of her purring, felt its vibration on my fingertips, then, thinking about creation and other miracles, rose and went back into the house, making sure to fasten the screen door's latch behind me. I stood there, looking remorsefully at Pussywillow, who was scratching feverishly at the door. This ardency was mesmerizing; I knew about this sort of thing; I leaned against the wire mesh, watching.

Suddenly, the porch light went out. Ted must have turned it off from another switch located somewhere inside. I stood there in the dark, not knowing where the other light switches were. Probably, I could find my way to the bedroom. As my sister had remarked, when she began to pick up on what my post-Frank life was like, I could always find my way to a man's bedroom, even in the dark. Even, should the need arise, without eyes to see, like a homing pigeon or bat. Accordingly, putting Pussywillow out of my mind, I groped my way into the bedroom where, in the dim light, I could see Ted was already in bed, covered by the fresh, white sheet; his eyes were closed. Well, that was fast. I whispered, "Are you faking?" and started to giggle. He opened his eyes and smiled."I'm waiting for you," he said. "Hurry up."

"You're squeaky clean," I said, "I need to catch up with you. Shower. Now, where's your robe?" I'd been working on fashioning it into my own second skin. *Robe,* I muttered, and started to open his closet door.

"No, no!" he said. He sounded alarmed, but then Ted always sounded alarmed."Not that one, the robe's in the closet in the hall." I went to get it. He called out to me, "Did you find it? I'm going to put up a second clothes hook in the bathroom, for you. You can always hang the robe there." Yes, I told him, I'd found it. It was red and shiny. Hugging it, I started for the shower. I'd be washed in the blood of the lamb.

After that I remember that we made love, or tried to, the solace of bodies, fumbling and sweet. And that I fell asleep wrapped in Ted's arms, under crisp sheets, replete with him.

And that in the morning, I found myself on the very edge of the bed, in another life, under a heap of thrown covers. On the far side Ted lay with his back to me; he was quiet, even asleep he looked tense; his fists, I saw, were lightly clenched. Gently, I touched him; he flinched.

"What's the matter?" I whispered, reaching for him.

"No," he muttered, "No ambulance."

"What ambulance?" I said, joshing, "Ted, wake up. You okay?"

"Sirens," he said. I watched him; somehow I knew not to touch him.

"I dreamed," he said, twitching away, his voice freighted with reproach, looking into some middle distance only he could see, "that an atom bomb fell on Iowa City, and I was badly burned."

Chapter 5

Sweet Nothings

Time-out for pillow talk, a habit which crept into our lives, reinforced by the returning bitter cold. The cold, the harsh Alaskan wind it carried with it, the snow, the shivering—all were conducive to the sweet nothings Ted and I exchanged, as we huddled together each weekend inside his house—or igloo, as I'd taken to calling it; he would laugh nervously, seeming not to mind. Arising from sofa or bed, one of us would murmur, "Let's put a fresh bandaid on it; it'll be a pretty scar," and then lean down to stroke a temple. Some hours later, a kiss and some heavy breathing would be interrupted by a tender whisper from the other: "What do you think will happen with Simeon?" followed by, "God, I hope I don't have to get my own lawyer." Sweatier caresses got punctuated too: "Of course, I'll read your book... Soon... Shh... there..." The silences were filled by simple gasps, accompanied by things unsaid: the hope, for example, that I might be promoted from a hook in the bathroom to a closet of my own. Or half of one.

We'd follow each other around from room to room—kitchen to dining alcove, bedroom to den—as Ted showed me things, artifacts from previous lives, before Georgina and, later, before me. We'd joke lightly about being joined at the hip.

And then, with light melancholy, he'd tell me stories about his Kentucky childhood, of his well-meaning but unenlightened parents, about the house where he grew up, whose agglomeration of rooms had a jigsaw-puzzle quality; as with the family puzzle, pieces were missing. Though he was helpless to fill in the gaps, he would tell me what he knew. I was dear, sweet, generous to be moved by his openness, to praise that quality that Georgina couldn't see—and he went on: Certain rooms, he explained, were off limits, one could enter them only at certain times and not for long. There were dividing lines; and only those were clear. "It was like the war between the states," Ted said wistfully. The Yankees, in the person of his mother (a transplanted New Englander), took over a couple of the upstairs rooms which then became off limits to him or anyone else. His father, whose geographical origins were less clear, was by default a representative of the Confederacy; he staked a claim to a large downstairs room in the back of the house. That was his exclusive turf. Sometimes, Ted mused, they'd seem to switch roles; it was hard sometimes to know which camp was which, or who had moved where; still, he remembered the separateness. And that one needed the child's equivalent of a passport or visa to cross a border from one to the other. He became animated, almost excited as he told me this. So, he'd taken to reading, an activity not requiring migration, one that could take place safely, each time, in the same easy chair. Yes, he'd read many books; no, he couldn't single out titles; there was no point, since he'd had no favorites. He liked them all.

He took to collecting things too, stamps first, then coins. Small things that that didn't take up space, that could be easily consolidated. Here lay the origins of his neatness which, he told me, I didn't need to envy—it wasn't a virtue, merely an adaptation. Besides, the collections were abandoned before they got very far. He'd lost interest in stamps, he explained, and not long after in collecting altogether. It no longer calmed him; he became agitated instead, and it escalated, until one day he woke up knowing nothing except that he'd become terrified of loss. He couldn't remember what happened to his hoard; he hoped it didn't have value, since probably it had been thrown away. (He blamed no one. He didn't take sides.)

Joshingly, I said, "I think you just needed a new hobby. Maybe you still do."

He said fondly, "I've got you." He sat there contented, and reached for my hand. I smiled, but said nothing. I didn't want to be a hobby. Let Pussywillow be his hobby, Pussywillow who, provided she stayed put in the basement, was now allowed in out of the cold.

I didn't know what I wanted, exactly, except a firmer assurance that our inseparability was serious enough not to be restricted to weekends. Val had pointed out, early on, that weekends only were more intimate than the other way around. But Val was making herself scarce; and there were long stretches between reassurances. She would surface sometimes—return a phone call, keep a date, or break one—but something was wrong. Probably, if Ted's hints post-pigroast could be trusted, it had to do with Andrew; and I thought if I pressed him probably he would tell me more; something told me its name was Edith. But I badly didn't want to know about this, whatever it was, though I loved Val, in fact treasured her. I'd palliate my guilt by reminding myself that the distance being fashioned was as much Val's doing as mine. Val, I'd tell myself, had put *herself* off limits; there was a force field surrounding her (force field being a tidy concept I'd picked up in my diligent viewings of *Star Trek*) that actively discouraged questions, let alone hugs. She'd be huffy, or remote. She had excuses, the kind you could see through, like her curtains were on fire. Perhaps we colluded in my not knowing. That was something I did easily, I'd had a lot of practice, though then I didn't know it. I missed her. But I didn't really need her. I had a new cocoon.

And a new purpose: to see how I could get the weekend to bleed into the week. Something I could accomplish, perhaps, without Ted noticing. It might take time and patience, but I wasn't going anywhere and patience becomes a whole lot easier when one stopped wanting; I'd taught myself not to want my father, and, after that, not wanting Frank was a snap. So I was sure that what I didn't want now could be arranged.

Even if not easily. For Ted seemed to have a built-in curfew wired into his brain circuitry. I would kid him about it—the hour each Sunday night when, rain or shine, dishes done or not, passion mounting or ebbing, when fate, like clockwork, turned us into pumpkins. I entertained fantasies of reprogramming him through various schemes: I could, for example, read up on techniques of behavior modification, guided by a bibliography no doubt easily obtained from the Psychology Department. (It might help anyway to widen my circle of Iowa City acquaintances; it would reduce the risk of being surrounded entirely by people whose expletive of choice was "Jeepers".) Or I could let Ted see me home, then after a decent interval return to the house, tiptoe in with Pussywillow through the back door, and present myself to Ted as a delightful surprise in the morning. Or—

I didn't act on any of this then. Perhaps I didn't really care, another way of saying I was still sane. Whatever my plan, it would be implemented along more traditional lines—drawn from one or another of the standard *M.O.*'s for the late-20th-century coquette.

What I didn't count on was Pablo. And I didn't know it would become unthinkable to bide my time.

The Sunday night preceding the events in question unfolded like any other. Ted and I each, it seemed, wanted our Sunday evenings to get sawed-off with grace. It was my belief that we as a couple would this way become, as the saying goes, *stronger in the broken place*, that we would work up gradually and naturally to expanding our time together; it was like building muscles. Meanwhile, it was important that neither of us scared the other away. No scenes, no fuss. Good manners protect everyone. I kept all this to myself, simply taking for granted that it was shared; and that we were united in perfecting the arts of curtailment so that finally we could curtail *it!* Moreover, once our unusual masterwork was realized, we would have added to what we had in common. This was important, since we had started from scratch.

Accordingly, we evolved an additional set of sweet nothings, this one reserved for domesticity and leavetaking (which seemed to go together) just as the earlier one had been set aside for sex. We were presiding, I believed, over the enrichment of our lovers' shorthand. It went like this:

Sample dialogue, between Ted and me, from 9 to 10 P.M.

"You got everything? Your toothbrush? You sure?"

"I'm sure. You sure you want to drive, Ted? You look sleepy."

Uncommonly long pause, followed by (in a tone of voice whose gallantry and quaver could have been lifted from Nathan Hale), "After all, I can walk home." It came out apathetic.

"No you can't," Ted said briskly, "there's a biting wind out there. I'm driving you home." He was running his eye over my things, cataloguing as I stuffed them into a shopping bag, one by one, "You want to leave that nightie *here*?"

"Why not?" I asked, lightly, fingering it. It was frilly and translucent, an oversized handkerchief.

Ted said, "You don't need nightclothes here. You can wear nothing. Or my pajama top. Or my robe."

"I know," I said, folding it into the bag. Was I leaving him anything to remember me by?

He was hurrying me. "Get a move-on, get a move-on," he said, in his sexy Kentucky drawl, adding, "She who hesitates is lost." He grinned. Once or twice before he had said this to encourage me in bed.

"Ah, Ted," I said, and went to him. I nuzzled against him, lightly kissed his neck; he quivered or (depending on spin) twitched, and some patting and stroking ensued. I listened to his breath quicken. Postlude. Standing there, we began to whisper to each other, familiarly, helping ourselves to the various private nonsense syllables we'd fashioned as endearments over these weeks, concluding with *Teddy Bear* and *Baby*. For good measure, I breathed them both again. He started.

"Intimate vocabulary," I chuckled, pausing to catch my own breath, "A growth industry."

Ted broke away. "What do you mean by that?" he asked, his face flushing.

"I'm sorry," I said.

Ted said, "I hate remarks like that."

I had no idea what he was talking about. "Sorry, Ted," I said earnestly, "really—it was a joke."

He exhaled. "Okay," he said, after a couple of beats of silence. "I'll accept that."

Fine—but I didn't know what I had done, except, apparently, hit some secret nerve that came, on cue, alive with pain. I wasn't prepared for this; Ted, of all people, an open book, easy to read. I was deeply unwilling to apologize again, but I sensed Ted wanted it, even expected it. He liked being forgiving; and we aim to please. So, I took a deep breath. "I didn't mean anything," I mumbled. I added, "I never wanted to hurt you." The novelty of this remark, coming from me, struck me—it was something I'd seldom said and meant even less. But I sounded sincere, even to myself; I had tried so hard with Ted; and the stakes suddenly seemed high.

"Never mind," he said, more chipper. His unflappability, as I took it to be, was coming back. "We'd better scoot," he said, grasping my shopping bag by its handles and lifting it off the bed. He saw me into the car. He held the door open for me, and made sure that I fastened the safety belt, a new and, he said, welcome Iowa City law. Ted valued safety.

As we drove through the dimly lit Iowa City streets, we were, both of us, silent; I sat beside him, wearing my pasted-on smile, underneath seething with impatience and confusion. I'd wanted him to explain, to pour out one of his interesting stories, one that would shed light on this unusual flareup of ill temper. I had a bad track record with thwarted curiosity. So, I decided to take a chance on my honest and straightforward modes, both underutilized. "What was *that* all about?" I asked, throwing caution to the winds. (This yielding to impulse, combined with candor, was proving a little heady.) I coaxed, "Come on, Ted, you know what I mean by 'that'—you know, back at the house?" He was tight-lipped, embarrassed. We parked in front of my house; the motor idled; and I pressed him; when I wanted to, I could be persuasive, I knew. I reminded him, winding up, that I wasn't Georgina. Then I listened; and kept my cool.

It turned out that he thought I'd been mocking him, as if I'd been, for example, ridiculing his performance in bed. *Baby*, as delivered, had offended him. So had *Teddy Bear.* Both put-downs.

"How can you think that?" I murmured, melting, drawing on the sounds we shared of reassurance. Ted, Ted. I could repair this; it just might take a little time.

The next morning, like other Mondays, was given over to preparing for the Freshman Composition class I taught each Monday afternoon. This had entailed a self-taught crash course on names (long forgotten) for parts of speech. Words like "gerund" or "participle" (sometimes conjoined with "dangling") whose functions I'd long left to instinct and trust. That morning, scanning the grammar handbook I'd furtively purchased some weeks before, I felt a little sick, as if the words disjoined from their sentences were like bodies separated from their limbs.

Ted. How could he think that? Mocking him, after last night and the nights before that, when I'd tried so hard to care, without pretending. I wondered if there were some gap in my expert's knowledge of the grammar of bodies. Why else take my affectionate high spirits for taunts?

I flung the grammar book aside and tried to steel myself for going through the newest batch of freshman essays. Even if this *was* a state university (with lower standards), did these children all go to high school on Neptune where punctuation was an encumbrance, where it was unnecessary either to spell or write?

The truth was, though my interest in their work was fitful, I felt a vast affection for them; though I never said it to their faces, from time to time I'd refer to them as children, and often thought of them that way. They seemed, in fact, to be tapping into some lode of mother-love I hadn't felt before. And so, taking care that my gestures at least were assured and generous, even if my thoughts were elsewhere, I reached for their papers. I would feel better about reading them once they were gathered in my arms.

All I'd done so far with this week's set was arrange them on my desk more or less alphabetically—*A to K* and *L to Z*—in two passably orderly piles. Riffling through them, I discovered that some were missing—three, possibly four, from each pile. You would think I'd lost a jewel. (Precious as the rings Frank had given me, before we were married, that I'd worn always, even when it hurt, like the times when Frank was meeting his public—receptions, campaign rallies, other photo-ops—and would bring me along to shake hands, many hands.) Now, my throat was tightening, the rush of syllables in my brain were emerging as gasps, as I tore around the room looking for the missing papers, which were rapidly becoming emblematic of all losses—and all the times I'd broken trust (now with the students, before with others too numerous to count).

Panicked, I rang Ted, who wasn't home, of course; he was in class, dispelling superstition; briefly, I considered dashing over there to search (as a mark of his openness, Ted kept his door unlatched), weighed that against the likelihood it would make me late for class, and decided to head for my office instead. That made more sense and would at least give me time to collect myself before facing the children, a prospect that now frightened me.

But the papers didn't turn up at the office either. As I sank into my swivel chair and leaned my head on the desk, I had a fresh pang of longing for Ted. It occurred to me that Ted would understand; he knew about loss, he'd been down the same road; and his understanding would ground my panic. I could leave word for him with the Religion Department secretary, Edith, the Bucher woman. (The Bucher woman. Like *That Hamilton Woman*, it had a nice ring; and it probably wouldn't hurt in any event, to put her on notice that, when it came to Andrew, my loyalties lay with Val, and when it came to Ted, the sign in my yard, in large invisible letters, read *No Trespassing*.)

Accordingly, gliding down the corridor on my way to class (with the materials I hadn't lost nestled in my arms), I paused at the door of the Religion Department office to give Edith, graciously, her instructions. I had the idea that an example of my innate refinement might keep her officiousness (or meanness) at bay.

Pablo was leaning over Edith's desk when I got there, at eye level with her. I couldn't see what they were gazing at, since it was not exactly at each other; perhaps there was something fascinating on the desk. Whatever it was, Edith folded it over when they saw me. They looked up, guilty or startled, as if I'd interrupted some exchange of the garden variety secrets I'd learned were native to the state.

With a curiously contained petulance—it seemed to be her trademark—Edith accepted the note I'd scribbled to leave for Ted. Pablo smiled his disarming smile. I lounged in the doorway; my getaway shouldn't seem indecently quick. Pablo said, lazily, "I've just come from the library. The periodical room, in fact." This was pointless information; I was careful not to shrug. "I didn't know there was one," I said pleasantly. "The University Library?"

"Oh yes," said Edith. "It has a morgue too. Where they keep old newspapers, press clippings."

"I know what a morgue is," I told her. Thinking *Can I go now?* "I'll be late to class," I murmured.

"I'll see that Ted gets your message," said Edith. "Why don't you stop back?"

One syllable more of this politesse and I would utter something I'd later regret. I donned what I hoped was my *don't mess with me* mask; I'd been taught just how to wear it by Frank, coached to perfection, though that didn't do me a whole lot of good when I needed it with him—on the night he'd come home, six years ago, six or seven hours after his arrest, when I awoke to find myself in an armlock. I'd heard a low mutter, earlier, his, then his brother's, and one I couldn't place at first, then identified as the lawyer's. A door closed, and there was a long moment of silence, broken by Frank's familiar steps. I'd gotten up from the bed, still in my clothes; and in my stocking feet—I had no idea where I'd left my shoes—I ran to meet him, nearly colliding with him in the doorway. He stood, more or less unmoving. He didn't want to talk, he said; he couldn't. He'd explain later. Later. Trust him, he said. I put my arms around him. My hands moved over his back, I pressed him against me, then I stood back a little and took his hands and saw the traces of ink on his fingertips and the marks left by the handcuffs on his wrists. He pulled away, and laughed. "Oh, for God's sake, don't do that, kiddo. I'm not up for that." I laughed too, then, companionably, to show him I was game, a good sport. But I felt ashamed of myself and my gestures; Frank's rebuff told me they were hollow and stagey. He didn't want to be touched.

I didn't know where I was or how long I'd been asleep. My hands were being pinned, between headboard and bed, over my pillow. His tongue was working in my mouth; I could feel his agitated breath. We struggled; and I realized that my legs were tightly pressed together and that if I could talk, I would be begging someone to make this stop. I felt the clamp on my wrists loosen but understood within seconds that one hand now pinned them instead of two, and just as effectively. His mouth briefly came away from mine, and I heard him say, hoarsely, "Open them, what's wrong with you?" and the hand that had been at my wrists was now clawing at my thighs, wedging finally between my legs. "Now," he said, "come on; Now. Do as I say; Now." His voice was cracking.

"Please, don't, you're hurting me."

"Don't be ridiculous; Come on; Now." I willed myself to open my legs. "Help me," he said, "Give me your hand," and I did and he pushed into me, and as he began to thrust, a triphammer rhythm matching the wild hammer of his heart, I wondered if he knew who I was.

Well, in a way he did me a favor. This was valuable information—it was important to know that my sense of well being had depended totally on the man Frank wasn't. Talk about blessings in disguise. He'd come disguised as my first love. Frank was full of disguises.

Now the truth seems obvious—that no one had compelled me to marry him. No one had commanded me, go forth and be hoodwinked. But you can't see when you keep staring, enthralled, at the light, shining directly in your eyes, that blinds you. Nothing was obvious then. Your pupils contract. *Frank, I did better that night in the pitch dark, the night you raped me. When I knew we didn't know each other, that intimacy was an accident, and flesh just the means to an end. We'd been thrill-seekers.*

"Earth calling Rae," said Pablo, snapping his fingers, summoning me at warp speed back to the present. For a confused moment—as if something had gotten scrambled in the transporter beam—I thought he was Frank.

"I never left," I said airily. Time-travel didn't count.

"Could have fooled us," Pablo said.

Could and did. Fool or get fooled.

Which meant: If the students asked me about their papers, I could draw on my superior ability to cover-up. So long, Pablo. You don't get resurrected into my life, Frank. Sorry about that.

Blotting them out, I went down the hall blinking against the wavy out-of-focus after-image of Edith floating before me. I blotted that out too. Just as well, as Val's friend, not to see what Andrew saw.

Leaving class two hours later, I felt sure for the time being I'd induced in the children a raptness that would keep them from asking questions I couldn't answer, from asking for anything I couldn't give. I knew how to dazzle. If my original teachers, Edward and Annette—and Frank—had taught me anything they'd taught me that.

Someone had slid a sheaf of papers under my office door.

The student papers! I thought—found and brought back by a good Samaritan. Dropping my books on the window sill, I stooped to gather them up: Clips of two newspaper stories, with a note.

One, ten years old, poorly copied, had a blurred but recognizeable photograph of a couple I used to know. Me with Frank, taken in a lifetime now discontinued, from the *New York Times* announcement of our engagement, with a sidebar featuring an admiring profile of

Frank. The accompanying photo looked like a movie still, with the girl radiantly happy (her hair only a little unkempt), and beaming at the man beside her. And why not? He was unsettlingly good looking, tall, with wide intelligent eyes, and a knowing smile that promised things and made guessing what they were a pleasure. You knew he would be rock solid in emergencies. A war hero, who used his statewide (and rapidly growing) celebrity not to promote himself, but to champion civil rights. He was ambitious, though publicly modest. Right—and my cue to stop reading.

Only those closest to Frank—like me, like his brother, Whit, like his savvy well-connected lawyer, Noel Borders—knew how closely he monitored the abundant rumors about his candidacy for higher office and how passionately he orchestrated them. I loved being an insider then and, though it had been years, I knew how to be one, schooled early on by my father's love for me.

BARNARD ALUMNA TO WED ASSEMBLY SPEAKER, read the headline of the other story, the one heralding my entry into the limelight. The article reported that I'd abandoned my plan to serve in Africa with the Peace Corps to marry the Speaker of the New York State Assembly, whose father was dead, whose brother and closest aide was Whitney, and whose mother oversaw the family philanthropies. The groom-to-be's two married sisters had some distinctions worth mentioning too, and it was noted that the Speaker himself figured prominently in speculation about the next New York gubernatorial campaign, or the one after that. Reading it again now, ten years later, I remembered the rush of happiness I'd felt, entering this family, and my astonishment and delight when the happiness didn't go away. I was walking on air. Looking back, I think that in the thick haze of my triumph, I'd conjured a belief that my father was, in some mysterious way, being returned to me, and that my marriage to Frank Chase provided a channel for his message.

On the night four-and-a-half years later when they came to arrest him, my first thought was that Frank's crime lay in his goodness, that is, in his commitment to the outcast, his dedication to the fight for equal rights for *all* Americans, whatever their differences. That his political enemies (who included some of the country's most virulent bigots, among them powerful senators with their constituents) were getting at him with trumped up charges to discredit his leadership, to silence his eloquence, to put a halt to his activism. The civil rights organization he'd launched was growing, it had a catchy acronym and a board he'd recruited of business and industry leaders, some whose names were household words, it ran ads that drew major attention, it supported and helped organize rallies and marches; the contributions Frank was soliciting had begun pouring in. One could feel no more ashamed of Frank's being handcuffed on our doorstep (with reporters and photographers recording each move) than we could feel that the arrests by southern bullies dishonored Martin Luther King.

But his crime *was* a crime, unpretty, a lot simpler than that, and he did commit it. The details emerged in the days that followed—that for more than a year he had been siphoning money from the nationally solicited contributions to his organization to a personal campaign fund. This, using the mails to defraud, was a violation of federal law. He was tried and convicted, with his sentence to be served in a federal minimum security facility, located in Pennsylvania. After the trial, the few people still able to overcome their disappointment, or disgust, to muster enough compassion to talk with him or me—to return phone calls or greet us on the street—said they'd heard it wasn't such a bad prison, as prisons go. Right. I stood by him, playing it out as long as I could; his lawyer, and his brother, asked me to. I visited him once. It was real, the prison, and not nice, though the grounds were pretty. I made a devil's pact with myself: I would lie for myself, I would even lie to myself, but I wouldn't anymore lie for him. I would—and I did—beam myself into another life. And I was in it now.

Frank's picture appeared in the second clipping too. I glanced at it—it was the same face, perhaps older. The story, from yesterday's New York Times, reported Frank's release from prison last week. I picked up the note, and deciphering its pointy scrawl, read, "English—Hey, you know this guy?" It was signed: Richter.

So much for my own privately fashioned witness protection program. I looked again at the story. It was short, on an inside page, sandwiched between a Lord and Taylor ad and a squib about a minor accident on a West Side construction site. With any luck at all, not a lot of people would read it. I remembered what my mother had said to me, at last, after the trial.

"Get over it," she told me briskly. I wasn't, she said, the first person to discover that people, one's chosen loves included, were sometimes not what they seemed. Not exactly heartwarming, her counsel, but I could live with it; I thought she was being shrewd and practical and giving me, finally, some useful advice. Out of prison Frank need not exist for me any more than he had before. Not thinking about him might have begun as learned behavior, but I'd been a quick study, hardly a novice at getting on with my life. And these two clippings scarcely constituted a paper trail. Now, if I needed to, I could paper this over with Ted. Papers. Ted. My brain in overdrive, telling me what to do.

Which was to make my way purposefully to Ted's house, through the Iowa City streets. En route, I marveled at how calm I was. The plan: At Ted's, I would conduct an efficient search for the missing student papers. I was already picturing the places they could be—on the dining room table, perhaps under the sofa cushions, or on some shelf. Of course, their disappearance had been superceded by Frank's reappearance—but that was happening in another country, whose citizenship I'd long ago renounced. And about which I knew I'd better mention something to Ted before Pablo or anyone else did. Not that I was really cowed by Pablo; a paper tiger, for all his swagger. Probably one could safely reduce his rank to mischievous child. But Ted I took seriously; he was an adult, with compassion for adult pain; for so long, his own had persisted. I started thinking, rehearsing mentally, how I could broach this with him. Something charming about my new and improved weary load. Something offhand about an ex-husband.

Ted was not there and the papers had turned up neither on the dining table nor beneath the sofa cushions since I'd let myself in through his unlatched front door a short while back. Stepping into his foyer, for a moment I'd felt proprietary, even as I reminded myself that Ted was a private person and this wasn't my house; five days out of seven, it was the place he occupied alone, and without him, it had the look of a lovingly-maintained cave. If given a chance, I believed, I could let in the light. As I explored the house's nooks and crannies (taking care not to dislodge anything) they seemed less and less to be likely hiding places for anything of mine. The cabinets into which I peeked (in the kitchen and pantry) seemed to contain layers of stash, neatly arranged like geological strata, from mini-epochs of Ted's life. So, I thought, smiling a little, he's still a collector. (My own fossil specimens, three illustrated newspaper stories about Frank, were in my satchel waiting to be thrown out, maybe burned.)

Through the window, I glimpsed Pussywillow listening raptly to the sound of her own meows—the usual entreaties, and too plaintive for my comfort. They made me want to go to her—but venturing outside seemed too close to trespassing. Indoors, my mission was clear and my presence benevolent. I think I had begun to see myself as The Good Exorcist. In Ted's absence, I felt as if I were in the house of his childhood, where you constantly risked running afoul of border patrol; where, without notice, any room could turn into Checkpoint Charlie; I might banish those ghosts.

Skimming along the surfaces of his things, I'd been struck, again, by his unfailing neatness, the tight orderliness of his life's layers. In my marriage, I'd been dutiful, all spic and span, all spit and polish, but the family I was born into considered me to be naturally untidy, as if born that way and when the marriage was over, they thought I'd reverted to type. Whatever type that was; I'd been a lot of types. Though I was comfortable with my looseness and dishevelment, I envied Ted his neatness, and he knew it. What he didn't guess was how badly I wanted also to shake it up. From the kitchen, I walked directly to the bedroom and its off-limits closet I'd set my sights on (as a short-term goal for the relationship) and opened the door.

And beheld its contents—a jumble of clothes and papers, magazines and books, albums and chipped cups. And garden tools. No wonder he hadn't shared it with me—nothing here could enrich the language of sweet nothings. (What could you say?—"You never told me you had such a lovely rake"?) I was so pleased with this spectacle of chaos—Ted probably concealed it even from himself—that I forgot to feel the twinges of guilt that go with snooping.

Not that I was snooping, exactly. The door no longer functioned as a containing wall; of their own accord, things had begun falling off hangers and sliding off shelves. I reached for an album that had tumbled to the floor, along with some loose photos, sat down beside it. In the jumble, I saw family photos, glimpses of childhood, and began leafing through it, eagerly, until I came to one particular packet, cordoned off from the others, that seemed to be part of a series.

Bodies—adult, male—with the faces attached to them hidden in the vise of another body's legs or, literally, masked. Identifiable parts belonging to one body were tied with rope or entangled with the parts belonging to another (maybe more than two; it was somewhat hard to count). Leather sometimes bit into flesh. An arty sheen of sweat covered the naked torsos and flung limbs. These masked and struggling bodies belonged, all of them, to men, all contorted with excitement, real or simulated, thrashing with pleasure that looked like pain.

I closed my eyes; I saw the motel room with a doctor propping my parted legs on two stacks of books, adding a Gideon Bible from the night table to one to equalize them, and telling me before the abortion not to scream—this token anesthetic was the best he could do. I saw the worn face of my mother when she came to get me after the trial.

She said delicately, shrugging, "At least Frank didn't have another woman."

I said, "No—he just had another self."

I saw the green line going flat on the monitor when my father died. I saw Frank holding me in his arms, saying something dirty and loving as he moved inside me, laughing at my alarm and delight at this pleasure which he knew overrode every fear I'd felt in my life. Frank, glowing. I was all rapture and reflex in bed, he told me.

"Take my word for it," he said, "it's great."

"I wouldn't know," I gasped, "I have no basis for comparison."

I watched Frank electrify crowds with the same ardor and confidence, and bring them hope. I saw Frank, later, looking out at a vacant world—disgraced and baffled, angry and impatient at my shame, wounded when I said—someone has to feel it. Goody two-shoes.

Then Frank, enraged—driving into me, hurting me, pinning me so that I couldn't move. Telling me, with stabs, who he really was, that his drive and ambition were cover for raw and frantic need, that he would seize what he wanted however he could get it, that when he was hurt or afraid he would punish. I was helpless; like the money, I had become loot. I looked again at the pictures of these men with hidden faces, who except for their sweat and nakedness, seen through smears of light and shadow and obscurely photographed rope, scarcely seemed human or alive. They couldn't move either. You couldn't see behind the masks whether it was pleasure they were straining after or pain they fought. Maybe neither. Maybe they were all pretending.

It came to this; things got torn apart, only pieces were left, and you didn't know how they fit together, if they ever fit together. Like these pictures on the floor beside me. Pick one up. Squint—and you might see dismemberment. Pick up another, hold it to the light away from you, change the angle. Squint—now you see the shower scene from Psycho. Put it down. Look away—see the image of the man in Korea whose head was blown off before Ted's eyes. And you still can't move.

Thirty minutes later, that's how Ted found me.

"No," he said, watching carefully as I got to my feet; he was not angry. "About the closet, leave it alone. I'll put all those things away later. Go sit down. You look like you need it."

He followed me over to the living-room sofa, under whose cushions nothing was hidden, though he was scrutinizing them; probably he guessed that I'd looked; he sat down beside me. He'd been meaning to tackle that closet anyway, he said, he'd kept putting it off, and now, "thanks to you"—a throwaway line—he would get to it sooner. No more excuses. "Time," he said, "to face the music." A blessing in disguise. Assurances I wanted badly to take at face value.

Ted sat beside me quietly, neither looking at me exactly, nor looking away. His voice seemed steady, his manner easy and natural. He offered no judgments, invited no questions, though my sense was that he would not necessarily deflect them. As we sat there in a lengthening, bland silence, I understood that this was all being left up to me. And I was a gambler; I plunged ahead.

Yes, of course that's what it was—pornography. Ted was matter-of-fact and perfectly cheerful. No, he said, laughing, he *didn't* collect that sort of thing, *of course not*, though the originals of these and a few other pictures like it would probably become collectors' items, if they weren't already. He'd had a friend, he said who, as part of a graduate school internship, worked at the Kinsey Institute; these were some stray duplicates of pictures from the Kinsey archives; the originals had historical importance. His friend thought Ted would be interested in looking at them and sent them along to him, since, as duplicates, they were about to be discarded anyway. The friend was still at Indiana, completing his doctorate in zoology.

What was Kinsey doing, anyway? Investigating the range of human sexual behavior, including animal contacts and homosexuality. These were from that archive. I must, of course, have noticed that the subjects were all men.

"No kidding," I said with mock surprise.

Ted seemed not to know I was kidding. "They had *penises!*" he exclaimed, looking indulgent and amused. "You mean it? You didn't notice?"

"Of course I noticed," I said quietly, adding fliply, "even though I've conducted most of my research in the dark."

"And," he said, brushing provocatively against my hip, "that's not the only place where you keep your eyes closed."

He swivelled and, facing me, announced that *he* was curious; he wanted to ask *me* some questions, and they came, fast and furious, now and then punctuated by Ted's high-strung guffaws.

"No," I said, fibbing primly, searching for a voice modulated to approximate the ring of truth. "I didn't pick up that it was porn right away," I said and went on. "It looked like any picture, just couples, couples embracing—you know, regular couples. That's how it looked at first." No, I did not find the picture erotic. "Guys find things like that kicky," I said sagely. "They go for visual aids."

"And girls?" he asked.

"Women," I said, emphatically, "like to be touched."

He looked away. "Kicky," he mused, thoughtfully, "I don't know that word."

"Well," I said, hoping to redirect his attention to me with a seductively evil chuckle, "actions speak louder than words."

But his gaze was fixed on something that was, at least to my naked eye, invisible. He had edged away from me on the sofa. My eyes filled, in a moment I'd blink, and everything would be a blur; then maybe we could compare notes. Is it a blur for you too? Does my blur match your blur? And so on. I felt a stab of desire, and found myself for an instant hungering to be touched by Frank.

I'd been content—until I met Frank—to be concerned with words and their meanings nearly exclusively; in the rarefied and ascetic climate of our home, words were currency. Then Frank came into my life and with his supple and astonishing body introduced me to a new and thrilling set of meanings. He was partial to a special look I had, he'd told me, a mingling of irony and tenderness that went right to his solar plexus. He got a big kick out of it. That this look apparently vanished in bed delighted him even more; in bed I was wild, a small animal sprung from a trap. So he said. I remembered the sweet familiar lassitude that overcame us afterward; I remembered the awful intimacy of his arrest.

"What's wrong?" asked Ted. You could say this about Ted, he was strikingly attuned to trouble.

I looked up and blurted out, "I've had a rough day." I heard myself not being flip, my voice cracking, and suddenly, without premeditation, I broke into raw sobs.

"There, there," he said. "Shh, shh—don't cry, my good girl." He patted my shoulder. "Don't cry," he said. Did I want to talk about it? Yes, I wanted to, I needed to, but I didn't know how to begin. "Shh," he kept saying, "don't cry, don't cry. Tell me what's wrong, shh, shh." So, finally, after comforting me with sibilants, a little ribaldry, and some broken-off not-quite-words, he made me smile.

I was amazed at how attentively he listened. For a while, his hand rested lightly on my shoulder, which he would squeeze from time to time. For a while, he held my hand. Then, turning toward me so that he almost faced me, he didn't take his eyes off me; we didn't touch, it didn't matter, his gaze was steady. I took out the old news clips to show him the photographs, one picture being worth a thousand words. The words took over; the story possessed me, as it always had. I choked it out, not caring that it was unpretty, that my grammar faltered, my syntax came unwound, and that unchecked and ragged, noisy sobs would break without warning into the story. He kept bringing me back, asking me questions. "And *then* what happened—and *then*?" not condemning, it seemed, the detritus of my life and the collapse of my pride

He told me to rest for a little while. He brought me some tea. He set out some cheese and crackers and offered them to me, as he had at Val's and Andrew's on that first night. "I must look awful," I said, aware of tears, streaked makeup, twisted skirt, matted hair.

"No," he said abstractedly, "you don't." He'd been pacing. I wondered if he was going to come back and sit beside me; the story wasn't finished, but perhaps it was as much as he could stand and who could blame him? I said something. "No," he said quietly. "We're just taking five."

He ambled out into the hall, then into the bedroom; in my peripheral vision I could see him gathering up some of the spread out clutter from the closet, picking things off the floor.

"I thought you were going to leave it," I called out.

"I am leaving it," he said serenely, "Sit tight—I'm coming right back." And he came back, with an armful of the things he'd gathered, which he placed on the coffee table in front of us, in a neat little pile. "Go on," he said.

And I went on—Frank's arrest and imprisonment, the abortion (no—I'd never told Frank), the doctor who just vanished when it was over without telling me, bleeding on the motel lobby's leatherette sofa until a motherly friend, named Andrea Cowan, came for me; she rode in the ambulance with me; probably she saved my life. Girl always gets rescued in nick of time. I stopped and smiled at Ted. But he pressed me to go on, wanting to know more, go back and if I'd left something out, just fill it in, the chronology didn't matter. He especially wanted to know what Frank had been like in bed, about Frank's lovemaking. "Yes," I said quietly, remembering. "Frank was a good lover, my first."

I don't know what I'd been saying exactly as I unburdened myself of this story (my secret for so long) when I saw Ted, intently sorting through the pile of the artifacts on the coffee table, looking at one object after another, retiring most to a pile for storage; they'd go back into this closet or that. One or two he seemed to be holding on to. "What are you rescuing?" I asked him, smiling, "Besides me?"

"A portrait," he said, fingering it. A photograph (like Georgina's, it had been hidden) modestly framed, of a young man.

"Someone you went to school with?" I asked.

"Yes," he said and rose to set it on the mantel alongside the pictures of his children.

"He looks familiar," I said.

"Yes," said Ted.

I asked who it was.

"I'll tell you later," he said.

"He reminds me of someone," I said. "It's a good face."

Ted nodded. Then he said, "Let's get you home."

No, I thought, I can't, I've told him everything, everything. "Ted," I said softly, reaching for him, "I want to stay here." I kissed him—not on the mouth—something about the way he'd tilted his head.

"Tomorrow's a work day," he said. "Not a good idea. Okay? I'll drive you. You need to rest."

I don't need to rest, I thought, I need to hold you—and I need you inside me.

"Come," he said, rising, sounding rueful. "We need to skedaddle."

It was so Ted. How could you try to disarm, seduce a man who'd listened for hours, so accepting, to a heavy story and who said things like "skedaddle"?

I told myself I would put a good face on it. Try to damp down my bitter disappointment. Don't want so much, I told myself, it's risky, and look how much he's given.

"I'll call you," he said, as we pulled up in front of my house. I saw Mrs. Gillette's light go on. "You get a good night's sleep, now," he said, "You hear?"

"I hear," I said. He was not usually so southern. Then he kissed me, on the forehead. Like the neurologist. I swallowed.

"Rest well," he said, as I got out of the car. Don't be a child, I told myself, why should it hurt so unbearably that he won't walk you to your door—so with a wave and a smile, I turned to go into the house. Climbing the stairs to my room, I heard Ted's car starting, I heard Mrs. Gillette cough. I heard him driving away.

I lay down, not bothering to take off my clothes. And then it came to me. I knew who the man in the picture reminded me of—the man named Ricardo, who had been my father's friend. R, my initial too. Ricardo.

Chapter 6

Overshooting the Runway

Forget sweet nothings. There came a time when I told myself that nothing itself—plain and simple—was what I longed for. If nothing were a thing, something I could get my hands on, I would hold it close and wrap it around me like a blanket. Neither heavy nor light, neither soft nor scratchy, without attributes, I would let it cover me forever like an old friend.

But the conversion of nothing into desired object, something I'd covet, took place slowly, and not so you'd notice, in the psyche's undergrowth.

On the days after that Monday, I wanted *things*, lots of them, and actively. I wanted not to have blown it with Ted. I wanted the story of Frank to wash away, now that it had surfaced and I'd shared it at last. I wanted the life I had built here in this white-picket-fence town to go on and, steadily, to get better. I wanted friends—Val. I wanted Val to be happy and for Andrew to leave Edith and return to her. I wanted to be generous—even to bear Edith no ill will; I practiced hoping, that once it was over with Andrew, she would find someone new. Practice doesn't always make perfect.

I wanted not to hate Frank, who had, as the saying goes, paid his debt to society. I wanted, finally, to release him along with the secrets I'd surrendered to Ted.

For all of it to serve as a transaction of purification.

I smiled, thinking I didn't want to become too forgiving, not as forgiving as Ted; I wasn't that virtuous. But a new improved me might give us a little more balance as a couple. I thought about changes I could make in other realms (even if they seemed minor league)—like cutting my hair or, following fashion, not shaving my legs (a cosmetic trend now reaching Iowa City). I wanted to remake myself, to be a better person, perhaps even to be nice. I didn't even question that Ted was essential to the equation. Because I'd told him something, I believed I'd told him everything.

You call this overshooting the runway.

It didn't begin that day—or the next—or even the day after that. But as we got closer to the weekend, something knotted up in me each day that Ted didn't call. I wasn't going to let that get in the way of all my earnest resolutions about self-betterment. But my earlier elation—like the kind of euphoria you feel right after a death, when you sense the person very near—was fading.

On Friday, I called him. "I'm not calling to borrow a cup of gin," I said brightly.

He laughed. "I didn't think you were."

He asked me how I was. I asked him how he was. We went on like that for a couple of minutes.

I wasn't going to bring it up—I was brought up in a decade when you didn't Talk Things Out—and I was certainly out of practice. For a long time it had been either slash, burn, and take no prisoners—or silent seething. Middle ground bordered on enemy territory

"Ted," I said finally, to the man who knew everything, "I'd like to see you."

I heard him say, "I need to think."

He said, "I just need a breather."

He said, "I'll call you, honey."

"No," he said laughing, "not the generic honey—"

"I know," I said softly. I did know how to be gracious and compliant.

Albany dinner parties. Frank's right hand. It's like riding a bicycle. You don't forget.

So I resolved to let Ted's breather run its course. Meanwhile, I'd embark on lesson one of my self-taught elective, Intermediate Self Improvement. (I decided I'd already taken the Introduction course and that it counted, even if I'd just barely squeaked by.) Lesson one in Intermediate was about handling vicissitudes—life's ups and downs—without either turning into a hellcat or basket case. I'd heard that what you were supposed to do was go about your business—even if some wagging Iowa tongues had begun wagging about you and your Hidden Past. Even if the town crier was Pablo Richter, whom you had dismissed incautiously as a harmless child. And while going about your business you must have Faith that things will continue to go your way—your only obligation is to go on being good.

You have a family heirloom called blinders that will stand you in good stead.

I retrieved my novel from the closet and gave thought to retitling it something with *R*, a name or maybe just the letter itself. A pun on *are*—on being. It was shorter than *Persephone in South Dakota* and seemed too to be a key—or anyway prevalent—initial (mine, Ricardo's). I'd been thinking about Ricardo, whose face I could see faintly, like the face of the man in the photograph Ted had placed on the mantel, alongside the picture of two small daughters. I could summon those eyes that, along with my father's, seemed to see things the rest of us couldn't, secrets I once decided had been entrusted for safekeeping and national security to J. Edgar Hoover. I remembered my father, with a faraway look, alluding also to a friend he'd had before Ricardo, before I was born; his name was Roger. This was when he told me my name was good. Roger was a classicist who after the friendship ended had—my mother told me reluctantly—gone on to become famous. Two great friendships.

"Why just two?" I asked her.

"It was all he wanted, it was enough for him," she said pensively. "So many other things absorbed him; there was no time."

So, after they were gone, what remained was a plethora of R's. I rather liked the idea of disappearing into an initial. And with a new title, the novel could, like its author, break with the past.

I called Val, and stammered something about how sorry I was for my neglect. "I've missed you," I said. *I haven't meant to treat you like a luxury item,* I thought.

She said, after just a beat of silence, "No apologies required." She went on—*she* could have called me, after all—but she hadn't wanted to intrude on the unfolding idyll with Ted. I explained that the idyll was just now in recess. I told her why. "Sometimes they do need a breather," she said, softly. "Let him be. Let Teddy be," she said. And yes, she'd heard about Frank; Pablo, she thought, should mind his own business.

Gently, I said, "We haven't talked about you," and held my breath, wondering if she would tell me to mind mine.

She didn't, not in those words. "Oh, I'm fine," was—I think—the way she put it. I told her I'd like to see her and waited to be rebuffed.

She laughed, and said, "That can be arranged."

I started preparing my class, conscientiously, and well in advance. As I inscribed my comments in the margins of their papers, I tried my best to call their various grammatical errors by their rightful names. About the papers still missing: I weighed, without coming to a decision, the pros and cons of telling my students the truth.

I even showed up once (or twice) at the class I was supposed to be taking and, whether or not he recognized me, was cordial to Lars.

I answered my mother's and sister's letters and returned their calls, dividing my time equally between coasts. I was civil to my sister's husband, Keith Benedict (the botanist) and found pretexts for thinking up questions to ask him about flowers. I'd ask both of them about their baby, due, Marta would laugh, "any minute." My voice would tremble.

I made plans to call the Chamber of Commerce to get the current population figures for Iowa City, so that I could remind myself more forcefully that there were people who resided there other than Ted. I tried that one out on Val, over coffee, one night after the movies.

(*Alfie,* with Michael Caine. British. His character kept calling women "birds".)

"Of course I'm kidding," I told her. "I'm fine," I told her. "He needs his breather." I was glad, I told her, cheerfully, to wait it out. He was "thinking"; that was important, it was mysterious; like Edward, he needed to be left alone.

But I had already divined the content of Ted's thoughts; they were about marriage, I was sure—because I was thinking them too.

Though I was telling Val pretty much everything these days, I kept that one to myself.

The end of the second week approached without either sightings of Ted or word. I practiced forbearance. I thought I was getting better and better at it. I told myself it wasn't that hard. I shared with Val a wordy progress report on my path toward goodness.

"You mean so far so good," she drawled, when I paused finally for breath.

I laughed. I said to her, "You sound just like Ted."

She gave me a keen look. "Honey—just how gone on him are you?"

"Don't worry," I told her, "I'm monitoring it."

"You love him?" she asked.

"No," I said, remembering only later that I'd decided to be done with lying.

I told her about my book's proposed new title, going into some detail about Rs. "No, I never knew Ricardo's last name," I said; I was bewildered myself that this was so. "I told myself he was a spy, you see," I said, thinking back, "working for J. Edgar Hoover. Ricardo was supposed to be his code name. Maybe it really was—and there never was a last name." I added, "My mother would know." I decided not to tell her I had reason to believe that Ricardo was a sore subject with my mother; sometimes she pretended she didn't know who I meant. "My idea was," I said, "that my father was Ricardo's contact. And that they were both FBI agents."

"G-Men," Val said, knowingly.

"Right," I said, picking up the *Daily Iowan* to see what was playing at the movies. We were sitting in a booth at the Airliner. *Puff, the Magic Dragon* was playing on the jukebox. We'd fallen into the habit of going to movies together—*A Hard Day's Night, The Group* from Mary McCarthy's novel about acutely disappointing sex, Woody Allen's *Everything You Wanted to Know About Sex*. And something French with English subtitles and the universal language of heartbreak—*A Man and a Woman* with Anouk Aimee, or it may have been *The Umbrellas of Cherbourg* with Catherine Deneuve. In either case, I cried buckets—Val said we could have used an umbrella for my tears. She stayed dry-eyed, I noticed. But when I murmured something about Andrew, and reached across the table to take hold of her hand, she abruptly pulled back. "Val," I protested softly, "You haven't wanted to talk about it."

She looked at me and said quietly: "Neither have you."

How did she know? It was true. I couldn't look at her. There was a tear, which you could mend but not undo.

In Val, though, the habit of repair died hard. Leaning forward, she was already saying earnestly that she had in no way intended this as a reproach; it was, she insisted, simply an observation. Actually, she said, she didn't like to talk about herself; or dwell on things; it was not her way. She cherished her involvement with other people, listened gladly to her friends, like me; and she couldn't change herself. My way was probably healthier, she said wistfully. "You're so open," she said.

Open, like Ted. That would be nice—if true. What would Val say if I let on that "openness" had mostly served as my cover? My way of telling all had mostly been my way of telling nothing. That I had a long way to go.

I said cautiously, "I'm not sure the openness shoe fits."

Val laughed. She said, "You sound like Teddy."

"I miss him," I blurted out. I'd been wondering, in fact, if the time hadn't come to supplement forbearance with some modest scheming. I said, "This is a real question. Do you think," I asked, raggedly, "that there's anything I should do?"

Within the week, I came up with something, in which Val—reassuring me, perhaps humoring me—professed to see the possible hand of God. I think she would have hesitated if she'd had any idea how literal I had become. But I didn't exactly know that myself. I hadn't noticed, in my meanderings about town—to and from my room, to and from class, going, in Iowa City, hither and yon—that I'd begun looking for signs. In short order, I found them.

They appeared in the form of a rash of announcements—in the *Daily Iowan,* campus posters and the like—that a distinguished elderly classical scholar was coming to town to lecture on the Greek deity Hecate. He was bringing his wife Minna, who also had a reputation (though it wasn't clear for what); and they were to be guests at an elegant faculty reception after his talk. His name was Roger Rawlings. I wanted two things: to discover if he and the friend of my father's youth were the same man—and to see if Ted could be prevailed upon to come with me to the lecture or take me to the reception—or both.

"Get Ted to take you to both," Val advised. "If he *was* your father's friend, Teddy will be impressed. And if it isn't the same man, let him bring you anyway. Emphasize your abiding interest in Hecate."

Hecate was, in fact, a figure in some of the Persephone legends; I had some impression the two had hobnobbed with each other in the underworld. I wondered too if Hecate might not be some kind of kindred spirit; she was, after all, in charge of the dark side of the moon...

Everything was coming together—it seemed almost too good to be true. In a concession to common sense, I put the question to Val: would it be too much of a coincidence for this Roger to be that Roger too?

"There's a saying," said Val, "that coincidences are God's way of remaining anonymous."

That *could* be taken for encouragement. "Spooky," I said, trying to keep it light.

"Teddy would put it another way. *God helps those who help themselves.* If you like that better."

"A cliché," I said, dispiritedly. In the absence of Ted's heartfelt delivery, its roteness struck me.

And so I called him. "Hello!" he barked. It was as if alarm were Ted's natural condition. And then, when he realized it was me, I thought I heard his dear, familiar sigh of pleasure.

"I've missed you too," he said. He added, a little ruefully, "I've gotten awfully used to the sound of your voice."

I suppressed the impulse to say he could have back not only the voice but also the body that went with it. Instead, I drew on some prepackaged lines about the friends of my father and Persephone. They were rehearsed—though not over-rehearsed. (I wanted the *sound* of spontaneity—on the real thing, more work was needed.) My delivery was low and even, while a teleprompter in my head shrilled, "*Stay light! Stay calm!*"

Winding up, finally, I said, with an offhand little laugh, "It might not be the same person."

"I'll bet it is," he said confidently. "I'll bet it is. Anyway, you should find out. Meet him; maybe get a chance to talk to him about your father."

My invitation to the lecture was accepted with alacrity. So was his to the reception.

When I put down the phone, my palms were sweating. I was almost thankful that I remembered how to breathe. "Don't tell me again that God helps those who help themselves," I muttered, to no one.

One hurdle cleared with relative ease—once my heart stopped pounding. My ache for Ted was replaced, in the days that followed, by a mellowness, something unfamiliar that I might have called contentment if I'd been able to give it a name. I found myself thinking not so much about Ted (who was, I believed, coming back into to my life) as about my father. I began revisiting the blissfulness, the gaiety, even the exaltation, of my love for him.

Something about "the forerunner"—a refrain, I thought, from a novel by Evelyn Waugh—kept going through my head. Whatever it had been, I made it my own. "He was the forerunner—"

My father: the forerunner to Ted, I thought, skipping over Frank entirely.

I have a vivid memory of going through some papers in my father's study, not long after he died, feverishly looking for something (I no longer recall what it was), and finding a brand new, crisp manila envelope labeled, in my mother's handwriting, "The life of Edward English". In that dizzy, dissociated moment, I believed that his life, somehow, really was there, placed in that envelope for safekeeping. But when I opened it and reached inside, nothing was there; the envelope was empty; and in the wave of despair that washed over me after that, I bitterly fought the knowledge that he was not recoverable. It seems I won.

Roger and Minna Rawlings. They came into the auditorium to the sound of excited whispers by approximately two-hundred accredited intellectuals. "Aren't they a couple of grand nobodies," I murmured to Ted, who was sitting beside me. It was exactly the sort of thing my father would have said; he hated pretension and carried his own distinction lightly. Ted looked a little startled and didn't crack a smile. "My father hated crowds," I whispered, squirming in my seat the better to get a disapproving look at them, as they watched Roger Rawlings take the stage. For some reason, Minna was right up there with him.

"I think he's been ill," Ted explained. "She stays near him, just in case he needs anything. A lot of the time he's on oxygen."

I nodded. It would be easier for me to like Minna if I could think of her as a nurse. Across the auditorium, I studied them. Upstage right, a chair had been provided for Minna to occupy during her husband's talk. I watched her take his arm, protectively, before she took her seat. She might, once, have been a beauty; you could tell by her smile and the way her eyes lit up with pride when she looked at him; now, I thought uncharitably, she had the silhouette of age. She was formidable looking, but impressive otherwise only if you knew who she was. I decided not to tell Ted that my mother was much prettier; it didn't seem germane; but I watched them, proprietarily, as they arranged themselves on the stage, as if I'd always known them, always had an inside look. Minna, like my mother, wore a look of composed discontent. And then, I studied him, I saw that he was indeed frail, almost startlingly so; now he was stooped, but you could see the tall and handsome—almost beautiful—man he once was. His stance and manner were diffident, especially compared with Minna who, I thought, seemed to swagger. He rose and, with a faltering step, approached the lectern; I saw the man my father did not live to be; imposing, though shy and not quite at home with himself, and with a shock of white hair that, to me, looked like a halo.

He was being introduced by Andrew, filling in for the Classics department chair who was said to be ailing.

"Hangover," Ted whispered.

"Oh," I breathed.

Secrets spelled for me intimacy. It almost didn't matter what kind of secrets they were. I'd get a kick out of a purloined social security number, Ted would tease. I thought this was sweet. He'd been a little stiff and formal when he'd arrived to pick me up. I'd been shy too. Now, he seemed looser, more relaxed. We were almost in sweet-nothings mode.

"Of course Val's not here," Ted said gently, as if he were correcting my spelling. "He's here with Edith."

I have little idea of what Roger Rawlings said about Hecate who, as described, struck me as being more like Minna than the wraith I had envisioned as being perhaps kin to me. I think what I was doing, as he spoke, was incorporating these figures of myth into one big family constellation, to which I also belonged; and with that belonging, you had—almost—the power to bring back the dead.

I remember how close to Ted I felt then, how proud, how deeply consoled.

When the talk was over, the select group of invited guests—including Ted, with me on his arm—repaired to one of the elegantly appointed rooms the University reserved for important functions, like the reception for Roger and Minna Rawlings. The room gleamed, the high polish of the wood and silver caused them to reflect each other; at a distance the upholstery was discreet, up close it was plush. As the hall filled, the mood became at once more celebratory and hushed. It was as if the guests, filing in and milling about, felt the room itself did honor to anyone who crossed its threshhold. It was lit by candelabra; and as if following the local prime directive, guests were gazing upward with awe.

I was awash in fear and excitement, though I would have died rather than admit it, even to myself. Instead, I was busy telling myself how unimpressive this was, that it was, for me (who had scaled heights) a major anti-climax. I'd been, with my husband, a guest, even sometimes a guest of honor, at gatherings more important and halls more splendid than this. At the governor's mansion, for instance—where, if things had turned out differently, I might have, one day, lived. The airs these people gave themselves—you'd think this was Buckingham Palace. I tried to think of a way to convey to Ted that I knew exactly how close to rinky-dink this was—when I realized suddenly how badly it would hurt his feelings. He was proud to be here, and happy, it seemed, to be here with me—and he was being entirely kind. I'd allowed myself, meanwhile, to go all misty and dewy-eyed over the man, Frank, my once-upon-a-time escort to all those fancy places, who was probably now having to check in with a probation officer and wouldn't even be allowed to vote.

I smiled at Ted, and squeezed his arm.

Ted was saying, "I'm trying to clear a path for us to meet them. You want to, don't you? Do you think he *is* your father's friend?" He was propelling me along, greeting people he knew en route, asking me questions about the Rawlings. He'd already decided, apparently, that this was no case of mistaken identity and that I was going to fall into the arms of these two long lost friends who'd never seen me before in their lives.

My throat was dry—and as we advanced toward Roger and Minna, with Ted holding onto my hand, all at once, I knew what I was frightened of and I became nearly sick with excitement. I might find what I was looking for—and if I did, it was as close to the noble skeletons of home as I would ever come—*Edward, my father, carry me there.*

I must have said it aloud. "Why are you looking at me funny?" I said to Ted.

He said, "Why are you muttering? It sounds like you're reciting poetry. Why not practice saying simply hello? Look—we don't have to do this."

I said, "It's all right. I'm just feeling shy."

He snorted. "Shy! Like Gene Tierney in *Leave Her to Heaven*! Didn't you see it? She lets her husband's crippled brother drown, then when that isn't enough for her, she kills herself—and she frames him for her own murder! I think there's a scene where she throws herself down a flight of stairs."

I said, "That doesn't sound very nice."

Ted said, "That's exactly my point."

I said, "Well, I hope I get to see it sometime. Maybe you can fill me in on the rest of the plot later. Now, don't you think we should practice talking about Hecate?"

Suddenly, both of us were cheerier. Ted hadn't meant to give me a hard time. He knew I was nervous and that his ribbing calmed my fears.

We arrived at the edges of the cluster of people surrounding Roger and Minna. He was talking animatedly. Though I couldn't quite hear what he was saying (and wasn't exactly listening), he struck me as immensely courteous, with—despite his natural formality—an easy charm. Minna was at his side, protective, and gracious, after her fashion. I was content to wait patiently, standing there with Ted. I didn't want to force this encounter—I was almost ready to acknowledge that I might not want anything beyond this. Given another minute, I might have suggested to Ted that it would be okay to just forget this—I would just as soon be at home with him, in his bed—when Roger Rawlings reached across the intervening bodies for my hand.

"Who is she?" he said urgently. "I want to meet her." His warm hand clasped mine. I'm not sure he was able to hear, over the turmoil of voices, as Ted introduced me. Then the knot of people seemed to loosen and he drew me toward him. Ted introduced me again, repeating my name. I was briefly surprised that Ted hadn't said I was his fiancée, then reminded myself that even if this *was* likely, we were just emerging from our lovers' quarrel. Ted hadn't yet mentioned it to me, and (remembering Frank) it was imprudent to script the future.

"English," Minna said, regarding me alertly.

Looking into Roger Rawlings' pale green eyes, I said, "My father was Edward English. I think you may have known him?"

Unhesitatingly—it seemed not so much impulse as reflex—Roger Rawlings leaned forward, I thought to embrace me, which he did, loosely. I began to pour forth details about the family I was born into, as if it were a separate country with a history, with names, places, and dates. I invoked my mother. "Her name is Annette," I said. "She's still alive."

Letting go of me, he shook his head. Suddenly he looked tired. "I'm sorry," he said, stepping back. "I'm sorry."

Minna put her hand on my arm. I heard her say, "My husband is ill."

"I'm sorry," I murmured, echoing him. "I'm sorry."

There was a shift, as if the crowd had become a single organism, with the individuals composing it having in unison yielded their autonomy to a collective, whose function was to form a protective rim around Minna. A portable oxygen tank had been brought for Roger who was being lowered into a chair.

"Let's go," Ted said. "Let's *go*." His hand was on my elbow and he was steering me toward the door; not breaking step, he was responding tersely to my questions. His responses were along the lines of: "No, it's not your fault. Don't be foolish. I told you, the man has these spells. He'll probably be all right, he's come through before." Then, in what sounded like despair: "Rae, how would I know that? I'm not a doctor. Please. Step lively, now."

He drove me back to Mrs. Gillette's. He parked; we sat in the car for a while. "You don't have a choice," Ted said. "You have to think of it as sheer coincidence. Even if he knew your father, why should your bringing it up cause him to collapse? I don't know why he hugged you. Maybe you're huggable," he said with a wan smile. "Or maybe," he went on, "he had you mixed up with someone else. In answer to another question, he said moodily, "I don't know what I thought of his wife. I don't know what I think of any of this." Please, he said helplessly, don't ask me any more.

I looked at him, saw he was frightened, that it would be reckless to invite him upstairs. Boundaries had been drawn; we could be wearing the uniforms of opposing armies, Yankees' blue, Confederates' gray, it didn't matter who wore which and this wasn't the right time to find out, to test Ted's famous openness. Not tonight. Tonight we weren't on the same side. Even with my blinders, I could see that.

Upstairs, I turned on the light, and tried to tell myself this room, that I'd lived in now for some months, was comforting.

Maybe *I* needed a breather too. Something I hadn't considered before. An interesting idea. A breather gave you license to empty your mind of absolutely everything as well as the freedom to wear underwear that was mended or tattletale-gray. I was tired of men and the constraints they made necessary, tired of their secrets, which weren't interesting and hadn't been since my father took his own with him. Besides, what ever made me think that Ted, any more than Frank, was, for me, last chance café? I congratulated myself on how easily I could shed obsession and went rummaging and poking around the room, doing something the rest of the world called straightening. What I might take away from the relationship with Ted was an insight, having to do with the simple *convenience* of being neat.

And then, as the landscape of the room changed, I saw them: my missing student papers. They were on the night table, where—unless some trickster had been slipping in and out of my room—they might have been all along. Talk about signs. *Here* was a sign, probably of something good. Recovery of loss. Restoration. And I knew that was something I could share with Ted. Forgetting all about breathers, I picked up the phone.

As soon as I heard his anxious sleepy voice, I felt remorse. "I didn't mean to wake you," I said. "I just wanted to tell you all's well that ends well." And I went rattling on, telling him triumphantly about my find—the missing papers. "I know," I said, "it doesn't exactly rank with finding the lost continent of Atlantis." I paused here for an appealing little self-mocking laugh.

"Rae," he said, plaintively, "I was asleep."

"I'm ringing off," I said quickly. "I just thought it was strange, *nice*, that they were right there in front of me the whole time. I wanted to tell you." I was thinking about the search for the bluebird of happiness, which I'd been told about by Maeterlinck via Shirley Temple, and the discovery that the bluebird of happiness all along has been right here at home.

"You have a way," Ted was saying, "of not seeing what's been right in front of you the whole time."

"I do? What do you mean?"

"Not now. I want to go back to sleep. I want to hang up."

"Just like that? You can't just say something like that and then get off the phone." Suddenly, I was seized by the idea that he was not alone. "*Ted—?*" I started blurting it out.

He said, "You have no right to ask me that."

I heard my own sharp intake of breath, a gasp, as if it was coming from someone else. Later, I was to call it the original pain. Then, I was just beginning to know how much it hurt.

"Don't take it personally," he was saying kindly. "It has nothing to do with you."

"How can I *not* take it personally? It has to do with me, me and you. What are you talking about? You're not making sense." Words tumbled out of me as I tried, at high speed, to recap our shared past. He didn't need reminding, he said. He kept saying, "I know."

"But we have been personal to each other!" I cried. "I've told you things I've never told anybody. Ted, you're my touchstone."

He said quietly, "That's a very sweet thing to say."

"The last time we really talked—that Monday, when I told you about Frank, the man I was married to—"

"Of course I remember," he said.

I was trying to slow down, trying anything so as not to sound frantic—it was probably too late—somehow, without knowing it, I'd lost the hang of guile. "We were so close! You were so kind! That Monday—it was only last month!"

I realized suddenly that I'd been begging. I was out of breath. Mrs. Gillette's house was very still. I put my hand over the mouthpiece, so that he'd think I was calm.

"Rae," Ted said wearily, "there is no lost continent of Atlantis." Bleakly, he added, "Monday's gone."

Chapter 7

Search Party

Gone.

Still, it's neither written on samplers nor posted on billboards that it's necessary to take things lying down. When in doubt, you can take action. Or try.

Needed: a plan. An ally, one you can trust. Plus, since without Ted I was now stranded—wheels.

Val and her car. If she agreed, that would make two out of three. But to conceive and carry out a plan, you need energy, a good strong jolt of it, the kind that springs from hope.

Not that I went about any of this so methodically. Nor was I cool. Hope, for me, was hot, like a new kind of fever. Like a fever, it plummeted and spiked.

The truth is, I don't like to remember this. Not remembering had been, for me, an article of faith. I'd wanted never to hurt this much again. I deeply disapproved of hurting, I hated pain. By loving

Ted, I had opened myself up to it once more. I'd obliterated Frank by following up the divorce with a comprehensive emotional annulment. And it worked. (No thanks to the motley crew of shrinks I'd consulted, briefly, in that period, who had some bee in their bonnet about how the cure for pain was to relive it.)

I had no wish to cure myself of Ted. I hadn't loved so many men—Edward (if one could count one's father, and why not), Frank, Ted. Getting over them had hurt more than loving them was worth. Therefore, what made sense was to fix things so that you didn't *need* to get over anyone—because nothing would be over. If it is, you undo it. Goal: to get them, him, back.

That's what took planning.

Which was difficult because I didn't have a clear head. Pain distracted me, and fear.

Accordingly, I went to bed. From there, I set up the strategic planning headquarters for what I called my United Federation of Planets mission—to boldly go and bring back Ted. I was spending a good deal of time in bed. I had the idea that the frequent shutdowns of consciousness brought about by sleep would beckon clarity back.

In among these bouts of sleep, the plan began to take shape. I told myself I had a legitimate need for more information—and a legitimate need to unearth it, by whatever means. Surprise Ted in the act, if there was one, whatever act it was. Later, it occurred to me that my notion of shadowing Ted had probably originated with Pablo. He had planted the idea the day we met when he'd offered casually that he'd had me followed. At the time, I'd decided he'd been bluffing. But it didn't matter; he'd found things out about me anyway. Clearly, Pablo was wise in the ways of prying and stealth. These days, the word for what I had in mind might be "stalking".

Then—it served my purpose to think of it as garnering intelligence to which I was sure I had a right, in keeping with the cloak and dagger talents I had once conferred upon my father. I didn't expect to like what I'd find. I didn't know what that would be, though I regularly reviewed the possibilities: Ted was with someone. Ted was alone. Ted was in trouble. Ted didn't know he was in trouble. I needed to know it, to ferret out whatever it was, so that I could rescue him.

And I had to find out if I had a rival.

Moving quickly, I checked in with Val to advise her that she was part of the plan. She was startled. "Are you sure?" she said. She seemed to harbor doubts about deviousness. She asked me if I didn't think there was a difference between a plan and a plot. She had concerns about consequences.

To reassure her, I decided to quote Lenin: "You can't make an omelette without breaking eggs." (I had some idea that Lenin might have been one of our ambiguous household words, in the period of my childhood just before I had my father going to work for the F.B.I.) To Val, I tried to explain my reasoning. I pleaded with her to understand that a reconnaissance mission, such as the one I had in mind, was in her best interest too. After all, she didn't have to take Andrew's desertion lying down. Why should we both wait helplessly, and in the dark? We should find out where these men were and how they spent their nights. Knowledge was power.

No, I didn't believe that curiosity killed the cat. (Never mind about what happened to Persephone. It depends on what you mean by marrying down—she married a god, after all, didn't she?)

I could have been more delicate. I might have done better by not roping Val into it, by acting as if what I had in mind was a normal evening out. You know, supper, the movies, and then just some driving around for a late-night once-over of the serpentine Iowa City streets. With follow-up forays to be scheduled later.

As if my devotion to her had not gotten mixed up with my need for her car.

I wore her down. She went along with it, finally. Perhaps she saw how it galvanized me and was relieved. Probably it helped that I was easier to be with, since I was once again under the impression that I was a lot of fun. And then—she too was angry.

"It's good to have you back with that nice fighting spirit," she said to me on the morning that I finally crawled out of bed. (Still unmade, and on which she was now sitting.) I was standing in front of the mirror across from her, vigorously brushing my hair.

"It's the will to live," I said.

"Well," she said easily, "you've always had that."

"Oh," I said brightly, "I've done my share of recreational suicidal brooding."

I saw her face change, fleetingly, heard a gasp. Instantly, I directed my attention back to my hair. "Now," I said, looking at her reflection in my mirror, "how does that look?" I announced, "I'm making a comeback."

So would she, I told her. "I'm counting," I said, still gazing at the mirror, "on having made real inroads on your aversion to sneakiness." She told me later that my enthusiasm for covert operations had been infectious. *Edith,* we snorted. What's *wrong* with Ted, we'd hiss. I told her that my aim had been to give her, finally, the courage of her rage.

Later, she said, it was not hers after all, it was the courage of *my* rage and she was giving it back.

Meanwhile, in the short term, I stayed focused on the plan, whose purpose was clear though the implementation wasn't. But I was sure the details would fall into place once we got started.

I was just the other side of a line which, if crossed, would return me to where I was in those early Iowa City days before I met Ted. Think (if you want to pretty it up): *bare, ruined choirs.* Otherwise, think solitary confinement in a clammy women's prison.

On a Saturday night, two weeks to the day after Roger Rawlings' Hecate lecture and the ill-starred reception that followed, Val picked me up in her jeep. We drove downtown for an evening movie. She didn't say much; I believe she'd begun to think fleetingly about divorce; now she seemed focused on her driving. *Downtown,* I hummed, under some impression that I was Petula Clark. The movie was a revival, *Jules and Jim,* French with subtitles, which each of us had seen and liked before. I was looking forward to some calming bouts of inattention; it would put me in the right frame of mind for our first mission—planned for later that evening—when we tracked Ted and, time permitting, Andrew. We went in and took our seats.

But the movie oppressed me. I sat glazed and enervated, bewildered by the memory that this was something I had once enjoyed. Had I seen it with Frank? With Marta? With my mother, in whose wake the ghosts of all of Europe trailed? Whatever made me think I had any taste, or tolerance, for triangles? That I could watch this threesome and its murky rivalries with anything like pleasure? The Jeanne Moreau character! That crazy girl—with her divided nature, she tore apart two men. Then those two theatrical plunges into the river, who did she think she was kidding? Did she think after the first one that she was beautiful, even under that sopping dress? I'd managed to fall asleep during the early sequences, but the noises of the movie's World War I battles woke me. I'd had it with war stories, starting with Frank's; I'd overdosed all my life on warring factions; and I was sickened by the idea that Jules and Jim, who loved each other, wore the uniforms of enemy countries. That if in line of duty their paths crossed, they'd have to kill each other. Always, something would come between them. Everywhere you turned, there would be the unrelenting, suffocating presence of an unwanted other. And then that car, with Jeanne Moreau at the wheel, her second wicked plunge into the river, this time taking one of the two men with her. (Jules or Jim, I had trouble telling them apart.) You get rid of one man, inevitably you break the other. Like my father, without Ricardo, his friend. "It may be okay to kill yourself, but," my father once said, "it's not so okay to take with you someone who hasn't volunteered."

That was just about enough; my threshhold was exceeded. "I'm going to the bathroom," I whispered to Val, indicating that it would be nice if my getaway could be engineered before the credits. Which it was; Val and I arranged to meet in the lobby. Then, as I tore up the aisle by myself I saw him, and though I recognized no one beside him, I was sure that he was not alone.

We emerged from *Jules and Jim* somehow stripped of our bearings. Neither of us could remember where she had parked the car. Somewhere on State Street, Val muttered, "But where—?"

"There aren't that many jeeps in town," I said. "We'll find it." I added, "I should have been paying more attention."

"You were doing your singalong, you were too busy humming. Don't worry, we'll spot it," she said brightly, gazing down vacantly at the sidewalk, as if the object sought were a missing contact lens. Then she said, "I think what we need is food," and the next thing I knew she had us heading toward the Lotus Garden, Iowa City's lone foreign restaurant, for some dispiriting Chinese.

I don't remember what it was that night. Probably chow mein. Or egg foo yong. I played with my chopsticks, studied the formica, and tried not to smell the chop suey which you could inhale with every breath.

"It had charm," Val was saying. "It was even better the second time around." She had liked *Jules and Jim*. "The music was nice," she went on. "And," she observed, twirling bamboo shoots or noodles, "it was true to life."

"I hope not," I said. Not my life. "Ted was there, in the theatre, you know," I said with a certain bravado, "did you see him?"

She hadn't. She asked, "Was he there with anybody?"

A thrill of hurt went through me then, hearing her say it aloud. Looking down, I said, "I couldn't tell."

I couldn't look at her. I wondered if the movie's outlandish situation mirrored *her* life, but I wasn't going to say it because I didn't want it to be true for her either.

Her life, which we never talked about.

Ted would have said, "What's the point?" And probably he would have gone on about blood from a stone, and pulling teeth. He would, it suddenly occurred to me, have been describing himself. Who would have thought *he'd* turn out to be tightlipped, even secretive? Georgina, maybe. That's who.

And at the movie—Who? Who was he with?

"It is an excellent picture!" said Val. "It was then and it is now. It doesn't change each time some member of the audience goes through a bad patch in her life."

"I suppose it's like a feeling for a person," I said, hearing in my voice a certain clinical dispassion. Her heartiness was making me uneasy. "Boyfriend or girlfriend, husband, wife. Feelings, people, they come and go."

I heard a choking sound. "Yes," she said, crumpling a tissue. "I've noticed."

The jeep was parked on a side street around the corner from the Airliner. "I could've sworn—" Val said.

"I know," I broke in. "We thought it was on State Street. No wonder we couldn't find it. I thought Iowa City was a psychological maze, not a logistical one." I shared with her a conclusion I'd come to—that if Ted and I had any difficulties, Iowa City was their direct cause. A cure could be effected simply by leaving. Together.

We drove past Edith's place first; it was nearer and I thought it would be considerate.

"Drive around the block," I advised, hoping I was coming across more as Philip Marlowe than Nancy Drew. "There's a light in her window, but I don't see Andrew's car."

A second look produced no evidence either—no car, no bodies, no signs of life.

"You think it's worth staking out Ted?" she said. "You might just do better with scuttlebutt—you know, the Iowa City grapevine."

I suggested that the local grapevine was not to be trusted, since it bore poisoned fruit. Besides, I said, I was worried about Ted, which was true. But the moment I said it I became afraid for myself. The streets were dark and abandoned, the trees, lit by moonlight, cast misshapen shadows. And my apprehension grew as I talked about the pressures Ted was subject to—the Department, his dissertation, me (a throwaway line), the two lawsuits.

"One's been dropped," said Val. "Simeon's. Hadn't you heard? The lawyer said his doctors thought he was too fragile."

"Oh," I said. I hadn't heard. In passing, I noted that the relief I felt for Ted was being overwhelmed by the steadily increasing current of my fear. I asked Val whether the parents' lawsuit had been dropped too. She didn't know.

"Please," I said, trying to be light. "I know this is a pretty sorry excuse for a posse." I couldn't quite see if she was smiling. "At the theatre," I said. "Val, I *don't* think he was alone."

"You're hoping you'll see him, aren't you," said Val quietly.

I thought, *I miss his house, I miss his car* (jokingly, I'd say I knew even the landscape of its dents), *I miss the cat he is allergic to and loves—I miss—*

"The house is dark," Val said, squinting. She'd parked half a block from his house. One could hardly make out its outlines.

"Do you think there could be a light on in back?"

She couldn't tell, she said.

I urged her to drive past his house—but she said she wanted to go home, that she was afraid we'd be noticed. "Just once," I said. I said, if we didn't stop or slow down we wouldn't be noticed. I wanted just to make sure no one was there.

But in the shadows of the driveway I made out two cars and I knew one wasn't Ted's.

Query to self: Happy now?
I waited for Val to say, "I told you so."
But she said nothing. Nothing.

Later, probably much later, I came to understand what happened between Val and me. But at the time I was not doing well with cause and effect—and I had no idea that she didn't want to color-coordinate our sorrows, that she wanted to possess her own. I couldn't borrow hers—did she experience sharing it with me, or anyone, as a second theft of Andrew? And I saw her begin to back away from me. She clammed up that night. She insisted simply that she wanted to go home.

She let me off at Mrs. Gillette's—the scene, lately, of too many abandonments. If I stayed in Iowa City, I decided—watching her drive away—I'd move, I'd get away from this place. And I went upstairs to work some more on abandoning myself.

On the ride home from Ted's, I'd thought she'd been driving uncommonly fast, with sudden swerves; the jeep seemed scarcely able to absorb the shocks of the road as I listened to the harsh sounds of tires crunching gravel. In clipped monosyllables, we'd chatted about *Jules and Jim*. I didn't blame the movie, I offered, I blamed my mood. Forgetting I didn't like war stories, I asked her if she'd like to come with me to see the revival the theatre posters announced for next week—something called *The Desert Fox*, a nice World War II movie about the heroic German Field Marshal Rommel and his victories over the allies in Africa. He'd been on to Hitler, in on the failed plot against him; he had (the word my mother liked) "integrity". I had seen it some time back on television and, knowing what would happen—that he'd be compelled at the last to bite into a cyanide capsule—I'd wept.

"A cyanide capsule?" Val said. "I don't think so."

I shivered with an unease I couldn't place; after that there was the censure of her silence, which told me that our other plan, begun jointly at the evening's outset, was dissolved.

Fine. I'd create another, quickly, even if I couldn't take or bring someone with me, and before I could feel Val's loss. I had a talent I could fall back on, called going it alone. Try and stop me. I dare you. "I double-dare you," I murmured, climbing the porch steps.

But alone was unbearable, upstairs in my room.

I skidded. Options were shutting down, words separating from meanings, bodies one way or another fettered, like the tied up captives in Ted's photos and Frank in prison, men unavailable for cheap or costly thrills. With Val, the distance (my creation, I knew) baffled me. My calculations had gotten me nowhere. Impulse was the court of last resort. And so I called Pablo, and asked him to take me to the movies. The film I had in mind celebrated a key World War II architect of enemy victory, whose redemption took the form of death by cyanide—

He broke in, "I know who Rommel was." Then he said, with a cordiality I knew was counterfeit, "I'd be happy to. Thought you'd never ask."

"Cunning," Pablo said to me.

"What?" I asked absently. The seats he'd guided us to were too close to the screen. I'd hesitated, telling him I wasn't sure I wanted to be *that* immersed in the life and career of General Rommel.

"Cunning," he repeated. "I mean you. What you want," he notified me, "is to be strategically positioned to scan the audience for Gobisch. I can save you the trouble." He was looking at me, it seemed incuriously. "He's not here."

"What I don't want," I murmured, "is a stiff neck. And I want to be able to see."

"Sit back and relax," he said. "You'll see everything you need to. You'll see just fine." He pulled me back. Leaning over, he whispered, "Our first date."

I said, "I take it you jest?"

"Take it any way you want."

The lights dimmed; and the commanding figure of James Mason, in his smartly-tailored officer's uniform, came onscreen.

I sat back and "relaxed" as instructed; relaxing, after all, was close kin to tuning out, something I knew how to do. After a while, I felt his arm steal across my shoulders. A first. So far, I'd only been with politicians, doctors, and academics. I wondered if Pablo's poetry was any good.

I paid modest attention to the movie, disciplining myself not to sneak glances at the rows behind us, trying to take Richter's word for it that Ted wasn't there.

Pablo did *not* leave me off at my door—at the room I'd come to experience as a holding pen for individuals awaiting transfer to Hades or jail. We drove back instead, to his gingerbread cottage on the outlying road, down from Val's. I knew it only by reputation—Ted and Andrew, chortling and issuing warnings calculated to frighten small children the night we met. In fact, the place was welcoming, viewed from a distance and close-up, and just as cozy within. In the front room, the wood furniture was covered with colorful throws; his one or two upholstered pieces had fabrics just as eye-catching and bright. Their original patterns and designs blended in; the material had a reassuring graininess, inviting touch.

"Not what I expected," I murmured. I settled myself in the rocker, which he'd had a long time, he told me, well before President Kennedy made rocking-chairs a fad.

Did I want herbal tea or something stronger? I'll start with herbal tea, I said. Safety first.

He sat across from me. We sipped. I looked around, trying unobtrusively to case the room. He had open shelves everywhere, no cupboards, even in the kitchen, no sense of things hidden behind closed doors.

"Wander around if you like—prowl. Explore," he said expansively, gesturing toward the nether reaches of the room.

I shook my head. "I don't need to do that," I said. I felt suspended, lulled into a sense of well-being I attributed to the tea.

"You're at home with yourself," I said, finally, nesting in the rocker.

"You could say that," he said.

There was no mistaking the summons, later, when it came.

He'd guided me into a small back room which seemed set aside for sleep and storage interchangeably. On the floor lay an oversized futon, at an odd right angle to the wall. "You sleep on *this*?" I asked. Was it comfortable?

"You'll see," he said, and went about peeling off his clothes, and indicating I should do the same with the rest of mine. He didn't seem to be a connoisseur of underwear—my bra and panties were wadded up on the floor where he'd tossed them, as if it were the next best thing to a hamper. He had a practiced way of lowering lights, positioning limbs, and the rest of it. I did my part, so that it would be crystal clear I knew the ropes, too.

Drawing myself up later, I moved carefully, delicately, so as to indicate that I was both sated and refreshed. "That was nice," I said, softly. I didn't want my silence—or anything else—to betray that it hadn't been. I pondered whether the verb *to fuck* could be worked seamlessly into my next utterance. (As in: my husband—the former future governor—and I would say this to each other tenderly from our respective pillows all the time.) Not as in: Pablo, you fucked me. "Three times," I breathed, beaming him what I thought was a big, wide smile.

He looked at me, then shrugged. He was rooting around on the floor for his clothes. "Who're you trying to kid?" he said, impassive, as if the sole issue was accuracy. He got up and started to pull on his pants. "Not much fun for you. Not once, not twice, not three—what now? How do I know?" He said, "Come on, lady. I don't know who you've been with—or maybe I do. You do an okay impersonation, but we don't all get fooled so easy."

In the circumstances, I decided to postpone insisting I'd never had to fake it before. Huddling on the futon, I watched him alertly, to see how far he was going to take this business of getting dressed before making any moves of my own. I waited too long.

"Okay, what are you doing here?" he said.

I said, "I was invited. Right now I'm getting dressed." And I started to.

"Yes, well, 'invited,'" he said, watching me. "I agree, you weren't exactly dragooned. What are you up to? Anything? I mean besides trying to even the score with Gobisch. Or that ex-husband of yours. What are men to you, a set of clues? Your own customized trail of breadcrumbs? At the end of it, what do you think you're going to find, goodness, beauty and truth?" He looked at me coolly. "You're not good at this, you know. I don't mean the sack, the sack's incidental. You don't want to come—oh, I know, you don't mind if you do, but the real payoff for you is information. Don't feel obliged to respond. I'll understand—as Gobisch would say—if the cat's got your tongue." He studied me, as if curious to see if any of this was registering.

I was damned if I was going to cry, though I knew he wanted it, it now was the focus of his desire; and he had the skill. I respected skill.

I didn't look at him. He made no effort to approach or comfort me. Which took a certain kind of integrity—the integrity of his consistency. When I knew my voice would hold steady I told him so.

"Just like Rommel," he said. "English, I'm not going to get mixed up with you," he added, putting on his shoes.

"That makes two of us." I'd had enough presence of mind to have gotten into my clothes. But he'd unmasked me—and I despised that. As I patted my creased clothing into place and applied other finishing touches, I said brightly, "Well, thank you. It's been a lovely evening. The tea was delicious. I got laid," I threw him a look I hoped with all my heart would tell him how little I cared, "and I had a good cry."

"I've done one without the other."

"You can still catch up," I said. This was acceptable phrase-making. Good, I was thinking, just take it slow and easy—self-possession can't have wandered far.

"First, I'll have to think of something sad," he said, "like the death of Black Beauty."

"You *are* a poet," I said, and adjusted slightly the waistband of my skirt.

He stopped the car about a block away from Mrs. Gillette's. I wondered if *he* wasn't outmaneuvering some surveillance. "Let me give you some advice," he said. The motor was running. "I have an idea where you're going," he said, "and you're going there all by yourself."

"It's only a block," I said huffily, peering into the street. "And it's getting light. I can certainly walk." I opened the car door; he made no effort to stop me.

"Oh you'll get home all right. This time. But you're heading for a bad place. And ma'am, I ain't going to follow."

"Well, git along then," I said, as a way of letting him know that I could drawl too. "I have no idea what you mean, but thanks for the warning." I shivered. For the first time in several hours, I was unable to hold my thoughts of Ted at bay.

"You're welcome," he said, and added, "it's just across the river, babe."

"What river? I still don't know what you're talking about," I said. He sounded as if he was drafting some poem.

He said, "You will."

Chapter 8

Across the River

What lay across the river was an imposing hospital complex which included the medical school and the Psychopathic Hospital. It was really called that—and the Iowa City grapevine hummed with its news. The Psychopathic Hospital was where Duane Wheeler conducted his deviance research and treated his designated patients; where Simeon Levey was said to be recovering (slowly); where Lenni Olmstead went whenever she felt a break coming on (brought about, people agreed, by Lars' betrayals); where Pablo's casualties would arrive, slumped in one passenger seat or another. Pablo's car was a virtual ferry service; it was said he could make his way there blindfolded.

A lot of this I pieced together for myself, initially via armchair research (phoning around here and there), conducted in the cramped safety of my apartment. It was Pablo's bait. But it gave me something to do. I didn't have to just wait around for the fulfillment of Pablo's mysterious prophecy; or to monitor helplessly the workings of my disordered heart, or to nurse certain effects like the periodic hang-overs I was now enjoying in my room.

The room: a hotplate. A refrigerator out in the hall. One window, facing some back yards on North Gilbert and other streets adjoining North Linn. Yards snow-covered or slicked with ice in winter, and in the heat of summer, shriveled and parched. Inside, a melange of over-upholstered furniture—worn armchairs with mismatching ottomans, in different shades of beige—rounded out with hooked rugs of faded rose predating World War II. One twin bed. A tall old-fashioned bureau with a dull wood finish. A small bathroom, trapezoidal in shape, which might have been fashioned out of a couple of adjoining closets; instead of a tub (which it was probably too small to accommodate) it had a shower stall whose filmy walls must, once, have been pink.

About the shower: *I* could get clean in it, but the shower itself—its peeling walls, its cement floor where pinkish flakes clustered around the drain—resisted all my scouring; it wouldn't yield up its stains.

The place was not going to be photographed by *House & Garden* anytime soon.

Not that I was exactly camera-ready either. I was, as I sank into that room, already working on my disappearance. I almost believed that in the unlikely event of an on-location photo-op for me (say, as an ex-wife with a possible newsworthy notoriety), the camera might record the ottomans and smudgy shower stall but would register no trace whatsoever of me. Maybe if you looked really carefully, I thought—in a passing fit of vanity—you might discern a lustrous void.

Among my other props: my television set (bought second hand), and a handful of recordings of sad songs (Dylan, Baez, Buffy Sainte-Marie.)

And a recent addition: a privately stocked bar, fashioned from orange crates, with martinis for watching Adam West in *Batman*; scotch for the five o'clock evening news with Walter Cronkite; one or two syrupy liqueurs set aside for late-night desserts, when one tended to forget the stuff wasn't candy. The supply, which was available for sale only at the Iowa City liquor store, had been purchased by Ted and me to share, before our break. Now I had it all to myself. Stunning—how quickly it cut a swath through loneliness.

The telephone: another key prop. More and more, it was my pipeline to the world and it had become the nearly exclusive conduit for our ragged and increasingly rare exchanges, Ted's and mine—so that, literally, I couldn't see him and he couldn't see me.

Nothing had changed, Ted said, when I told him this. He said I had *never* seen him. The telephone, he said, had merely brought that truth home.

Home. The word was filtered through the static of his voice—pitched for argument, hoarse, impassioned.

Pretexts for contact between us were dwindling. He'd call, once in a while, chatty and disarmingly friendly—conversations that would end abruptly, as if governed by a timer. I'd call usually about something I'd forgotten early on at his house, overlooked in one of those let's-pack-up Sunday night inventories. Earrings nudged out of sight on a nighttable. One pair of black stockings, draped discreetly over the bathroom's inside door-knob. A set of tossed tortoise-shell combs that had landed alongside a wastebasket, the result of a short-lived attempt to wrest my hair into a French twist.

I refrained from saying I missed him, that in his absence he loomed larger than ever, that I'd memorized the sliding cadences of his speech, the see-saw motion of his hands, the odd blend of compactness with fragility in his body.

It was late one evening, during one of these exchanges, that I decided to question him, circumspectly, about the local river.

"Must be the River Styx," he said genially, and added, "we also have the Iowa River. You know, that stream in the middle of town with the jerry-built bridge."

Why did I ask, he wanted to know. Had I taken to exploring the countryside? He didn't think so. Yes, he knew about all of those hospital buildings and the nest of healers inhabiting them, including the types from the Psychopathic Hospital. In fact, he said resonantly, Georgina and Duane Wheeler had done some of their after-hours screwing there. He knew because he'd shadowed them late one Iowa night. It was quite some scene! He hoped never to have to go through anything like *that* again! Otherwise, as far as the Psychopathic Hospital was concerned, he was not a primary source. "A lot of sick people there," he went on. "I don't see how anybody gets well. You can't tell the doctors from the patients. It's the blind leading the blind. I wouldn't take my cat there. And you wouldn't *believe* the musical beds."

"My goodness," I said dispiritedly, hoping to remind him that I was still there, wondering how to disrupt this onrush of words.

"And its *name*," he barreled on, "I don't know why they don't just call it *The Snake Pit*; it has the same quaint 12th century ring."

For a split second, I reviewed options and concluded I had none. "Just a sec," I said. "I'll be right back," and I put the phone down, went over to the rickety liquor cabinet, and poured myself a couple of shots of scotch. I was pleased to notice the efficiency with which my brain coordinated with my wrist. Alcohol and the telephone made a bracing mix.

A beat or two later, we were back to why I had asked, and I elected to tell him, in an account rich with details featuring Pablo. "It was when he finally dropped me off. He told me I was heading for some bad place. He said—across the river. I had no idea what he was talking about and then I found out about the hospital."

Please, Ted, I thought, *say something.*

"I don't know why he said that to you," Ted said after a pause, speaking slowly and in a deeper register. "Women he gets mixed up with end up there. It's what he's used to."

"But I'm not mixed up with him," I countered, between ladylike sips, wondering if I could represent it as a night that, though full of indecent pleasures, meant nothing. I gave it a try.

"Okay," he said indifferently when I was finished.

"Really," I said earnestly. I wanted him to be jealous but not too jealous; I was conscious of his fragility.

"It's none of my business," he said evenly. Then he added, "Sorry if that disappoints you."

"Surprised," I said, and began readying myself for some serious refilling of my glass.

"I'm not jealous of Pablo or anybody else, if that's what you're looking for," Ted said. He was speaking with the deliberateness he brought normally to formal disputes about, say, the existence of God. "If anything," he added softly, "I'm relieved."

I whispered, "Why?"

"Because I can't give you what you want," he said. "Maybe Richter can."

"Very gentlemanly," I said a couple of refills later, "handing me over to Richter."

"You handed yourself over," he said. Then, drawing from a storehouse of mental hygiene truisms, he went on animatedly about how people should take responsibility for themselves and their actions. I listened fitfully, amazed at how powerfully his words, even the clichés, hurt. I said so.

"Maybe the thing about clichés is that they're true," he said. "Did that ever occur to you? The truth hurts."

He reminded me that he'd warned me away from Richter. That I repaired to him anyway was my lookout, especially now, since, as everybody knew, I was on my own. He paused for a deep satisfied breath.

If this was true, and I couldn't exactly argue with any of it, some things were clear: that one of us (at least) had relocated to another planet, that it might be me, once again following footprints that were not there.

"Tell me something," said Ted lightly. "I'm curious. Why *did* you check out Pablo? Is it that hard for you to contain yourself between men?"

"I guess so," I said, icy. "I don't keep dirty pictures around to distract me." I added, "Or portraits of beautiful men." I had the telephone in one hand, my glass in the other, the fifth of Teacher's (transferred from the orange crate) within easy reach on the table in front of me. But I was light years away from Iowa City; I was with the forerunner, and I rattled on past Ted's quick intake of breath. "It's like the hard *G* in Gingerbread Man," I muttered, mispronouncing it faithfully, as I had as a first-grader testing my father. "I was double checking," I told him. "You warned me against Pablo. I just wanted to see if you were wrong." I waited for him to ask me if he had been.

"You're drunk," he said with disconcerting relish.

"You're talking in riddles. What *is* all this about a hard G?"

"It's simple," I said. "As on the street across from where I live: *Gilbert*. As in *great*, or *grief*, or *gone*. Or *gay*." I paused. What an interesting, unpremeditated moment. Simeon had said much the same thing and it had landed him in the hospital. Simeon. I remembered the last time I saw him, pinned and struggling in Lars' arms, spitting the accusation *faggot* at Ted—then going slack and helpless as if he did not belong in his own body as the ambulance with paramedics arrived to cart him off to the hospital. I'd never seen him before, but as he lay there weeping I recognized him. I was tuned to outsiders, it seemed, though I hadn't planned to be (leaving the specialness of my original family, led by my father, aside). Even Frank, the ultimate insider, was segregated when he went to prison. Frank, who was more at home in his body and, I'd thought, with himself than anyone I'd ever known. And I'd loved him for that; his touch, his talents, were a guarantee that I would belong too.

He'd cut quite a figure, even in prison—tall, tanned, well muscled (from lifting weights). His regulation khakis, the same as those worn by all the men and hardly a uniform of distinction, actually became him. I remembered the way he greeted me when, finally, I was allowed inside the prison grounds. My own steps were sure, perhaps stately; to get through this I was thinking of my wedding; okay, it'll be over soon, and here comes the bride. He met me more than halfway. As his arms went around me, with tenderness and force and I felt a sweet familiar lassitude, I knew he'd come courting.

It was a performance carefully modulated, over in a moment, the reckless, quickened breath and racing pulse. Like a dancer whose movements have all been rechoreographed, his arms fell gracefully away from me to his sides; and he stepped back. The guards were watching. We were restored to propriety. You had to admire him. First time out, and he'd got the hang of things. I wanted to ask him: *Why weren't you self-preserving before this?*

Maybe there had never been a charmed inner circle with Frank at its center. Maybe something else had drawn me to Frank; maybe his secrets; maybe outsiders always had the inside track with me.

Maybe it had always been my task to comfort them, to give myself over to them so that somewhere they could feel at home. Now, as I watched myself, I became conscious that it, too, was from the outside looking in. I saw a body of evidence grow around me. Enough to convict me. The tricks I could count on having up my sleeve dwindled, my confidence in the drawing power of my charms waned. Contact with Ted had ceased. There were no phone calls after that one, when he'd told me where the hospital was, and when I thought I had entertained him with that stutter of G's. *That* conversation had been our last. The current of connection to him had gone dead. And sex, along with sleep, became a thing of the past. Just like that.

And I still thought I could fix both, sex and sleep, just like that.

For this, my first court of last resort would be Frank.

News of whom had last surfaced, courtesy of Pablo, via clippings from the school library's newspaper morgue.

But now I didn't need Pablo. I could and would manage this effectively on my own. I knew what I needed. Nobody. Nothing except a cheap thrill followed by a night's sleep. I supposed that Frank, the man who had disappointed me in every other way, could furnish that. As the wordsmith Ted Gobisch would put it, you can kill two birds with one stone. Or try. Even if you miss. Or that what you kill might not be birds.

As a short-term habitue of the library, this is what I learned: first—that Frank, apparently based in New York, was writing a book on prison reform. Second—that people seeing me out and about for the first time in a while said they were pleased to see that I was once again taking an interest in life. Wrong. A person was as safe as her secrets, and I wasn't going to tell them that my interests had come to be much more specific: sex and sleep. Sensation (even fleeting), followed by oblivion (maybe not so fleeting). One—or the other—if I couldn't get both.

Other priorities: research first, *then* field work. Research wasn't supposed to take very long, just long enough for me to pin down a few facts, like an address or phone number that could lead me to him; my timesaving would be matched by my discretion. I was impatient to get to the field work. Facts were slippery and elusive, and had never been my sort of thing anyway. On one of my trips to the library, rifling through a weekly news magazine of the period (soon to cease publication), I came across Frank's photograph, recent, in color so vibrant it seemed ready to waft from the page. Anyone expecting prison pallor and a lean and hungry look was due for a surprise. Weight-lifting, gardening, and outdoor tennis had all made him flourish. Frank. I recognized those looks. Unretouched. Mr. America. With brains.

Pulling out my compact, I sneaked a glance in the mirror. Talk about pallor. I looked awful. I looked like what I'd expected Frank to look like, as if he and I had changed places.

I returned to the magazine. Scanning the article accompanying Frank's picture, I skipped the passages about Frank's upcoming book—which though not yet written was going to be wonderful—and made a scratchy note of the name of his publisher. Research. It might be enough for the curious and resourceful to go on. Throw in, too, a little wasted. I closed my eyes against rising tears. I blotted them furtively with my hands. Let people think I was rubbing my eyes or thinking. Though thinking was what I hadn't been doing for a while; probably I was even rusty at faking it. Better open my eyes. I stared again, long and hard, at the photograph. I took in the full lips parted, the calculation behind the ease of the smile, the too practiced directness of the gaze. What had I expected to find? It hadn't changed.

Gathering up the remains of my research materials, I returned them, with the magazine, to their shelves. My hands shook; the pages rustled. I felt as fragile as paper. I made my way quickly through the aisles of the periodical room, hoping not to encounter anyone I knew. Kindness and indifference would be equally hard to bear. I'd have to suppress the urge to seek advice; even if there were someone to ask, I couldn't; it's off limits when you're going it alone. Besides, I knew I'd be told to trim my expectations, and how could you explain that's not for me, it's what other people do. I'd put them off. "I'll sleep on it," I'd say—forgetting that I couldn't sleep.

I left the library.

Some days later, on a morning normally set aside for routine errands (Tampax, birth-control pills, bobby-pin refills) I took a detour and crossed the bridge over the Iowa City river, then wandered onto the hospital's wooded grounds. A large lettered plaque fronting the building I gravitated to bore its name. *Psychopathic Hospital.* If you managed to miss that, you could stroll into the lobby, which was chock full of such clues as arrows pointing the way to locked wards with euphemistic names. Scanning the lobby directory, I noted one standout familiar name, Wheeler's, a reminder that you could no more escape from loneliness in this town than you could escape the connection, however unwanted, to practically everyone else in it. As to the *Psych Hospital* (its nickname), I was just leaving. It didn't hurt, though, to get a look at the place where people like Simeon could go if they were going up in flames, if they were lucky enough to make it to the river.

The student health service, where I went next in search of sleep, was also located on hospital grounds, though at a safe remove from the Psych Hospital. But, they asked when I got there, didn't I know that doctors' visits were by appointment only? Unless, they added, I was an emergency. Hesitating before the reception desk, I weighed options: to stalk away after snapping "Forget it" versus the equivocal "I might be," and it was that which I found myself saying through involuntarily trembling lips.

In the struggle *not* to pour your heart out, if you're going to lose, I suppose you could do worse than lose to Dr. Marybeth Woodhull. Her skills lay in drawing out patients (probably mostly women) who were tightlipped and broken-hearted. After taking a medical history (which featured the usual question, the one I couldn't answer, about one's father's cause of death), leaning back in her squeaky swivel chair, she asked, "Is he running?" She nodded knowingly when I said yes. I looked at her, trying not to marvel at this seeming uncanny insight.

"This can't," I said, "be the first time you've heard this."

She said, "It isn't."

"That's too bad," I said, clearing my throat, "I get a kick out of being first." I added, "That's a joke," when she didn't smile. "I'm dealing with it," I said. ("It" being Ted, whom she claimed not to know.) I went on, "My problem is simply that I can't sleep." I paused there. I didn't think I was going to be able to convince her that it was my only problem. "I'm a writer," I said, trying not to think about a certain ex-husband beating me to it. "I need REM sleep, you see. I need to *dream*." I was hoping she wouldn't pose the amateur's usual question—*What are you writing about?*—the answer to which would have been that these days I was only a pretender, that the pages in question were about a willful girl's descent into hell, and that the account was presently sequestered under shoeboxes in a closet.

She didn't ask me about my writing; Dr. Woodhull knew better than that. Instead, she said, she could write me a scrip for a few pills but that I would have to check in with a psychiatrist at the hospital and run my state of mind by him too.

"At the *psych* hospital?" I said, raising my eyebrows, "That *zoo*?"

She said, "You can do it right now." Reaching for the phone, she said, "I'll make the appointment for you." And she said, handing it to me, "You can get this prescription filled there too."

A short time later I was sitting in a nondescript, below-stairs office across the desk from a young resident whose name was Caleb Hollister. "You look about thirteen," I said smiling quickly as it occurred to me that he might not be experiencing this as a compliment; the smile was to offset that and to impress him with my mental health. "How old are you?"

"I'm not going to answer that one," he said, looking unruffled.

"I guess I could look it up in the A.M.A. directory," I offered.

"There you go," he said. He sounded more in charge than he looked.

"I think this is why I am supposed to be here." I waved Dr. Woodhull's prescription at him.

"She already gave it to you?" he said, glancing at it.

"Yes. She said I could get it filled here, at the hospital pharmacy."

He said he had some questions. The first was: Did I drink?

A little, I said, offhandedly, feeling let down on not being congratulated for my honesty.

"I wouldn't," he said. "The two don't mix."

I nodded. "I know." I sat back, a little more relaxed, a little more confident that I could finesse a lineup of sticky questions.

I told Dr. Hollister, easily, that I was fine about my breakup with this man who was wrong for me anyway, though, I added, he had a way of coming back.

Would I take him back?

I wouldn't consider it. Or if I did, I'd have to give it a lot of thought.

Had any of my thoughts been self-destructive?

I leaned forward, and smiled winningly. Dr. Hollister was nice. "Don't worry," I said confidingly. "Let me tell you my secret. I'm not planning to die." He looked startled. "But I don't tell people," I went on, "because they get jealous."

He smiled. He'd been disarmed. He said I was to check back with him next week, whether I felt I needed it or not. "And the pharmacy's down the hall," he said. He scribbled something on the prescription and handed it back.

And that was how I came away with five capsules of Noludar, a sleeping pill of the period.

And walked in sunlight back across the bridge.

But sunlight was a trick of nature. My room, I knew as soon as I entered it, was what was real. Cramped, small, limitlessly dark. The sympathy of Dr. Woodhull had only momentary power to brace one's spirits; Dr. Hollister's friendly banter and concern got you no further than his door. I deposited the vial of pretty pills ("one daily at bedtime") in the medicine cabinet and skipped my ritual encounter with its mirror. A re-ordering of priorities, noted without interest. Exiting from the bathroom, I came up against my bookcase. Took a moment to look at my books. Long time no see. From the adjoining orange crate, I poured myself a drink. Seemed like the next right thing to do. But before sinking into the armchair with its familiar worn upholstery to listen to selected sad music, I decided suddenly to try varying this routine. I wanted to change something, though I wasn't sure yet what. I deposited the drink down gently on some improvised side-table, and reached for a worn paperback book of poetry ("verse," it said on the cover) that I had been carting around since Barnard. A 19th century survey lit teacher had, as a concession to comprehensiveness, introduced us to Swinburne (Algernon, Charles), the life and work, which had always struck me as having a deeply seductive and intimate relation to endings. As knowing everything you wanted to know about them, as the source to turn to when you had no one to ask. Might go nicely with Noludar. The same teacher had explained that the poet's friends had become so troubled about him that they had formed a kind of society "to figure out what could be done for and about Algernon." That was thoughtful. Too bad I'd alienated any friends who might have been moved to do something similar for me.

Found the right poem, on the first try: *The Garden of Proserpine.* (Which, appropriately, as everyone knew, was the Roman name for the Greeks' Persephone.) It began:

Here, where the world is quiet;
    Here, where all trouble seems
Dead winds' and spent waves' riot
    In doubtful dreams of dreams...

It was even better than I remembered. I read on:

I am tired of tears and laughter,
    And men that laugh and weep;
Of what may come hereafter
    For men that sow to reap:
I am weary of days and hours,
Blown buds of barren flowers
Desires and dreams and powers
    And everything but sleep.

You had to say this Swinburne cat was right on the money. Skimming some verses, I read:

Though one were strong as seven,
    He too with death shall dwell,
Nor wake with wings in heaven,
    Nor weep for pains in hell;
Though one were fair as roses,
His beauty clouds and closes
And well though love reposes,
    In the end it is not well.

He had it nailed. When I came to the next to last stanza, I began to whisper it aloud:

From too much love of living,
    From hope and fear set free,

We thank with brief thanksgiving
    Whatever gods may be
That no life lives for ever;
That dead men rise up never;
That even the weariest river
    Winds somewhere safe to sea.

I held my breath. It seemed oddly triumphant.

I noticed, after a while, even through the lowered shades, that it had grown dark outside. Not a lot of scotch left in what was once upon a time (maybe yesterday, maybe two hours ago) a fifth.

Maybe, if I could get it together just enough to retitle my novel, I could call it *Was. Was* was, when I stumbled over to check, still on the closet floor. Where I left it.

I had another problem. I was to take one *Noludar* daily, at bedtime, and it had been brought to my attention that it was not a good idea to chase it down with drinks. "I wouldn't," Dr. Hollister had said. He wouldn't? I shrugged. I'd wait a while. The scotch would wear off. Then in the bathroom (pausing en route only to kick shut the closet door) I'd pluck a pill from the container and wash it down with something wholesome like tap water. After all, it wasn't cyanide.

I let some time pass—I don't remember how much (it had been a busy day)—and then I went and did just that. Leaving on the light in the bathroom, I came back into the room, leaned over to switch off the reading lamp, and crumpled back into the chair. Which didn't help. I was dizzy, something that hadn't been part of the plan, but often happened anyway. I thought about the privileged information I'd shared with Dr. Hollister, the bravado of it, that I was never going to die. Did I believe that the way we all believe it, because the alternative is unbelievable, or did I believe something else, that I was chosen, that as they said in the old gangster movies I could beat this rap? The death rap. There was the risk that I would fail—and I didn't like to fail.

It would be nice not to be so dizzy. But soon I was feeling a lot dizzier, and I wanted badly for this to stop, to have it over with, one way or another. I wondered if I was in trouble, bad girl for playing fast and loose with Dr. Hollister's orders. I'd ask him, if I could. I'd explain what I wanted which was either to feel fine or to feel nothing and ask what he'd advise. If I had any idea how to reach him. I thought of the local numbers I knew by heart, all two of them. I wasn't going to bring Val into this; I loved her and I'd hurt her.

I don't know how mindless it was, since the follow-up topped it, but then I did ring Ted's number, got it right even though the dial was too dark to see, and told him—this time no lie—that I was in trouble.

"*No!*" he said. "This is *not* my neck of the woods. Whatever it is, can't you see that right now I am very *dangerous* to you?"

I slurred something to the effect that I understood. I had called him only because once he'd been my lover and my best friend. There was danger and then there was danger.

"Anything," he said, his hoarse voice sounding disembodied at the other end of the phone, "anything I said to you as a friend would be very, very hurtful to you as a lover."

"I didn't know it was so easy to separate them." My own voice seemed to be coming from some other place. I said faintly, "There aren't two of me."

"There are two of all of us."

"I'm in trouble," I said, "and I'm all out of funny stories."

"You do sound funny."

I must have asked him something; a long explanation was forthcoming. He was saying, "I can't come over probably for the same reason you couldn't let go. I have no choice. Can't I get you to understand that?"

"I have a choice," I whispered.

He went on, "Yes you do. I've been an anodyne. I wore off. A habit. Kick it."

"If you say so." Anodyne. Now there was a word you could savor. Maybe he was right. I put the phone down and went into the bathroom and swallowed the four remaining Noludars.

He waited for a little while. Usually, I'd return to the phone.

When he finally came over, he found me lying on the bathroom floor. He shook me; I woke up briefly. "But it's okay, I didn't take you with me," I slurred, gazing, with eyes that didn't focus up into his stunned face.

Chapter 9

Dead Ahead

Suicide, though it lurked, had not for a long time been foremost among my aspirations. Also, I was inexperienced.

If you're taking chances with overdoses, it is prudent to leave the telephone off the hook. To have been talking to someone who knows your address.

Still, they told me later, it was a close call. With the Noludar family, you don't fool around. "You had no reflexes," said Caleb Hollister, quietly.

"Inert and waxen," was how Edith Bucher phrased it. I talked to her, to everybody, before Caleb Hollister advised me that it was unnecessary to interview everybody for their recollections. "Because it's painful," he said, having grasped that this was something I didn't know.

That—and that I'd had only an offhand and incidental relation to the possibility that I might die.

"You were white as a sheet," exclaimed Edith. "The sheet was yellow next to you." She certainly made it vivid. You could picture it, as if it were on a wide screen, with surround-sound. That I can picture it now I may owe to Edith, to those conversations, since for what I gather was a significant part of the proceedings, I wasn't there.

I have only a freeze-frame image of Ted in the apartment, but Edith and Andrew were there too. It was Andrew, taking Edith with him, who had rushed over when Ted called. It was Edith who'd scooped up the empty vial of pills, while Ted and Andrew half-dragged, half-carried me to the door. There is such a thing as dead-weight—and it is, as they told me, different from the other kind. They were, all of them, voluble and forthcoming, happy to fill in the blanks.

This is what I remember: that I hadn't expected to feel so sick. I woke up in the Emergency Room, grimy but otherwise white as bone. I was surrounded by interns, residents and other medical personnel some of whom, like Duane Wheeler, M.D., might have doubled as Georgina's lovers. Choking, I asked if any of them had and felt deeply disappointed when they all, including Wheeler, declined to answer. I vomited, and vomited again, into the portable metal basin they brought me and was too sick to feel shame or remorse or anything but grateful for that basin.

When I was finished someone handed me a pen; incredibly, they wanted me to sign some paper they'd shoved in front of me, which I did with a wobbly hand. It was a form of some kind, giving them permission to do God knows what. What was there left to do? They'd already pumped my stomach. It occurred to me that they might take my signature as license for them to call my mother. "Don't call her," I said; I was hoarse from the NG tube, my throat was sore. Somehow they already knew that her name was English, Annette. "She's out of the country," I lied. I wanted Ted and he was all I wanted. Lying face down on the gurney, I felt he was all I'd ever wanted. Later I told Caleb Hollister that I must have felt that all would be revealed if I just kept on parsing Ted. Now I sobbed his name, then sobbed some more. He was out in the waiting room, with Edith and Andrew; Caleb Hollister said later that they'd made a convivial trio—laughing and waving their arms, convulsed with the hilarity of it all, signs to Dr. Hollister, he said, of how upset they were. But I knew there were other reasons for their merriment: it was going to be a good story, was probably already on its way to serving as reliable entertainment at parties. In a culturally dilapidated place like Iowa City such stories were needed. Three television stations were all you could get and there were only two movie-theatres to go to and there was nothing for the natives to do except feast on intimate knowledge of each other.

Back in the emergency room, I was doing my part to contribute to the entertainment. The doctors seemed to be intently talking to one another. Now they were up to English, Edward. "You mean Edward English," I said. "He's dead. Feel free to call him."

"Isn't Gobisch's name Edward too?" someone asked, adding, "You seem to go for Edwards."

I slurred, "His name is Ted."

"His full name is Edward," Duane Wheeler said.

"Well," I said, "I certainly didn't know that and I didn't do it deliberately. Ted," I said, "is a copycat. And," I went on airily, "falling in love is, for some of us anyway, a copycat crime." I felt quite pleased with myself; I was still a phrasemaker, even though my life had become a spectator sport, separate even from me.

I peered at Wheeler; there was some kind of film over my eyes and there appeared to be two of him. Trying to focus, I said, "We've never met."

"I've heard about you," he said.

"I've heard about you too," I said miserably, turning away from him. *Oh, Ted.*

I must have said it aloud, because someone, who turned out to be Hollister, went and got him and brought him back to me. He stood before the gurney. I looked up into his worried face.

"The doctor told me to come see you," he explained. "He said you were asking for me."

"I just gave him the information," said Caleb Hollister coolly. "I didn't *tell* him what to do."

I reached for Ted's hand; it was smooth and cool; mine was sweaty and had a residue of snow and blood. "Edward," I whispered.

"I can't hear you," said Ted.

"They told me your name is Edward," I said. I sighed, "And I want to go home."

"Why don't you try and get some sleep," Ted said in his Kentucky twang.

(The next day, when he brought me my things, he said, kidding, that it was just about all he could do not to say, "Leave her to heaven." I think we both forgot sometimes that what we were watching wasn't a movie.)

"Stay," I pleaded. "I can sleep if you stay."

"Honey," he said. "It's been a hell of a night. I've *got* to get home. I'm hungry and I've *got* to get some sleep."

Horrified, I heard myself say, "I'm begging you," and closed my eyes against the memory of a six-year-old I'd once known, kneeling before someone named Norma whom I could hardly see.

When I opened them again, Ted was gone. Who could blame him, I thought, my head and heart aching. A young aide, trying to comfort me, told me he was sure Ted loved me, the proof being that he'd called me "Honey," and when I explained to him, in an English translated from the Narcotic, that it had been the generic honey, uttered with a practised exasperation, it was clear that he had no idea what I meant.

At some point in the long night I was wheeled into the ward where I could not sleep. This seemed to me the last straw, almost worse than not dying. I pleaded for a sleeping pill. "Just *one*," I'd implore, listening to my voice take on a distinctly crazy edge, watching my hands twitch and claw at the pillow. As the night wore on, I became aware, more and more, that my body had things in it—an IV, attached to a pole and hooked to my arm, other funnels, other tubes. I had nearly become a thing with moving parts.

"I am not crazy," I announced the next morning to the nurse, who had just come on duty. I thought it was information she could use. She looked like anyone, anyone you could call pretty; she could even have been me—the me of six years ago, buttoned-up, with higher neckline and longer skirt (and with parts concealed known only to Frank). Her prettiness seemed out of place in these surroundings. I wondered what was she doing here in the midwest, where nothing ramified, where the living scarcely cast a shadow, where the dead probably didn't even leave behind their ghosts. "I don't belong here," I said.

I was sitting on the edge of my bed, my legs were dangling, my bare feet brushed the floor. They were dirty. My shoe had come off last night, as I was being dragged through the snow to the car that would drive me to the hospital.

"You were whimpering like a puppy," Ted told me later, shaking his head.

On the way, Edith reported afterward, he'd complained that I'd dogged his footsteps all season. He'd told it to her and he'd told it to Andrew. They both knew a thing or two about women like Val and me who had no idea they had claws, who sank them into you and wouldn't let go. Retracting one's claws was, Edith advised, an important thing for women like us to learn how to do.

Their accounts, Ted's and Edith's were, I pointed out, dotted with feline and canine imagery. "All these puppies and kitty-cats," I sniffed, adding, "You'd think we were talking about a petting zoo."

"You were stumbling, you fell down," Edith said. "You kept crying for your shoe." She went on, dreamily, lost in the arts of narrative. I stopped listening. I remembered only my hands and feet being frozen, locked, it seemed, in the snow.

Now my hand was hovering over the neck of my hospital gown. I looked around; other patients were up and about. "My clothes," I said to the nurse. I glanced at her hospital badge with its photo i.d. Her name was Mariah. "Mariah," I said to her, "where are my things?" I hung my head and whispered, "I need some slippers." And a shower, I thought, though I wasn't sure I had enough pluck. And to think I used to be something of a daredevil—stealing into a Holiday Inn motel room on the outskirts of Albany for an illegal abortion; careening through the Pennsylvania countryside to visit Frank in jail; then sailing home to see about getting a divorce and refine the lies I was planning about having never been married.

"Your friends may have taken your clothes," said Mariah. "I'll get you a robe so you can go in to breakfast."

I got into the robe gingerly. Mariah brought me paper slippers and walked me down a corridor to a nearly empty dining room. She, or someone like her, was evidently going to dog my footsteps—someone stationed at a discreet distance, drawn from the hospital population of trained lookouts. Standing in a cafeteria line, a party of one, I spooned some scrambled eggs on to my plate and went to sit at one of the more sparsely populated tables.

"So this," I said jovially to a handful of fellow diners, taking a tentative bite out of the toast, "is what paper slippers taste like!"

No one laughed. Apparently, a different set of conversational skills was called for. Odd to feel excluded even here, at the end of the road. *Banished from the cemetery*—I mumbled the words. It was the title of a book I'd read in the heady early days of my marriage, while Frank was over at the State Legislature—running the world, fighting to improve the lot of Negroes and oppressed peoples of voting age everywhere. I remember almost nothing of the story, and paid little attention to it then, but never forgot the title, its beckoning melancholy. Even then, when as a new bride I'd never had a more robust sense of belonging, I loved it; I pounced on it, I let it roll off my tongue; it became my litany, an agreeable substitute for prayer. If I allowed myself to live, I would check out the book that went with the title. Now, one by one, the patients at my table drifted away. I looked down at my plate; the eggs seemed to meld with the crockery; I ate them anyway. I was hungry enough to eat glass.

After breakfast, the attendant escorted me back to the ward. I sat perched on the edge of the bed and waited for Ted, whom Mariah had said was coming, to bring me my birth control pills and clothes. I had begun to store up funny stories to tell him about my night of hospital adventure; if I made him laugh, and I knew I could, he would forgive me for whatever trouble I'd put him through and we could put this behind us and go on to other entertainments. I asked for a mirror to check out my looks. But Mariah hesitated, for some reason reluctant to bring one to me. I tried cajolery, for which I had a talent, unaware that just now I was considerably short on charm. Surely, woman to woman, she could understand my boyfriend was coming and that I wanted to look nice for him. "Please," I coaxed, "please." I went on like this until finally, perhaps to humor me, she gave in. Wish granted. Beware of what you beg for.

Rae, through the looking glass: not so funny. Not funny at all. How to describe her? Thatches of matted dark hair. Skin, permanently blanched, pasted over a face devoid of quiver or expression. If she died, you'd truly be hard put to raise her ghost.

So I had killed something. No one was there. At the end of this road was something yawning and vacant. Why did I think I'd seen it before?

"I didn't think this was a good idea," said Mariah, and quickly she took the mirror away.

After a while, someone brought me a comb. Mariah stood nearby while I struggled to effect repairs, unaided by a mirror. I dragged my fingers over unfamiliar snarls and tangles, clumps of Gordian knots, trying to peel off whatever was coating them, some sticky, gum-like stuff picked up somehow in last night's travels. I wanted back my clean and springy, pre-suicidal hair.

Whatever happens, keep on looking good. I wondered if that's what my mother, Annette, had thought, as she glided past me in her floral chiffon with her haunting fragrance of perfume.

Then Ted came with my things, all neatly packed in an overnight bag I'd never seen before and, in answer to my questions, told me all about the parts I'd missed in our nighttime trip to the emergency room.

"Then what?" I said, urgently. "And *then* what? Then what, Ted?"

We laughed together.

"We never did see that movie," I said wistfully, after he declaimed, *Leave Her to Heaven*. I thought I saw him look appreciatively at my legs.

Edith could fill me in more, he said.

"How come Edith?" I said softly, "I would've wanted Val."

"Not with Andrew along," he said sounding curiously upbeat. He said, "Those days are gone forever." Andrew, he was sure, would be happy to be interviewed too, and would especially appreciate that it might be for literary purposes. Andrew had often said he wished he could write. "By the way," Ted told me, reaching for his coat, "I don't know about that shrink of yours. It seemed last night like he was in a panic."

Caleb Hollister arrived just as Ted was leaving. I told him what Ted had said.

"Never mind all that," said Caleb Hollister abruptly. His next question was oddly pure. "How do you feel?" he asked simply. It seemed that he really wanted to know.

I stayed on in the Psychopathic Hospital for two weeks. Dr. Hollister said he wished to protect me from my environment, where the goings-on sounded scarier than any movie. "You're safer here," he said. That explanation upset my mother, who phoned from Seattle where she had gone to be with my sister and the new baby.

"The baby's name is Emmy," she said, trying to subdue a joyousness which I thought she suspected might hurt my feelings. My mother cautioned me not to get friendly with the other patients. "Keep your distance," she advised. Don't tell them this, don't tell them that.

What other patients? I had no heart to make new friends, let alone share my secrets (or betray my family's) with them.

I did, however, connect with Simeon.

It was on my third day, after occupational therapy, where I had just been assured that it was no disgrace to fail at lanyards; there would be, the therapist said, another chance. I'd drifted into the patient lounge, to wait out the twenty minutes or so till lunchtime.

I saw him in profile, from a distance, before I knew who he was. Something about him compelled my attention, the way his head was bent, the way, I saw as I got closer, he held the book he was reading balanced on his knees. He was curled up on a window seat, every so often looking up, smoothing back his hair, shifting to look out of the window, then turning back to his book, as if to verify these simple facts of his existence. He was skinny, fragile, with a restlessness below the surface that could break him unless carefully contained. He could have been one of my students, less rumpled than most and with a deer-in-the-headlights look that added to his intensity. All at once I knew who he reminded me of—my father—and then a second or two later I recognized the tattoo on his arm. I walked up to him, wondering whether to interrupt him, or not. I knew it would be tactful just to pass on by, not to furnish him with any reminders of what had brought him here. But then I was here too, with him. Look where heartbreak gets you—or curiosity.

He turned. "I'm reading," he snapped.

"The light must be good here by the window," I offered.

He said, "People need to be quiet when they read. Haven't you heard?" He paused. "You know? Light without sound? *Alone.*" He gestured toward the book, then set it down closer to the window where I couldn't see it, letting his hand rest on it protectively.

I said, "I just wanted to say hello."

"Do I know you?" he asked.

"I'm a patient here," I said, casually. "So we have something in common."

"I'm being discharged the day after tomorrow," he said, looking at me directly. "What about you?"

"I was just admitted," I said. "Two days ago."

"I guess then," he said, "after the day after tomorrow we won't have anything in common." Then, with a dismissive jab at the air, he went back to his book.

He wasn't what you'd call warm and toasty. Or friendly. But, then, I was used to unfriendly men. You might say I had a way with them. I'd long believed their standoffishness to be a kind of cloaking device to hide their affection.

"What are you reading?"

He said, "A play by Tennessee Williams. Which is none of your business."

"Which play?" I asked, leaning too close as I tried to inspect it, throwing a shadow over the page. He snatched it away quickly, barely in time for me to see he had covered the dust jacket with brown paper, fashioned from a paper bag, like a child's kindergarten cutout.

"I don't mean to pry," I said, gently.

"Okay. Pry. It's stolen property," he said through his teeth, "Satisfied?"

This was interesting; and I smiled at him encouragingly. He went on to explain that it was way overdue at the library (which he said was run like a terrorist state where students were treated like serfs). Since unaffordable fines had accumulated, he had no intention of taking it back and, finally, rules sickened him. The lunch bell rang, mid-peroration. He wasn't hungry; continuing on a rising note, he said the food, in addition to the regimentation, made him sick too.

He said all this eagerly, with a relish that was infectious, and though I was hungry, I said fervently, "Me too. Nothing interests me less than lunch." Detaching from a live wire like Simeon had never been my style. I could cadge some food later, something like a leftover roll. I told him I liked his spirit.

He said: "It's *Cat on a Hot Tin Roof*, by the way. The play. If you must know."

I smiled. With a southern lilt (deriving, I assumed, from my father's southern roots), I plunged right in. "It's my favorite play! I love Maggie, the cat. She has such great lines." In the belief that I was quoting one, I rattled on.

"That's Brick's line, not hers," said Simeon. "I'm partial to his lines about mendacity. Are you done?"

"Almost," I said. Not wanting at all to stop, I began to rush through more passages I knew by heart.

He broke in, "If there isn't anything else you've memorized, I'd like to get back to my book," he said.

"I didn't want to disturb you," I mumbled, backing away.

Swatting at a dust mote, he said, "Like hell you didn't."

"No, really—" I protested. I sounded insincere even to myself.

"I know where I've seen you before," said Simeon. "Last Halloween. You were one of those Workshop chicks—at that kosher barbecue, right?"

I nodded. "A pig roast," I said. "Not so kosher,"

"And you only just got here? I've been here ever since. You must be made of strong stuff. Get ready for a long stay. The snake pit's not for overnighters. I hope you packed your steamer trunk."

"You're not serious. You're kidding, right?"

"Wrong," said Simeon, "Dead serious. I never kid."

He'd shouted *faggot,* I remembered. That, and his crying. Was he kidding then?

Who's kidding who?

"I'm fine," I notified him. "I'm going to be discharged *very* soon." Then, feeling slightly sheepish about my bravado, I added cautiously, "It wasn't exactly a nice party."

"Gory," said Simeon, with a shudder.

Yes. Never mind the pig—like the spill of blood from Ted's scalp, when Simeon slugged him. Why, Simeon had nearly sent Ted to the hospital! Still, bringing it up just then seemed a pretty bad idea. I took a deep breath. "So," I said, "what brought you there?"

"My religion professor invited me. You?"

"Your religion professor invited me." I added, "Something else we have in common."

"Why? Did you take a class with that atheist?" Simeon asked.

"No," I said. "Actually, I came as his date."

"Then," said Simeon, tonelessly, "we have nothing in common."

Simeon was sitting very still. He was huddled on the window seat, facing away from me, as if his previous animation had abruptly become an alien entity which vanished. This was a new Simeon—or a return of the Simeon I'd met earlier, the one who lay crumpled and weeping on the Olmsteads' lawn with the barbecue fumes drifting overhead. With his bristliness and febrile quality gone, he was mysterious, remote, a stranger. If I wanted to know whatever I'd imagined he could tell me, I would have to start from scratch, all over again. Not fair, to be required to make the acquaintance of the same person twice.

Every muscle in my body seemed to be aching. I remembered the tightness, the heaviness, the weight of deep exhaustion I'd felt in the moments just before Ted first kissed me—and then, how lovely it was, how I'd felt airborne, how convinced I'd been that somehow I'd wafted home. Now—as Ted might put it—I felt heavy as lead.

Simeon was muttering something; I strained to hear. "I can't wait to get out of here," he said testily. He sounded as if he might be coming back to life. He added, "I would have gotten better sooner in the Lubyanka."

"They didn't help you here?"

"Oh sure, Dr. Wheeler was a real help. He could write a whole book with the data he's been collecting about my childhood. As if I never get tired of talking about my mother."

"Duane Wheeler is your doctor?" I asked, surprised.

"Yes, he's my doctor. Why? You know him?"

"Indirectly," I said cautiously. "I've heard about the research he's doing. In prisons."

"Yeah. I heard about that too. He studies perverts."

"Deviants," I said learnedly. "That's more polite."

"Whatever," said Simeon. "Perverts. Faggots. Whatever I say, Wheeler gives me a hard time. Fairies. I told him he should pay more attention to the kids those guys prey on."

"You care about underdogs," I said to him softly, keenly aware that now I was not lying.

"I suppose so," he said, making gingerly eye contact. "But I wouldn't call them dogs."

I said, "It's a figure of speech." I added, "I care, too."

The silence held, a nice, enveloping blanket. I wondered if it signaled something even better than a truce.

Cautiously, I asked, "Does Dr. Wheeler really give you a hard time?"

"Yeah. He says he'll ask the questions since he's the one who's been to medical school. So he asks them. Why am I so sensitive about this? Why am I so sensitive about that? I'm a sensitive person. Apparently he's never met one before. He's a snoop." He added, "Like you." After a pause, he said, "You mind me saying that?"

"I've heard worse," I said pleasantly. "So, hasn't he been *any* help at all?"

"Oh sure. He gives swell advice. Practical stuff, to keep me out of the hospital. Like don't call people names."

"Good idea. Sometimes they're worse than sticks and stones. As in, they hurt more." Like my hurt when they said—and said again—that Frank was a crook.

Simeon shrugged. "Dr. Wheeler says it depends on who gets hurt."

Oh, does he? To Simeon, I said, "You mean it's okay to do it selectively? You just take it insult by insult?"

"I guess," said Simeon. "Sometimes you've got to protect yourself."

I blurted out, "What about not hitting them?"

Simeon flushed. I took this for contrition.

"You know," I said, "Mr. Gobisch could have wound up in the hospital too. Ted." I couldn't help myself; I murmured his name.

"Yeah, well, I beat him to it," said Simeon, in a low, controlled voice. "And Dr. Wheeler wants to keep me from coming here again. He wants me to get cured."

Of what, I wanted to ask, but was held back by Simeon's tumble of words.

He was saying, "So I'm moving on, I'm leaving this town. I'm going to the seminary, I'm going to study to be a priest."

I stammered, taken aback, "But what does that have to do with Ted?"

"That atheist can take care of himself. Dr. Wheeler says he's not my problem."

I cried, "But why take a swing at him?"

"Simple. It's in here," he said and began tapping out a rhythm on his book's plain brown cover. "In *Cat.* It's about mendacity—all those lies. That's what Brick can't stand." He paused. "Mr. Gobisch *lied* to me."

"Lied about what?"

"He told me there is no God, for one thing."

I said, "You must have misunderstood. He was just telling you what *he* believed. He didn't mean his students all had to agree."

"Not all of them. Just me. He didn't care about the rest."

"I'm *sure* you misunderstood."

Simeon said, "There sure are a lot of misunderstandings around here. Never met so many misunderstandings in my life."

"Like what? What else?"

"Nothing," said Simeon, resting his fingers lightly on his book. "Probably a 'misunderstanding'. He let me think I meant more to him—I thought there was more to our relationship."

"I see," I said, stirred, astonished by an impulse to reach out to him. "How *hard* for you," I said, bathed in an idea I was entertaining about the selflessness of my concern until I realized that the same thing was true, true of me.

As Simeon went on talking, animatedly, an outpouring, I listened, hoping my face was a mask, struggling to draw on my usually effortless ability to tune him, all of them, out. It wasn't working. I heard him, Simeon, talking rapidly, explaining that Dr. Wheeler appeared to have an unusual interest in Ted. In anything and everything Simeon had to say about him. "Jesus, we talk about Professor Gobisch as much as my mother," Simeon said breathlessly. In fact, he continued, Dr. Wheeler lately had begun *taping* their sessions about Ted. *Only those?* I spluttered. An unease was gathering, coming from somewhere, threatening to outstrip my curiosity, something to do with Wheeler, I didn't know what.

I persisted: but didn't Dr. Wheeler tape all of his sessions? Didn't he tape the other sessions as well?

"Oh, maybe," Simeon said, with a disconcertingly easy shrug. He couldn't, he said, be sure about that since it wasn't his habit to check on whether Dr. Wheeler had the premises bugged. But, he said, there was no mistaking the purr of the tape recorder when the subject was Ted.

"Yup!" he said, clipped and staccato, but trying anyway, it seemed, to sound like some movie cowboy. I wondered if he'd picked it up from Ted. Then, reverting to his native cadence (city-slicker, northern), he said briskly that if he was sure of anything, he was sure of that. He didn't know what Wheeler wanted, "aside from curing me," said Simeon, "whatever that means," but he seemed pleased that Wheeler, with his help, was getting the goods on Ted. He thought some good could come of that.

His eyes were bright. He had allies. Like his doctor who, in fact, he was about to go see. He'd become confident, though I didn't know it then, that he also had me.

Which I began to realize later that afternoon as he, emerging from Dr. Wheeler's office, came toward me with a newly resolute stride.

He had decided—with Dr. Wheeler' support—he told me, to reinstate his lawsuit against Ted.

He confided more about all this after dinner in the patients' lounge. A fishbowl. We hunkered down in what Simeon seemed to think was a private, inconspicuous corner.

No, he said, *his* lawsuit was not about his conversion to Catholicism; his parents were the ones wrought up about that. It was about morals—Professor Gobisch had exploited him. Blown hot and cold. Taken advantage. Toyed with his beliefs. His feelings—

I interrupted him. "Is all of that against the law?" If it was, I said, the prison population would soar, needs would exceed existing facilities. I stopped listening to Simeon and began the mental addition, starting with Frank and going on from there. Take the neurologist. Take Pablo. Take—was there anyone you *couldn't* call fickle? I certainly was no stranger to vanishing acts. Take yesterday, or the day before—pills, stomach pumped, sick over a basin—all gone in a flash. Take Ted, arriving at the hospital with birth control pills, tampons, other intimate sundries, then leaving, having deposited them at the foot of my bed. Why I knew people who didn't have to go anywhere to disappear. Then, dipping into ancient history, I remembered one who did: Ricardo. Ricardo won, my mother had said enigmatically in the days after my father died. Won what? And whatever it was, was it managed by remote control? After all, Ricardo had long since vanished from our house.

"He took your father," my mother said. So he was there, though he was not there, my father. I thought of a six-year-old named Norma Povich, my best friend one minute, the next minute an invader, snoop, overall hobgoblin my mother was turning out of the house. All told, there sure had been a lot of *now you see them, now you don't.*

I heard Simeon say, "It doesn't always have to be jail."

Jolted back from time-travel, I said, "What?"

"There are other ways to punish someone," Simeon said. Not all misdeeds were something you went to jail for. There were other ways, he continued, to stop people like Ted from hurting people like Simeon, people like me. Like telling people about him. Maybe, no longer allowing him to teach.

"I don't see why he should lose his job," I said. "That's going pretty far."

"Well, he went pretty far," Simeon said, flushing.

"Talking up atheism doesn't seem so terrible," I said. I was growing apprehensive.

"Well, there was more. Like the reason I called him—"

"When did you call him?"

"It's not when, it's what," Simeon said. He was staring intently at the floor; his voice was reedy. He mumbled, "I called him a fag."

I was about to say, briskly, "*What? I can hardly hear you.*" But I had heard him, even though his voice seemed to have dropped many decibels.

I whispered, "But wasn't that one of the misunderstandings?"

"Someone like him," Simeon was saying, "in authority, a teacher, can make you think you want something when you don't even want it."

"Who wants or doesn't want *what*?"

And *who* wants to know? Or doesn't? Answer, to both: *Me*. Time-tested remedy: *Stall*; buy time against the possibility I might one day have to decide which. Though I've had curiosity to spare, I wasn't wild about having it satisfied. Luckily, I'd had a lot of practice in appearing non-committal. I was good at fake composure, striking just the right tossed-off note. I came out of my colloquy with myself in time to hear Simeon winding up his catalogue of Ted's offenses against nature and the moral law, apparently all traceable to his mother. I managed an airy, "Did Dr. Wheeler tell you all this?"

"He asks questions, he draws me out," said Simeon, who as his discharge neared seemed to have an improved opinion of his doctor.

"Leading questions?" I asked, remembering how Ted had been worried that Wheeler was gunning for him, wondering whether Ted was right.

"Like the ones you're asking?" Simeon said, giving me a look. He went on, "Dr. Wheeler doesn't try to influence me. He wants me to make up my own mind. He wants me to stand up for myself."

"That's why the lawsuit?"

"Yes," said Simeon, leaning forward. "And you can help."

What he wanted, he explained, was a letter from me supporting his case; the letter would feature personal details I could contribute about Ted's character. "And *proclivities,*" he added.

What proclivities? That he kept a cat he was allergic to? That he was inordinately neat? I said I didn't think I could help him there. Neither of those things had legal teeth.

I kept to myself that Ted wasn't the first man in whom I'd been bitterly disappointed, who had hurt me, who had betrayed my expectations. It couldn't be said, across the boards, that their characters were all bad, though there were conspicuous exceptions—like Frank. Besides, I'd had my fill, and more, of legal labyrinths and public scandal.

"What about Mr. Gobisch's pornography collection?" Simeon asked. "You must have seen it too."

The shock of this made me wary. I wasn't going to ask him how he knew about those photos. I had just stumbled on them.

But I didn't have to ask. Simeon went on, "He showed me those pictures. He *showed* them to me!"

Simeon said, "They think it would really strengthen the case if you could say you saw them too."

"Who're 'they'?" I asked, fervently hoping to bypass the subject of photographs.

"My lawyer," Simeon said. His voice was sturdy. "And my doctor too, of course."

"Doctors and lawyers. Well. You can't get much more protection than that."

"Right," said Simeon, speaking in this different, richer register, in which I made out the vibrant notes of a relief I was not feeling. While Simeon was forging links with others, in pursuit of a goal, I was being remanded back to isolation. Which felt so familiar and inevitable, you would have thought it was genetic, a condition of my birth.

My father. How alone he had been on the day she, my mother, made the urchin Norma leave our house.

"She's not normal," my mother had said. She'd gone, but she left her strangeness or whatever-it-was behind. So, though she was gone, the stain of her wasn't. Apparently, that's what abnormalness was—a stain, which manifested in our house later that night: A father I'd never seen before, sobbing. Sobs loud enough to reach me in my bedroom and propel me toward him as they echoed through the house. (Not like Simeon, who wept in silence.)

"Don't leave me, baby," my father had cried. It was close as he'd ever come to clinging to me.

"I won't leave you," I said, and I never did. What had broken his heart? I'd thought it'd had something to do with the thing in Norma that my mother saw, the thing which moved her to expel Norma from our house. As if that would take care of it, the abnormalness—like spring cleaning. But what was also wiped away was whatever made our family special—beautiful, great and, because we were us, unceasingly happy—because my father didn't seem happy after that.

"Why was that, do you suppose?" Dr. Hollister asked me a couple of days later. "Do you think it was Norma he missed?"

"No, she was *my* friend," I said. I thought, but didn't say, *"He missed his."*

I'd entrusted myself to my father. *"I don't want not to be,"* I'd told him, committing myself to him, not knowing I was setting myself up for a lifetime of second thoughts.

Now Simeon was saying, "You could get even with him."

"Who?"

"Ted."

He explained, "So then you wouldn't have to come back here either."

"I won't have to come back. *I'm* not sick."

"Then why are you in the hospital?" Simeon asked. He said, "I know why."

"I doubt that," I said. "I don't want to talk about it."

He reminded me that he was being discharged tomorrow. That no discharge date had been set for me. What loomed before me, he said, was a future in a Psychopathic Hospital located in a jerkwater town—

"I can leave anytime I want to," I said. Nobody could tell me I belonged here—in a culture of lanyards with bad food.

"Nobody belongs here," said Simeon, decisively. "So will you help me?"

"I'm not sure," I said, adding coyly, "What photographs are you talking about?"

"You know what photographs," he said. "Don't you?" His shoulders sagged; the bravado seemed to empty out of him as quickly as it came; he was looking down. I was glad he wasn't scrutinizing me. But I didn't need his disappointed, reproachful look to tell me what I already knew: that few people could match my ability to join my native recklessness to an equally deep-seated knack for hedging bets. Try a lifetime of that; and if your goal at the end of it is to come to a dead halt, you'd have to say I was a smashing success.

"Simeon," I mumbled, "I'll think about it." If all else fails, you can count on my wanting to please.

He said, "Don't you want to get even?"

I didn't do well with direct questions. Something he couldn't know; I asked so many. I said, "You know where to reach me? Care of the English Department?"

Rising to his feet, he looked down at me and said, "How about here?"

Chapter 10

Lanyards

"You say that a lot," I told Dr. Hollister.

What he'd said was, "How do you feel?"

"You're allowed to answer," he said, and added, "I'm not just being polite."

"Okay, fine. But I want to know what you think about *that*." Impatiently, I pointed to the letter I had drafted for Simeon's lawyers, enumerating Ted's flaws. He'd set it down, still folded over, alongside a sheaf of other papers on his desk. I was anxious for him to read it. I wanted him to, I said, before I sent it. Which I hadn't—yet.

"That's wise," Dr. Hollister said, evenly. He said he would read it later. For my treatment, he said, he had other priorities. They were different from Simeon's. Simeon, he reminded me, had his own doctor.

I asked, conversationally, "Do you think Dr. Wheeler's treatment of Simeon has anything to do with Dr. Wheeler's distaste for Ted?"

"Distaste?" He looked surprised. The same look of surprise he'd shown when I reported, returning to the hospital from my first all-day-pass, that the tomato soup Edith and Andrew served their dinner guests (the Olmsteads, me) had been laced with vodka. "Vodka?" he'd said, his eyes widening. "Just a splash," I said. "I figured I had to tell you," I said.

His conditions for the pass had been, "No pills, no booze, no suicide." He said, "You figured right."

Now, he said he didn't know anything about a supposed aversion to Ted on the part of Dr. Wheeler or, for that matter, anyone else. He said, decisively, "Never mind that."

"You say that a lot too," I said.

He smiled. "Right."

I had been in the hospital all of one week. In this, the third of our crisply conducted sessions, Dr. Hollister seemed determined to draw a firm dividing line between my treatment and Simeon's; somehow, they had merged in my mind. He said, "What might be good for Simeon might not be right for you. Like the priesthood," he added, "or suing Ted."

Abruptly, I requested an overnight pass. I told him I was ready.

He said he didn't know about that. He wanted to know what I would do with it. He looked disbelieving when I told him I wished to tidy my apartment.

Instead, he wanted to talk about my letter to Simeon's lawyers about Ted. He shrugged off my reminder that he hadn't yet read it. Why, he wanted to know, did I want to join forces with Simeon on this?

"Ted hurts people," I mumbled. "Simeon. Me. Something has to be done."

"I think you did it already," he said. He added, "You got even." He went on, "Let's call it your overdose. Even if it hurt you worse than it hurt him. Don't you imagine it also bothered him?"

"I don't really remember it," I said. I asked hopefully, "*Did* it?"

Dr. Hollister seemed to think the studied aplomb Ted manifested that night in the emergency room meant that it did.

"Does that displease you?" he asked.

"No." I said confidently, "I wanted to ruin his evening."

"Did you consider that you would also ruin your own?"

"I think I thought it would be worth it."

"You could have died," said Caleb Hollister.

"You're telling me I can get even without getting dead?"

"You can put it that way," he said, unsmiling. He seemed worried that I might be up for trying it again.

"I've always thought it was better to leave than to be left," I said airily. "You can always find some other welcome mat."

"Maybe—but it doesn't," Dr. Hollister said, "have to be the one the Hemlock Society sets out. You could have died," he said again. "Did you want that?"

I cut short my usual stagy shrug. I said softly, "It was an indecipherable life."

"It was yours and it got saved," Dr. Hollister said. "So you have a shot at deciphering it."

That sounded hopeful, though I didn't know what that would take, or how powerfully unwilling I was to do anything that would threaten my inheritance, a certain lovingly fashioned, carefully maintained code—to record your life in hieroglyphics.

For starters, I couldn't relinquish the lawsuit. On my occasional day-passes, in the guise of ordering my apartment (in fact, too scary to revisit) and my life, I frantically tried airing, with anyone who would listen, the question of whether or not to help Simeon sue Ted? I re-ran pros and cons with an assortment of listeners, distinguished by the persistence of their curiosity. An exception was Dr. Hollister, who struck me as a lightweight because he had no axe to grind and delivered truisms like, "Having some things in common with Simeon doesn't have to mean you're on the same side."

And there was another exception. Val.

She picked me up at the hospital early in the second week and we drove, very fast, in her jeep, back to the farm. On the way, to my relief and surprise, she talked mostly about herself. About Andrew, she said emphatically, "No, I do not want him back." The sooner her divorce became final the better, she said.

Guiltily, I wondered what she would say if she knew I'd just recently broken bread with Andrew and the Other Woman. Maybe she knew already, I thought, as the jeep spun along the road. The town was too small. How else to justify dining with the enemy? Only that if you stayed anywhere too long you became a betrayer simply because there weren't enough people to go around. Just like families, including the one you were born into, though not limited to it. Take Hades and Persephone, for example; stripped of their legend, maybe they too were just your average married couple with an interfering mother-in-law.

The grounds seemed bare, as we approached the farm, and the house itself was smaller than I remembered it, somehow jerry-built.

"It hasn't changed," Val said drily, once we were inside. "He took his clothes and his books. That's all." She was moving, with a kind of nervous determination, back and forth in her kitchen.

"You really mean that about not wanting Andrew back?" I said.

"I do," she said. Vows. "I do renounce you, Andrew."

"I admire you," I said. I myself, I went on, had known women who, for a wedding band, would walk through the fires of hell. She knew such women too, she said, giving me a look. She wasn't keen to be one of them.

"I grew up around army bases," she said. "You move on." She was surveying a melange of vegetables strewn over her kitchen table. She sat down, motioned me to join her, and set before us some husks. Grimly, she said, "Let's shuck some corn." Hardly missing a beat, she added: "You know, what you did was *square*."

Flushing, I murmured, "Isn't the word 'square' square?"

"Yes. It went out with the fifties. People don't say it anymore. They don't die for love, either," she said resolutely. "Not anymore." It was clear she didn't plan to.

I reached for some corn, grateful I had something to do with my hands.

"What about Ted? What will you do?" she asked, after a while. She went on to say that she really couldn't recommend litigation for persons looking for new experience; though, granted, it was a step up from suicide.

"I *was* thinking about a splendid trial," I told her. "Maybe something like *Anatomy of a Murder*."

"Better than a splendid funeral," Val said tenderly. "I suppose. It's rumored there are other choices."

Oh, I thought. I thought revenge.

But according to Dr. Hollister I'd gotten even with Ted already, on the night I'd turned to Noludars to make my point.

Not really, I told him. For revenge to count, I said, you should have your wits about you and I remembered so little of that night, it hardly seemed to belong to me; it was as if the experience had been hijacked. After all, for most of it, I'd had to rely on secondary sources, *other* people's words

Dr. Hollister said curtly, "The experience was yours. Whether you remember it or not. Sometimes we have to make do—in cases like yours—when the primary source is unavailable."

"You mean," I said, "when the primary source is out cold." (I managed to suppress a giggle—a quick judgment call.)

"I mean *unconscious*," he said, adding pointedly. "You had no reflexes." He'd said it before. Now there was a silence. He seemed to be waiting for me to look at him rather than the floor; I owed him that.

He said, after a while, that he agreed it was nice to have your wits about you. "But," he said, "your wits could be put to other uses."

"Other than what?"

"Other than retaliating."

The word was objectionable, I allowed; it didn't sound like something nice girls did.

What would happen, he persisted, if I just walked away from this, the lawsuit? If I let Simeon go his way and I mine?

"I'd be letting Simeon down," I said at once with a conviction that startled even me. "And wouldn't it be cowardly?"

"But what's in it for you if you hang on?"

"I don't know," I said. Somehow, while serving as Simeon's new reason for being, his lawsuit had become my life-raft as well. I went on to explain, "It's almost as if it happened when my back was turned."

Dr. Hollister broke in. "Forget Simeon," he said. "What would happen if you let it go? Let's put it another way—if you let Ted go?"

I said it's not the same thing.

He said, "But let's say it is."

I knew the answer to that one. I couldn't pretend that I didn't because my voice, breaking, betrayed me, and I said, "It would *hurt*." And then I heard myself say I'd walk through the fire to avoid pain. A neat trick, he said and added, you've already done that. I said nothing. I was contemplating a walk, trying to remember when I'd last taken one.

Mid-afternoon, on my next daytime pass, I made my way along the Iowa City streets, trying to ignore the trees in bloom overhead and the scraggly clumps of flowers sprouting, here and there, underfoot. It was spring; soon it would be very hot. I headed down a path, familiar, ghostly, to Ted's. Rumors were that he was spending his weekends, at least, out of town—where, nobody exactly knew. Doing what? They didn't know that either. It all had, spreading along the grapevine, the air of mystery. Meanwhile, around me, people were shushing each other, making elaborate efforts not to speak his name. Screening out their kindness, their tact, was one of my skills then. But I did sense that the concern wasn't all benign. Lenni Olmstead, in particular, presumed an intimacy between us which seemed to feed on my not wanting it. And there were others who continued to welcome me as a diversion. (Pablo, later, put it this way: "Without you," he offered, with a pleasant smile, "the annual local murder would have to take up the slack.")

I didn't know if I'd find Ted at home. I hadn't confided, to anyone, my plans for this visit; they'd discourage it, they'd ask me why—and

I didn't know how to explain I had no choice. Like a child, I'd say, "Becuz," and hang my head. I just needed to see him. (And in some way, I imagined, he still needed me.) Besides, I was sick of conjuring acceptable replies to various unanswerable questions beginning with "who?" or "why?"

Let someone else answer them for a change. Was anyone, beside Simeon and some lawyer speaking in legalese, badgering Ted for answers? The true, bedrock answers, which only Ted could give.

How can you make decisions—to stay or leave, cooperate with a lawsuit or not, without a word? Yes, his absence was wrenching; yes, it was bad form, cruel even, to disappear. But I needed a word. Maybe, I thought, above all, a word would set it right. In the hospital, it had come to me that I'd nearly made myself become a thing. But I was alive, and so was Ted. And whether or not he'd come back as my lover, he survived as a text.

He was standing on the steps of his house when I arrived, with his back to the closed front door. He started, as he caught sight of me. I called out, "Hello there."

"Well, goodness gracious!" he said. A diffident smile seemed at odds with his heartiness.

"You look as though you're just leaving." I was hanging back consciously, making an effort to be tactful.

"Yes, yes," he said. "But I've got a minute." He seemed to be waving me in the direction of his back yard. I followed behind on the path leading past the house. "If you'd called—" he said.

"Yes, well," I said, "I'm limited to the hospital pay-phones." I went on, "One tends to run out of coins."

"Oh," he said. "You're still in the hospital, are you?"

I murmured, "I'm getting out soon."

"Good God," he exclaimed. "Do you remember when pay-phones cost a nickel?"

I nodded. "I do."

He was looking around the yard. He seemed restless, distracted; his gaze fell on the garden.

"Oh," I said, "The garden looks lovely!"

"Tomatoes, bell peppers. I have other seedlings. Got to make some time to plant. We sure could use some rain."

I nodded. "We are having a dry spell." I couldn't catch his eye. Politely, I asked, "Are you looking for something?"

"No, no, not really," he said, with a nervous little laugh. "Sorry. I thought I left some garden tools out here. I guess not."

"You planting any flowers?" I asked, pointing toward the garden.

"Maybe," he said. "I don't know. I may stick to vegetables. You can come over for cabbage some time."

"Really? I can?"

"Oh, I don't know," he said. His hands were twitching a little. His hands, his gestures, seemed so familiar. "That is—maybe, if you're not eating your greens."

I laughed.

"Say—I don't know what I've got—but do you want anything to drink?"

"That would be nice."

He frowned. "I'll see what we've got."

"I'll settle for water," I said.

"You might have to," he said, heading for the back door which led to the pantry.

I called out, "Okay, then. At room temperature—with a twist."

But I was too late for comic relief. He was already inside the pantry.

As he kicked open the back door some seconds later, Pussywillow came bounding out.

I went to her, ignoring the water glass he'd tried to hand me. He set it down on the porch rail. "It has ice in it," he remarked moodily.

I had kneeled down, I was at eye-level with Pussywillow.

Ted said, "She's getting fat, she eats too much."

I began to stroke her, making the usual accompanying little sounds, *there, there, ah, mew, mew…*

"She doesn't go in for baby-talk anymore," Ted said sharply.

I looked up. "She's being responsive," I protested.

Ted frowned. "She's fooling you. She's just gotten good at going through the motions," he said.

I put the cat down and picked up the water glass; its ice had been melting. "We're going to have warm weather soon," I said. My lips seemed to be moving on their own, executing sipping motions, mouthing words, while I seemed to be standing apart, watching us. My mouth was dry. I didn't want to gulp my drink, but couldn't help it."Thirsty?" Ted asked conversationally.

I nodded, set the glass down, and blurted out, "A man I slept with once, the next morning, over orange juice and coffee, told me, 'The whole block can hear you swallow.'"

Ted smiled abstractedly. "I don't want to be like a pay-telephone, but we're out of minutes." He looked at his watch. "I have to be someplace," he said. He didn't say where.

I said, "Suppose I put in another dime?"

"Just one," he said.

"It's about Simeon. His lawyer's been in touch with me."

"Me too." His face grew hard. His words were clipped, "I don't think I should talk about this."

"Don't you want to know what his lawyer wants?"

"His lawyer wants what his mentally disturbed client tells him *he* wants. What do they want with you?" He paused, and added, "Maybe you shouldn't be talking about this either."

"They want a letter from me. Verifying—some things."

"What things?"

"Things." I had to make myself say it. "Photographs."

"I see." Suddenly, he seemed unmasked and I saw a face now full of pain. "I think," he said hoarsely, "I deserve better."

I said, "From me?" adding, silently, *even* from me?

"Yes. You."

"Ted," I began. Abruptly, he brushed something from his arm; it could have been a gnat or mosquito. I muttered, "I guess it's too early for mosquitoes."

Turning slightly away from me, his voice shaky, he said, "Your nickel's up."

"There's just one thing I want to know."

"Talk about a clinging vine," he said. "You never get enough," he said, "do you?"

"Just tell me—" I said, wondering how I could frame all that I wanted to know, in the brief sentence you get when your nickel's up.

"What, Rae?"

I whispered, "Did you ever encourage Simeon, I mean lead him on—or flirt?"

"Simeon is crazy," he exploded. "I no more did those things with him than I did with you!"

"You didn't encourage or flirt with me?"

"Of course not! I spent a lot of time watching you believe what you wanted to believe, hook, line and sinker. And there was nothing

I could do about it! Talk about the Dresden fire-bombing! If you remember World War II."

I stammered, "What about World War II?"

"Our side! They leveled that city. There was no stopping them. Pounded it, burned it to the ground."

"Ted," I cried, leaving Dresden be, "are you telling me you never cared?

"There's caring and there's caring. You can't care in a destructive emotional atmosphere."

I looked into his frightened face.

"Do you think that's what we had?"

"Yes. Don't you see? I *don't want* a relationship. Never did."

"You could have fooled me." A whistling sound was accompanying my breathing; it seemed unnaturally loud.

He said, "You don't have to be the fox in the chicken coop to fool you. Nobody even has to try."

I said, "I must have missed something."

(I could hear Dr. Hollister's words, *"Do you think it was Norma that your father missed?" I'd said, "Is this a riddle?"*)

Ted was again looking at his watch, as if studying it, memorizing its face. It suddenly struck me as urgent that I control the timing of my dismissal.

He beat me to it. He said, "I'll say goodbye to Pussywillow for you."

It was important not to react. Not in front of him. Blandly, I offered to carry the water glasses into the kitchen, rinse them out.

"No, no," he said. "Don't think of it. It's quite all right." He was looking at the sky. He was hoping for rain. "We need it. Of course," he added quickly, climbing into the car, "not before you get back to the hospital. Watch where you're going, by the way. You don't want to get run over."

He was revving up the motor, and telling me not to worry about the cat; he'd leave her outside, the house needed airing out. "*Vaya con dios, my darling . . .*" He started humming. Then, he laughed. "It's a *song*."

I said, "That's all you have to say?"

"It's small talk. We talked small talk, Rae. That's all it was. There was nothing else to say."

I was retracing my footsteps to the hospital, going back the way I came. Late, probably. The sun was going down and what had I learned? That all along a plaything for selected consumers, a toy, was what I'd let myself become? Nothing, that's what I'd learned, which was what I was planning to feel. Nothing and nothings, never mind sweet.

I was struggling to attain numbness when, as I neared the bridge to the hospital, I spotted someone striding across it, toward me, and waving. It was Pablo; there was no avoiding him; you couldn't sidestep him on the bridge. We stopped just short of colliding. He gave me a solicitous—oddly comforting—smile and said, "Aren't you out past your curfew?"

I said, "What makes you think so?"

He said, "I know the psych hospital's ropes. I'm viewed as a one-man escort service for the despairing and suicidal. The truth is I'm virtually the only one who hangs in there, who stays the course. I'm the guy who picks up the pieces the other guy left. Now, what are we going to do about your lateness?"

I said, "It won't be a problem."

"Okay, but you better have a good explanation. If you don't have one," he advised, "make one up. I'll help you."

"That's pretty generous."

"In fact, it is. Tell me, where were you—you look pale. Let me guess; you went to see Gobisch—for the beautiful farewell."

"I went to see him," I said, "because I have to decide whether to help Simeon with his lawsuit."

"You're going in with *Simeon*?"

"Not exactly going in, Simeon—his lawyers—have asked me for a letter. It could be helpful."

"And you're going to do it?"

I said, "I'm weighing it."

I met his gaze; he wore a look of honest concern. I was starting to experience his presence almost as benevolent, a kind of bulwark, standing now literally between me and the hospital. I wondered if I'd misread him; it wouldn't be a first.

"So it didn't go so well with Gobisch," he said softly.

"No," I said. My throat was tight. I said, "I had some idea we'd make peace."

"That was unlikely to happen if you brought up the lawsuit."

"I thought bringing it up would help me decide. I thought he'd give me an explanation."

"Explanation of what?"

"What happened between us. Something like that."

"And?"

"He said there's nothing between us. He said there never had been. Ever. I suppose I was hallucinating. I was even prepared to hear 'this can never be'—but not 'this never was.'"

Pablo nodded. "Let's figure out what are you going to tell the hospital."

"I'll tell them I needed to figure out what to do about the lawsuit. So I went to see him."

"Have you figured it out?"

"Maybe. I need to think about it some more. I'll talk to Simeon."

"Simeon," said Pablo. "My dear girl, you don't get it, do you?"

Impatiently, I said, "What don't I get?"

"You think Simeon is your confederate. Your ally. Listen to me carefully. He's your *rival.*"

"Do you think," Dr. Hollister had asked, *"it was Norma your father missed?"*

Did I remember this? Had he said it more than once?

"Ricardo won," said my mother.

Had there been a contest? Who'd been competing?

What—*who*—was the prize?

If you return after curfew, incidentally, your evening's telephone privileges get suspended.

So, it was morning before I could call her, my mother. Wedged into the hospital pay-phone booth, waiting for the call to go through, I tried to think of nice ways to ask questions that, if you didn't sugar-coat them beyond recognition, risked reprisal for gross violation of family taboo. My palms were damp; cold; I hadn't slept; nice girls don't wreck their mothers' hearts' defenses. Nice girls, like Edward and Annette's daughters, don't do a lot of things, like kill themselves or lie. Don't they? *Mother—what did you mean by that, exactly? Ricardo won.*

"I accept the charges," I heard her say in her liquid, melodious voice. Her lines, spoken so often as curtain lines, still had the timbre of intimacy. Always, whatever she said, I could hear her voice's music.

I blurted out my questions, unsweetened. "What did Ricardo win? What happened to him?"

Now, in her lilting voice, with its lulling rhythms, she professed astonishment. "But I never said that. I remember nothing of the kind. You're imagining this. It's one of your inventions."

"You said it. I know you said it. What did you mean? Why did Ricardo stop coming to visit?"

"Nothing special happened. Friendships fizzle," she said evenly. "Your father and I just went on with our lives."

"Did you send him away? Ricardo?"

"Why would I do that?" she said. "It was so long ago. I may have felt he was taking up too much of your father's time. I suppose he went on with his life too."

"But Dad liked him."

"Yes, well," she said absently, "it's hard to remember." She went on, "He wasn't a good friend for your father. He'd become a bad influence."

"How? How 'bad?'"

"Is this a quiz?"

"Yes."

A quiz she hadn't studied for. She said, "Why am I being asked to walk down memory lane?"

"Because," I said, "it's better than amnesia alley."

She said that wasn't funny. Family happiness had been at stake. Our very lives.

I said, "Is that so? And nothing's at stake now? Is that what you're saying?"

She said hoarsely, "I don't like being cross-examined."

"You *did* send Ricardo away."

"I believe your father did."

"Were you glad?"

"I supported his decision."

"Is that all?"

"I told you I didn't think Ricardo was a good influence. After a while that became obvious to both your father and me. We wanted to go on with our lives."

"Dad only went on for a few more years."

"He lived ten years. They were good years." There was a catch in her voice.

"But he didn't have friends."

She said, "He had us."

"But we didn't have him," I cried. "I missed him."

"Who? Ricardo?"

"I missed both of them. Dad was different without him."

It was getting very hot in the phone booth, but if I opened the door to let in some air, we'd be overheard, and I'd have to whisper.

She snapped, "Sometimes a clean break is best." Then she said, "Can we have this conversation another time?"

"*If* we have it." My voice dropped. "I'm not taking any bets." I was whispering anyway.

"You may have missed your father, but at least he was there. There are some things you shouldn't push."

"Mother." I was pleading with her. "Who are you trying to protect? Mother, I'm in the hospital. I swallowed pills."

"Ricardo wasn't normal, Rae," she said tremulously.

"Like Norma," I breathed.

"Who is Norma?" she asked. She seemed really not to know.

"She was with me in first grade. We were friends. I brought her home after school one day. You took one look at her and told me she wasn't normal. You made her leave the house."

"I have no idea who you're talking about."

"You don't remember Norma? My embarrassing mistake of a friend?"

"No. I was always nice to your friends. I had no problem with any of them."

"Then maybe it wasn't about Norma. Maybe something else was going on that day. Maybe Norma was just fine. Maybe you wanted to throw someone else—like Dad—out of the house and she was handy."

"I don't remember any such little girl."

"She existed," I said. "I didn't make that up. I remember you said she wasn't normal and I was so ashamed. I couldn't wait for her to go, and she'd been my best friend."

"And I would certainly would never throw out your father!"

"Then maybe it was Ricardo. Norma was a stand-in for Ricardo." Ricardo, who was also supposed to have not been normal, and whom she *had* cast out, perhaps even later that same night. My father would not have done that. He'd been sobbing. I'd found him, afterward, all broken.

"I'm sorry," my mother said, "that you had such an unpleasant experience, a rift with some little girl—what was it, 24, 25 years ago? In first grade? How in the world can I make that up to you?" The honey in her voice was gone, replaced by acid.

(I remember how she would swoop in, my mother when I was in first grade, wearing beautiful robes or dresses she'd made herself—exotic floral prints is what I remember, chiffon, cut low at the bosom. She'd dive low, tantalizingly near, and the edges of her clothing would brush over me lightly like feathers. I'd reach for her, my fingers would close on the hem of her skirt or her sleeve as she sailed past and away again. The hug-giving substance of her eluded me. And after Marta was born, my mother seemed not to *have* arms. What she'd had were wrapped around something small and indeterminate, swaddled in a blanket, that squirmed and had a cap stuck on top of it. Often enough, my mother had fingers, and sometimes a hand would appear and the fingers tug at something her older daughter was wearing, the sleeve of her coat or its collar, or the barrettes and ribbons holding my tightly braided hair. Or her fingers would light briefly on a shoulder, or the hand attached to the fingers would nudge gently along the small of my back, then vanish once again. I looked for my mother's arms all my life. It wasn't till years later—when Marta got married—that Mother's arms reappeared. She would hold me, hold onto me. *Oh, Ma...* But they'd changed, her arms, they were angular and compromised. They'd remained faithful to others, they'd been through the mill.)

"Tell me about Ricardo!" I cried, "*What was not normal?*"

"What was not normal," she said raggedly, "was that he was in love with your father. We couldn't have him in the house!"

"Mother, was Dad in love with him?"

She cried, "I had to protect your father! If it wasn't for me, none of us would have had him! Don't you see? You owe him to me."

I said, spitting it out, "No, I don't see! And I don't owe you anything!"

I stood, listening to her breathing, determined to outwait her silence, trying even to work up some fondness for that possibility.

Finally, she spoke; and though I immediately forgot her words, I was sure they'd been, just as I'd expected, cutting and cruel. I stumbled out of the phone booth, a nice, upright coffin. Cooped up, you've at least got an excuse if you want to make good on a recent pledge to neither move nor breathe.

Moving stiffly toward the patient lounge, I thought of Norma. "*Who do you think you are?*" she'd shouted at me in one of those moments contributing to my understanding that we were no longer friends. Maybe, I was thinking, she, Norma, had been right, all those years ago, to ask her question, not to believe a word any of us said. So what difference did it make what my mother said now? Whatever her words were, I sensed they were the source of a pain that I was becoming too strong to ward off.

Later, her words came back to me—those words I'd thought so cruel. They came back under the influence of a drug reluctantly administered by Dr. Hollister, who thought I didn't need it. (It was called sodium amytal, and I'd pleaded for it, having heard it had the magical properties of a truth serum, presumably the kind I'd encountered previously in spy movies or the comics.) But it wasn't like that at all, the truths elicited now were ordinary: an observation, for instance, that small towns had drawbacks, as did hospitals. That in the future, it might be smart to give both a wide berth.

Then, finally, I remembered my mother's words. "Come away from the dead," she'd cried. Which I'd thought meant *stay away from him*—her old message. Even now, I had thought, as rage flooded me, she wants him all to herself. Seductress.

I'd cried out, "What choice do I have now? Dad's dead!"

"That's right!" she said. "At last. It's time you noticed."

Then she said, "So leave him be. *Let him go!*"

Even after I knew better it was so hard to relinquish this. After the drug wore off—and, day by day, year by year, as I unbraided things after that—I was able, finally, to hear her words stripped of the meaning I'd imposed upon them. *Rae, she'd said, come away from the dead. Leave him be.* I would come to understand I'd tuned it all out violently, hearing only *stay away, forget him,* refusing the comfort that would come from hearing it for what it was, her anguish, her plea.

Chapter 11

R

Come away. Leave the dead be. Let them go.

Later that afternoon—after the drug had worn off—Caleb Hollister asked me why those words, my mother's, had struck me as so cruel. That was when I thought "them" meant "him." I tried to tell him: that it meant to give up, forget, abandon *him*.

The following morning, Dr. Hollister cornered me at breakfast in the hospital cafeteria with news. I was, he told me, to be released from the hospital.

"Released," he said.

"That has a nice ring to it," I said, trying to sound casual. The news had come as a shock; if it was a happy shock it was something I wasn't used to. At intervals throughout that morning, as I navigated through hospital red tape and paperwork, alerted my landlady to expect me, and arranged for a ride, a notion would tease, flicker—that there might be a difference between abandon and release. And later—that the distinction could have been discernible to my mother.

So I folded my belongings in the overnight bag Ted had never come to collect and, with Val, caught the ride I'd dreaded home. When we pulled up in front of the house on North Linn, Mrs. Gillette was there on the porch, waiting, she said, for the postman. While she thought of it, she said, she'd been holding mail that had been accumulating for me. She went inside to get it, handed it to me through the half-open screen door, then vanished back inside. As I hesitated on the porch, Val offered to come upstairs with me. I thanked her, but told her no, in keeping with a resolve never again to allow myself to be taken for a clinging vine. A clinging vine—that thing Ted called me.

So I kissed Val and let her go, not sure whether it was or wasn't like old times, and went inside, where at the foot of the stairs I was confronted by Mrs. Gillette. Gravely, she said she had something important to tell me.

Upstairs, she began, just outside my door, I would find a rain of fallen plaster. Two days ago, while she was dozing, someone rumored to be a graduate poet had found his way into the house and gone upstairs, where he tried to break down my door with his bare fists. The racket woke her. It turned out that the young man had mistaken this house for another one nearby where his girlfriend had barricaded herself. Owing to the speedy arrival of the Iowa City police, my door suffered only minimal damage. She thought she should warn me. I listened, rapt; I'd never known her to be this voluble.

She went on: she'd swept up some but not all of the fallen plaster; if I swept up the rest, she added, she'd be much obliged. It was nice that I was feeling better. That warmed me. Trying to be friendly, I murmured something jokey about the lovesick poet and his ardent attack on my door. She looked astonished.

She said, "Love? He *doesn't* love her. That's not love!"

I said, "Oh, I know!" and began to stammer assurances that I really knew all about such things, what love was or wasn't. She didn't look convinced. After a beat or two she withdrew, perfectly polite, back into the half-lit interior of her house.

One at a time, I took the stairs. I was clutching the packet of mail in one sweaty hand, and an overnight bag belonging to some stranger, possibly Ted's lover, in the other. In my head was a medley of voices, remarks from a committee of individuals who were not there.

Who do you think you are? (Norma Povich, age six.)

Talk about a clinging vine! (Ted Gobisch, three weeks short of forty.)

He doesn't love her. (Mrs. Gillette, age unknown.)

Come away from the dead. (Annette English, age sixty, my mother.) Who advised too, *Let them go.*

How did you do that? As in a clean break is best? The way she'd expunged Ricardo?

Ricardo. In a blur of memory I thought of Ricardo's graceful, sinuous body and his refined El Greco face. And I could see the man with the slight resemblance to him, in the photograph Ted had placed, tenderly, on his mantel… I came to a dead stop. Shifting the overnight bag to the other hand, I grabbed on to the banister to contain a sudden wild thought—Who did I think I was going to meet—Ted's lover?—at the top of the stairs?

On the landing I saw the fallen plaster, the crumbs of something that, in Mrs. Gillette's view, wasn't love but vandalism. Picking my way through the debris, I thought it was the sort of gesture Frank, once, had been capable of—and you'd have had a hard time, then, convincing me that it wasn't romantic. I unlocked my door, and stepped into the apartment.

I stood there, trying to acclimate to the heavy stillness; the apartment seemed empty, as it always had. Carefully, releasing my grip on the handle, I set the overnight case down by the door to remind myself that after I unpacked it I'd have to figure out what to do with it—depending upon whether it was a gift or a loan, if it was something I could use or would want to. Ted had not asked for it back. I ran my hand over it, the leather was smooth, the color a discreet tan with some kind of shiny trim and eye-catching brass locks. Someone had been planning to travel, though not far; it was just right for weekends. Which, people said, Ted had taken to spending out of town.

I decided the thing to do first was to go through the mail, beginning with some letters that lay scattered on the floor, covered with some flecks of plaster. Mrs. Gillette had, at first, just slid my letters under the door. Now, as I gathered them up, I saw an electric bill which carried a warning and a phone bill which I could scarcely afford to pay. These were among the trials of living; if I'd succeeded at the other, I wouldn't have to worry, someone else would be stuck with my bills. For some reason I muttered that aloud; somehow, turning this train of thought into an utterance made it seem especially unwholesome. I decided to postpone any further tour of this apartment which I had last occupied while researching unconsciousness lying on my bathroom floor.

What had I expected then, that night two weeks ago? All I'd wanted was for Ted to come over. At the time it hadn't seemed such a big step down from marriage.

Gingerly, I sat down on my nearly unrecognizably neat bed. I must not have expected to sleep in it again when I made it up that morning two weeks ago with hospital corners smartly tucked in. I settled Mrs. Gillette's loose pack of letters on the bed somewhere near my hip, and began to riffle through them.There was a note, addressed to me in a faltering and unfamiliar hand, that hinted of an old-fashioned elegance whose graceful loops and jaunty dashes had seen better days. It was a handwriting that seemed to be imitating itself, almost like a forgery. I scanned for the signature, held it to the light to authenticate it, saw that it was real. It was from Roger Rawlings.

> My dear Miss English,
>
> Your department was kind enough to furnish me with your address. I wanted to tell you that I do remember Edward English, your father. I recognized your smile. Like him, you smile with your eyes.
>
> I remember too that he was good. That's what I remember.
>
> Yours most sincerely,
> R. Rawlings

Good—So that's what the G in G-man stood for. Good. I'd always known that and would never stop believing it, though I had spent a lifetime refusing the possibility that it was good enough.

Gently, I set the letter down and glanced around the apartment, blinking against the light. With the blinds raised and daylight streaming in there was no way to evade the hard fact of the room's sameness. I preferred the dark when, even with my eyes open, I could remake it, give it different contours, conjure secret recesses and hidden corners where nice surprises could lurk. By day, there was only the repeated disappointment of finding it unchanged. There was so little in the room that was mine, unless you counted Ted's suitcase or my letters, bills mostly, strewn across the bed. Except for Roger's letter. I looked to make sure it was still there, retrieved it from the bedcover's folds close to my lap. I needed to draw up a list of the items or objects I wasn't sure what to do with—like this letter and Ted's luggage—and consolidate them under some heading like *R* for *Reminders,* until I could decide.

I unpacked the suitcase, a cross between a hamper and a drugstore notions counter: contents consisting of wrinkled underwear, birth-control pills and tampons—the sort of things you take with you to some half-way house. I went to the window, peered down at the narrow, tree-lined streets of the town, where I'd tried so fiercely and ineptly to sink roots. Maybe the thing to do was to steal quietly out of town—saying, later, that I'd been deported from the cemetery if anybody asked. Taking just the clothes on my back, leaving the rest. Including the loose ends—some things just stay untied.

But when I worked up the courage to explore the apartment, with its furnishings and props, I found it wasn't that simple. I was trying to keep relics too charged with memory at arm's length, at the same time that I wondered whether they'd become a permanent part of me, like appendages or skin.

There were exceptions, certain lightweight souvenirs, like books of matches from the disco out in Coralville, where go-go girls, wearing only glitzy pasties, danced in gilded cages. A novelty pen which Ted had given me in a tender moment. It too featured a dancing girl, clad modestly in ink until you turned the pen (that is, the girl) upside-down, which was the point—Ted showed me—upside-down, the ink would vanish, leaving the girl naked.

Then there were other things, not so frivolous, like books: a volume cross-referencing the Warren Commission's report on President Kennedy's death; a collection of papers on the medical benefits of marijuana (a gift or loan from Ted—I'd never been sure); and record albums, the usual, to cry by.

Turning to the bureau drawers: pretty lingerie, some never-worn, two new pairs of panty-hose, the recent replacement for stockings and garter belts; then, my wardrobe of stockings, fishnet and other, mostly black, and patterned (polka-dots, or diamond-shapes similarly arrayed). Bobby sox for what I imagined might be my rare moments of resting up from night-life. So much for underwear.

Turning to the closet, for outerwear and whatnot: slacks, skirts blouses, sweaters, a couple of dresses. Shoes, both brand-new and scuffed—and when I lifted them up, with a sinking feeling I try never to re-summon, the smudged, disheveled pages of *Persephone in South Dakota.*

I would like to say that I embraced the manuscript, clasped it, repossessed it—that I returned to it eagerly, all smiles. But that was not the case. The fact was I didn't do that then, any more than I retired all of my vices. I did retire some, trying to give priority to the ones that were life-threatening, but I took my time about it.

So I set aside too my profile of Persephone with its account of her trials. Her story now unnerved me, with its regulated descents and monitored re-surfacings. Afterward, after Iowa City, I moved from city to city and though I took the book with me each time, I kept it hidden. I let it linger for some time in one closet or another.

My first stopover was with my mother, who ran a good half-way house, and tried, in her way, to be kind. Still, direct questions made her shudder when she didn't walk away. She flinched even from queries framed as hints, conveyed in whispers.

One evening, before I moved on, I came across one of the dusty, manila-sealed envelopes that, typically, turned up in plain sight, even though they'd lain unnoticed and probably unmoved for years. I would open them, either to find nothing (despite such intriguing labels as *Honeymoon*), or to find old hairpins, rent-checks, and bills. This one seemed to have its contents sorted, held together with rubber-bands. One loose snapshot fell out of the packet—a picture of me as a baby with my father, vibrant and utterly relaxed, holding me close against his chest. So, as a baby, I must have been hugged and held. When I grew a little older, certainly when I was no longer a squirming toddler full of delicious wriggles and squeals, touching between us had ceased. His remoteness had held his loves in check. When he hugged me (in greeting, as I left or returned from school) his body would be stiff, rigid, really, inclined away from me. This is how I remember him, his touch. How ardent he must have been about me, I know now.

There were other photographs—and some letters. I glanced at those, quickly, recognizing my father's handwriting, then an earlier, more robust incarnation of Roger's. Were they love letters? To me, they seemed loving. Next, I took up the photographs; there seemed to be two sets, taken at different periods, of my father and the young Roger. Some of the early ones looked like studio portraits, posed. Taken later were candid shots, some of them out of doors in some rustic setting unfamiliar to me, though I recognized my mother in the background, looking beautiful, smiling—it seemed shyly—at the two men, standing together. Other photos were taken indoors, in an early apartment of my parents', one I'd never seen, though I immediately recognized its furniture. Perhaps my mother had taken these pictures; she appeared in none of them. They were of the two men, taken in different seasons, standing or sitting, dressed for summer or winter, gazing at the camera, I guessed, just long enough to have their picture taken before they turned again to each other. The last picture was of Ricardo. It was the only one. He was smiling, looking down—perhaps at the unseen, crouching photographer (whoever it might be)—and holding a squirming, inquisitive baby, me.

When she found me, poring over letters, inspecting photographs, she reacted as if they were contraband. Agitated, she said they were not meant for *me* to see.

"Then why are they here?" I asked her.

"Because *they're* not," she said, indicating the photographs' subjects.

After a beat or two, I asked, "Do you think they'd mind my seeing them—Dad, Roger, and Ricardo—if they were here?"

She said, "Times change. Things change. But they're *not* here. How can I know? Give them back to me." She was reaching for the letters and pictures. She said angrily, "It was a long time ago." She looked as if she might take them by force, but I held tight. Gripping them hard, as my mother looked at me, I could almost hear Ted's voice: *You never get enough. Do you?* And I loosened my grip.

"Here," I said, handing them over, adding, stagily, "I release them to you." To my surprise, she thanked me.

There was something else; I was not quite ready to go away empty-handed. I said, "*R* for Roger, *R* for Ricardo, *R* for Rae—" I asked her, "what was that all about?"

She looked away, then turning back to me, she said quietly, "I suppose he was partial to *R's*. Some kind of affinity." She went on, "I suppose it was as close as he could come to naming you for him, for Roger, maybe for Ricardo too. Though I think Ricardo came around only after you were born."

Came and went and hovered over us all.

I could feel her hand on my hair. In a minute I would shake her off. I said, "Curls too tangled? Color and texture don't please you? Looking for the gray?"

"No," she said, "I'm not looking for the gray."

It dawned on me then that she was stroking my hair.

But that was after I left Iowa City—where I still had unfinished business. A couple of loose ends. A pending lawsuit, and an answer, maybe even an explanation, due Simeon.

And an unclaimed valise.

I tracked Simeon down; that part wasn't hard. He'd obtained permission from the Dean to audit a course. I found him emerging from his classroom. We repaired to a coffee shop and, seated opposite each other in a tucked-away booth, we talked across a formica table. Yes, he liked his course. Art history. Dr. Wheeler had intervened with the Dean, had reassured him about Simeon's mental state.

"Oh," I said, "so you still see Dr. Wheeler?"

He said, "Old Duane? Yep. Not as often." He asked, "Do you still see your Dr.-what's-his-name?"

"Caleb Hollister," I murmured.

"I know," said Simeon. "Tell me, why is he so skinny? He looks like a wraith." Then he wanted to know, "Does he still say things like 'Jeepers'?"

I said, "I haven't kept track. Anyway, after this week I won't be seeing him. I'm leaving town."

Simeon said, at once, "But I need your letter."

I made myself say, "I'm sorry, Simeon. I can't help you with the lawsuit." My hands were clenched, I was holding tightly to the edge of the cold formica table.

"Can't or won't?"

"Maybe won't." I was hoping he wouldn't ask me why.

"Look," I said, trying to relax, making a conscious effort to unclench my hands, "I wish you all the luck in the world, Simeon. But I don't think I can do that. Just please don't count on me for that," I said prayerfully, hoping he'd understand.

"Any other restrictions?" he said.

"No. But I *am* leaving town."

"So," he said, "pinning Gobisch to the wall isn't part of your travel plan?"

"It isn't," I said. "That's right."

"Are you going to see him before you leave?" He was blinking; his eyes had filled. "Are you going to tell him you're *not* going to help me?"

"Probably not," I said. "He'll find out." And I reached for Simeon's hand.

Packing. In the discard heap, I tossed the following garments unearthed from my closet: party finery, unused, like a dress of neon pink whose hems seemed cut with pinking shears; that fashion statement must have lasted about four minutes. Panty-hose, torn, though recently bought. Keepsakes like underwear, now mended, dating from Albany shopping expeditions made with Frank in the waning shadows of the Statehouse. That sort of memorabilia. I didn't think they were right for my hope chest.

There was one thing more to take care of before I left. I took a long walk, its purpose, to return the overnight case to Ted. Maybe it was my answer to the question Simeon hadn't asked: *Why?* Why wouldn't I help him in the case against Ted, in which he believed, then, so strongly? The answer was that I was building a different case, having come to an understanding that the living have the right to be released too.

Photo © 2012 by Jessica Weber

Lucy Rosenthal is the author of the novel *The Ticket Out*. The recipient of a Pulitzer Fellowship in Critical Writing, she has edited the anthologies *Great American Love Stories, World Treasury of Love Stories,* and *The Eloquent Short Story: Varieties of Narration*. She is on the writing faculty of Sarah Lawrence College and has also taught in the creative writing programs of Columbia and New York University. She lives in New York City.